WHERE SHE
HAS GONE

WHERE SHE
HAS GONE

NINO RICCI

M&S

Canadian Cataloguing in Publication Data

Ricci, Nino, 1959 –
Where she has gone

ISBN 0-7710-7454-9

I. Title.

PS8585.I126W43 1997 C813'.54 C97-931081-4
PR9199.3.R52W43 1997

The publishers acknowledge the support of the Canada Council for
the Arts and the Ontario Arts Council for their publishing program.

The English translation of lines 5-10 from the poem "Antico inverno"
("Ancient Winter"), by Salvatore Quasimodo, © Luciano Rebay, are
taken from *Introduction to Italian Poetry*, ed. Luciano Rebay.
Reproduced by permission of Luciano Rebay.

Typesetting by M&S, Toronto
Printed and bound in Canada

McClelland & Stewart Inc.
The Canadian Publishers
481 University Avenue
Toronto, Ontario
M5G 2E9

2 3 4 5   01 00 99 98 97

for Erika

The birds were looking for millet
And were suddenly of snow;
So with words:
A bit of sun, an angel's halo
And then the mist; and the trees,
And ourselves made of air in the morning.

— SALVATORE QUASIMODO
"Ancient Winter"

~

In another order of things, less fraught, she might have said, Tell me a story, the way people did around a fire late at night. And I would have told her this: Back before you were born, before any of this had begun, a mother and son lived alone in a stony village overlooking a valley. Just outside the village stood an old chestnut tree where it was said that someone, some criminal or wounded lover, had hanged himself. The other villagers kept their distance from it, and wouldn't gather up the nuts it dropped, with their spiny husks, in the fall. But the mother was not so particular, gathering the nuts up in her apron and bringing them home to roast them. Afterwards, when things turned out as they did, when a daughter was born though there had been no father to make her, when the mother had died giving her life, the son had a dream in which a tree was growing up out of his belly, a great blossoming thing whose inconvenience to him, however, was only in the slight gnawing he felt in his stomach like hunger because of the roots inching into him.

Was I the tree? she might have asked then. Was I the daughter? And I would have said, It doesn't matter, it was only a dream, it was only a story.

Or I might have said this: On our farm in Canada, there was a chestnut tree that someone had planted behind the barn. Every year my father threatened to cut it down, because in all our time on the farm it had never once produced any flowers or fruit. But finally one spring, already long after you'd left us, it sent out a profusion of small white buds that turned to nuts in the fall. It was as if the tree had understood how tenuous its existence was, and had gathered up all its resources to hold out to us this offering, this bit of hope.

She would have asked, Was there really a tree? Did it happen that way? And I would have said, That was one way it could have happened. And the yes and the no, the precision things took on in the plain world, would not have mattered so much, only the story, that bit of hope.

~

I

I saw Rita again toward mid-September, in Toronto. Autumn was just settling over the city then, the light giving itself over to September's peculiar half-tones and the trees that lined the city's sidestreets showing the first tinctures of russet and gold. In little more than a month the autumn colours would already have given way to the grey-limbed monotony of winter; but now the whole city seemed on the brink of some revelation, some last redemptive sigh before the winter's cold and snow.

Rita had started school at the university downtown and was living on campus with Elena, their residence tucked away at the heart of the ivied island of quiet the campus formed in the city centre. It was early evening the first time I went by for her, sunset lighting fires in the leaded panes of the residence windows. Inside, trim young men in blue jeans and young women in cardigans and pleated skirts came and went, the air electric with the first tense promise of the beginning of term.

The door to Rita's room was open. At my knock she turned from the mirror she'd been staring into, the gold shaft of a lipstick bright in one hand.

"Hi, stranger," she said.

She looked indistinguishable from the young women I'd passed in the halls, fresh-faced and blithe, her hair pulled back in a ponytail to set off the red of her lips, the blue of her eyes, like tiny gifts. Outside the oppressive familiarity of our home town, what had kept us children there, all our sibling confusions seemed made small.

"So you finally made it up to the big city," I said.

"We haven't really had much of a chance to see it yet. With orientation and all that."

The room had already been arranged like a mirror of the one that she and Elena had shared in the Amhersts' house back home in Mersea, pink comforters covering the beds, small knick-knacks set out on bookshelves and sills. I remembered the visits I'd made to her at the Amhersts' after she'd left us, how the prim domesticity of her and Elena's room, its careful pretence that they were sisters, that they were daughters, had always instead seemed the reminder that they didn't quite belong there, were both only adopted, like orphans taken in by some strict but benevolent home in a Victorian story. Now, though, seeing this replica before me, I had the sense they'd been infiltrated, that what had been merely imposed had slowly become part of them. The room's lone discordant element was a Dali print Scotch-taped above a dresser, of a naked Leda and swan against a background of sea, its Raphaelite contours and hues seeming at once an embodiment of the room's tidy femininity and a mockery of it.

I'd remained standing at the doorway as Rita finished her preparations, uneasy somehow at the intimacy of going inside.

"Elena's not around?" I said.

"She went down to the caf." But I sensed Rita was covering for her. "She said to say hi."

"I make her nervous."

"Why would you say that?"

"Oh, you know. The gloomy half-brother always lurking in the wings."

"You're not *her* brother."

"Maybe that's the point."

We walked the short distance from the campus to Chinatown. Dusk had settled in and the streets there were awash in neon like in some gambling town or resort. I watched Rita taking things in, the tiny shops, the unknown vegetables and fruits arrayed outside, and seemed to understand for the first time that she was here in front of me, felt a flutter like a traveller in a foreign city seeing a familiar face in a crowd.

"My place is just around the corner from here," I said. "About a five-minute walk from your residence, actually."

"That's great." There was just the smallest bit of distance in her voice, the old self-protectiveness, the unsureness of what we were to each other. "We can see each other all the time then."

We had supper at a restaurant I'd begun to frequent in the neighbourhood, just an unmarked door at street level leading down to a small basement room whose walls were covered with chalkboard menus. The place's few rickety tables were already nearly filled when we arrived.

"This place is wild," Rita said.

We sat at a tiny table for two in an alcove at the back. For a moment the intimacy of being crammed like that into such a narrow space made us shy.

"So are you settling in all right?" I said.

"It's okay. I feel like a bumpkin half the time – everyone's parents are president of this or that or an ambassador or something. But it's good having Elena around. There isn't much that fazes her."

We talked about school, about leaving home. I could feel a niggling sense of obligation between us to bring up the subject of my father; but the more we skirted it, the more it seemed inessential. Though only a few months had passed since his death, already it felt like an eternity: there'd been the first torpor and shame afterwards but then a lifting, the thought, *Now it is over*.

There was also the codicil to his will that I hadn't told her about, his wish that I use my inheritance to help provide for her if she should need me to. He had neither fathered Rita nor been a father to her, had never really forgiven her for the betrayal she was the product of; but he'd carried the guilt of her to the grave. I ought to have brought the matter up now and made an end of it.

"Are you doing okay for money?" I said.

"I think so."

"I suppose the Amhersts are looking after school and all that."

I still couldn't bring myself to refer to them as her parents even though they had been that to her for the better part of her life.

"Mostly. Dad had some problems with the store for a while but I think it's all right now."

"Well, if you ever need anything –"

"Thanks."

The meal was served in a brusque onrush of sizzling meat and steaming vegetables. There were no forks; I expected Rita to struggle with her chopsticks but she handled them with an unthinking expertise. Always I felt this disjunction with her, the expectation of her innocence and then her instinctive at-homeness in the world like a reproof.

We talked a bit about her plans for the future. There was an uneasiness in me whenever conversation came around to the general shape of her life, the fear that some seismic injury would be revealed, some fault line leading back to her years with us on my father's farm. But she seemed like any healthy young woman her age, exploring her options, not quite certain what the future held but not afraid of it.

"Maybe I'll just live like you do," she said. "Travelling. Doing what I want."

"I wouldn't exactly think of myself as a role model," I said.

The room was a steamy bustle now of serving and eating and talk. Rita had pulled the band off her ponytail, her hair falling silky black to the shoulders of the sweater she wore. She seemed resplendent somehow in her unquestioning calm, in the anonymity of seeing her here in this world of strangers. It was a kind of wonder to be with her like this, without ambivalence: we seemed released suddenly into the miracle of our lives, to do with as we wished.

When we were walking home I invited her to stop by my apartment.

"I don't know. Maybe not tonight." I could see that she wanted to come, that she was thinking of Elena. "There's a pub crawl or something we're supposed to go on."

"Maybe some other time, then. I'll have you over for supper."

"I'd like that."

I left her at the door of her residence.

"It's good to see you again," I said. "Maybe things can be a little more normal between us now than they used to be."

"They weren't so bad before."

There was an instant's awkwardness and then we kissed.

"Goodnight, then."

I stopped off for cigarettes on the way home at the variety store on the ground floor of my building. The owner, a canny Korean man who went by the unlikely name of Andrew, drew a Kleenex from a box as I came up the counter and reached out to wipe a smudge of lipstick from my cheek. I expected some joke from him but he merely winked, rapid and mocking.

"My sister," I said.

"Ah."

It was the first time in the weeks I'd been frequenting his store that he'd been so familiar with me. He had a little ritual of goodwill with some of his regular customers, offering them a free selection from the display of penny candies he kept on the counter. Now, finally, he extended the gesture to me, waving a hand over the display with a casual flourish like some smiling tempter offering the world.

II

I'd rented an apartment in an old brown-brick low-rise at the corner of Huron and College, the building flanked by a rusting metal fire escape that people often used in lieu of the main entrance. Across the road was an institute for psychiatric research: at night, sometimes, from the sealed windows of the upper floors, where the inmates were held, came muted bellowings or sudden shouts or screams like distant jungle sounds; but during the day, amidst the noise of College Street, there was nothing in the building's blank façade to betray what it was. A few minutes' walk from my place and I was in the heart of Chinatown, with its restaurants and shops, its smell of spices and rotting vegetables, its broken packing crates forever stacked at the curbsides; a few minutes more, to the west, past Bathurst, and I was in Little Italy, though perhaps out of an instinctive devaluing of the familiar I seldom ventured there, aware of it only as something known and therefore inconsequential.

Despite the income from my inheritance I was sparing with my money, my apartment ample but slightly ramshackle, my furnishings scoured from second-hand shops. With school it was the same: because I'd been offered a scholarship I had accepted a place in a Master's program at my old alma mater, Centennial, on the city's barren outskirts, though when I'd left there to teach in Africa three years before I'd thought I'd shaken the dust of the place from my feet. Four days a week now I made the drive out to the campus in the car I'd inherited from my father, a cobalt-blue Olds, my one indulgence. Amid the tiny imports plying the roads now, the car seemed in its seventies extravagance already an anachronism, from another era, hulking and ghostly and huge like some prehistoric thing stumbled out from reptilian sleep.

I had dinner one night with a friend from my undergraduate years, Michael Iacobelli. He had married since I'd last seen him, and had a son, the family living just west of the Centennial campus in a house Michael rented from his father. The floor of his entrance hall was littered with baby's toys when I arrived.

"Victor, my boy. I expected you to come back with tribal markings or something. A little local colour."

He seemed to have aged a dozen years, grown frail, his hair, already thinning when I'd known him, now starting to grey as well, though he was only thirty.

"So it must be a bit of an adjustment coming back," he said.

"A bit. Though exciting too, a new start and all that." But I said nothing about my father's death. "My sister's in the city now, which is kind of nice."

"Yeah, I remember you talking about her," he said, though I couldn't recall ever mentioning her to him. "So I guess you guys get along pretty well, is that it?"

"Better than we used to."

"That's the funny thing about family. You spend all your life trying to get away from them and then they're all you've got."

Michael's wife, Suzie, was a non-Italian, on first impression pretty and bland like her name but then beneath the surface seeming to bristle, like Michael, with under-exploited intelligence.

"So I guess all this must look pretty boring to you," she said.

"No, not at all."

Michael brought up a gallon of his father's homemade wine from the cellar and we began to get slowly drunk. He told the story of a feud he'd had with his father over an old maple tree in the back yard.

"It was a beautiful thing, it must have been thirty or forty years old. But it was something about the leaves or the shade, I don't know what it was. So one day we come home from a camping trip and it's like there's a big hole in the sky out back, and where the tree used to be just this perfect pile of cut logs. The sad thing is he probably thought we'd be pleased or something when we saw how pretty it all looked, with the logs piled up like that. Maybe it's some kind of immigrant thing. Man against nature. He thinks he's a pioneer or something."

The baby cried once or twice from a back room while we were eating and Suzie got up to quiet him, Michael leaving her to the chore with the unthinking air of a patriarch. But then at the end of the meal he got up to clear the table, he and I doing the dishes together while Suzie sat with her feet propped on a kitchen chair having a smoke.

"So are there any women in your life?" she asked.

"Not yet."

"Maybe we should fix you up with Michael's sister."

"Is she any prettier than he is?"

"About the same, I'd say. Less facial hair maybe."

I had come up by transit to avoid having to explain my father's Olds. Michael offered me a ride back to the subway. In the car, he grew suddenly candid.

"I'm not saying I regret any of it. But it's not how I pictured it, the nine-to-five and all that. You're trying to do things differently. I respect that in you."

I felt a throb of affection for him, had an image of us standing elbow to elbow at his kitchen sink while Suzie smoked and the baby slept, and wanted to show him that I had nothing, had only my freedom.

"I guess we all make our own way," I said.

And at the station door he got out of the car to shake my hand as if seeing me off on some tremendous journey.

I seldom thought much any more about my father's death. It had remained, in a sense, the thing uppermost in my mind, and yet for that was perhaps more forgotten, already as unquestioned as air, something only the animal part of me made allowance for. I'd get a sense of him like a premonition whenever I got into the car, instinctively registering the lingering evidences of him still strewn about, the half-empty cigarette pack, Rothman's, still on the dash, the muddied church program on the floor; and sometimes it seemed our whole history together flashed before me then, that he was suddenly tangible there beside me on the car seat like on our old Sunday rides to mass at St. Mike's. But beyond that visceral sense of his presence, there seemed nothing more to know of him. It was my mother, instead, who I found myself going back to, as if my father's death had finally freed me to re-imagine her. Her own death, giving birth to Rita on our way to Canada, during a storm at sea, seemed the stuff of stories to me now, of other people's lives, not mine. It surprised me how vividly the feel of that voyage came back to me now, the sense of hovering over a chasm, poised between the world we'd left behind and the unknown one where my father was waiting, by then a stranger to me, long gone ahead of us to prepare our way. In my child's skewed understanding back then of my mother's pregnancy I had expected some demon to emerge from her, snake-headed and vile. But I'd been offered instead a simple blue-eyed child, a sister, and then my mother's slow bleeding to death like an afterthought.

I drove around the city sometimes in my car like a cruising teenager, following roads I'd never heard the names of out to their furthest, most banal retreats. It amazed me all the different congregations of things I knew nothing of, the unknown neighbourhoods with their different peculiarities and moods, the closed doors and the curtained windows. It was both uplifting and oppressive, the thought of all this life going on every day, every hour, with its own sense of importance and purpose; sometimes I seemed to hear all the million voices of it in my head like jumbled radio waves. And yet still I'd get the sense that the city was an outpost merely, just the endless repetition of what College Street looked like when I gazed westward from the corner window of my apartment, a long vista of dingy two- and three-storey storefronts like the main street of some dusty frontier town. At dusk, with the sun settling in between the buildings there as if at the visible end of the world, the street seemed still only an instant's remove from what it might have been a hundred years before; and I imagined then the wooden sidewalks and the clapboard rooming houses, the immigrant road gangs working bare-backed where the street trailed to mud to push the city out against the encroaching wild.

Outside my building I passed groups of children from time to time on excursion from some nearby daycare. Their leaders, usually earthy young women in denim and bulky wool, strung them out along the length of knotted ropes to keep them in line, moving calm and slightly distracted at their edges like a protective rim around their microcosm of prank-ishness and wonder. The children formed assortments like cross-sections of the world, black and yellow and white, seeming oblivious in their hopskipping bravado to each other's differences. Once, as I stood staring after a group of them, a small Asian girl toward the back briefly broke for-mation as she passed to perform a tiny jig for me, secretive and quick; and then in a twinkling she'd resumed her place, in giddy self-containment, casting back an impish grin before trailing off with the rest in the autumn sun.

III

Nearly three weeks passed before I saw Rita again. I seemed to be saving her like a reward I hadn't quite earned, but then as the days went by and I didn't call I began to feel a sense of guilt as if I'd been avoiding her. It had always been like that for us, this anticipation and deferral, and then afterwards always the sense of having to start again, of being able to take nothing for granted.

In the end it was Rita who called.

"I guess you've been busy with school," she said.

"Sort of."

I had her and Elena over for supper. I hadn't seen Elena since before I'd gone off to Africa, but she seemed unchanged, only more what she'd always been. As she'd grown older her blonde hair had gradually darkened to its present auburn; but otherwise she might have been simply a larger version of the girl who'd first befriended Rita in the schoolyard of St. Michael's years before, still lank and precocious and brooding, still carrying her attractiveness like a kind of dare.

"I was starting to think you've been avoiding me," I said, trying to sound genial, though the words came out like an accusation.

"Just waiting for an invitation, that's all." And she shot a look at Rita as if sharing a private joke.

I'd set up a table for our meal in a sort of anteroom to the living room that had sat empty till then. The room's high-ceilinged spareness imposed an odd formality on us – we seemed reassembled as if at the Sunday dinners we used to share in the Amhersts' house, with their atmosphere of enforced familial harmony.

"Your place looks great," Rita said.

"Thanks."

Not once during the whole meal did Elena look at me when she spoke, her eyes directed at Rita even when her comments were directed at me. I tried to engage her but each time her attention would shift, with always the same implication of hidden meaning – it was as if she'd set up a kind of force field around herself that couldn't be entered except through Rita. At one point, when I was clearing away dishes to bring in dessert, she got up from the table and began to wander around the apartment, inspecting things with what looked like genuine curiosity, the prints on the walls, the books on my bookcase, the knick-knacks I'd set out on my mantelpiece; but then she sat down again without a word.

At the end of the meal she got up almost at once to leave.

"I'm sure you folks would like to be alone for a while," she said, speaking directly to me for the first time, though with an undertone of almost menacing irony.

When she was gone, it was like a parent or chaperon had left the room.

"What was all that about?" I said.

"That's just Elena. She overreacts sometimes."

"What could she have to react to? I haven't seen her in years."

"If you want to know the truth," Rita said, trying to sound casual, though she got up suddenly and began clearing dishes away from the table, "she was angry because you didn't call. Like I said, she overreacts."

I felt strangely moved, as if I were being given a kind of permission, an order, to play a role in Rita's life.

"I really didn't think you guys took that much notice of me," I said.

"It's no big deal. Anyway you're right that she has a bit of a chip on her shoulder. From being adopted and everything."

"You were adopted."

"I just hide it better, that's all."

We finished clearing away the dishes. I kept expecting her to make some move to leave.

"Would you like some more wine?" I said.

"I dunno. I feel pretty drunk as it is."

"*In vino veritas.*"

"I'm not sure how far I'd want to go with that."

We carried our glasses into the living room. Rita took off her shoes and curled up at one end of the overstuffed couch I'd installed there, made small by its padded bulk.

There was a sudden mood of closeness between us.

"I always felt bad about that talk we had," she said. "Before you left for Africa. About our mother."

The subject had only come up that once between us, and then awkwardly, too weighted by that point by all the years of silence. But now it seemed imbued with a special allure exactly from having been so long avoided.

"That was my fault," I said. "It's not as if it has to be any big secret or anything."

"I always used to wonder what she looked like. I've never even seen a picture of her."

"Sort of like you, I guess. Dark-haired. Pretty."

"Thanks. Seriously though."

"To tell you the truth, sometimes I can't even remember. It was quite a long time ago."

I thought of mentioning her eyes – I remembered them as unnaturally dark, almost black, though perhaps only because I couldn't think of them now except in contrast to the blue of Rita's.

"It always seemed pretty wild to me," Rita said. "People having affairs in a village like that. I used to think there'd been a mistake or something, that people just didn't do that sort of thing back then."

She didn't ask about her father. That question had never been broached, seemed somehow less removed from us by time, less neutral. There was little I could have said of him in any case, a few shreds of gossip I'd overheard, a shadow I'd seen emerging from a stable door. In my mind he was not so much a person – someone with a history, a name – as an event, a thing that had happened and then been moved past.

It grew late. I offered to walk Rita back to her residence. We were plainly drunk now and yet the drunkenness had made us timid. Coming down the fire escape of my building Rita stumbled and fell against me, her hands grabbing hold of me as she struggled to regain her balance. I had an urge then to gather her up on my back like a child, so pleasant was the weight of her against me, so supple and frail.

"Are you okay?"

"Yeah. Sorry."

We walked to the residence in silence. The air had turned brisk, Rita's cheeks colouring with the cold.

"So maybe we could see a movie or something," I said.

"That would be great."

"How about on the weekend?"

"I think that's all right. I mean, I have mid-terms but I wouldn't mind a night off."

"I'll call you, then," I said.

She laughed.

"Promise?"

"Promise."

"If you don't, you'll have Elena to answer to."

And when she turned I thought there was a lightness in her step at the prospect of our seeing one another again.

IV

We began to see each other regularly, as much as two or three times a week, usually at my apartment and usually alone. I was always aware when we met of the shadow of Elena behind Rita, but we seldom spoke of her any more; and though Rita never betrayed the sign of any rift, I sensed that our time together was a sort of retreat from Elena for her, an unconscious shifting away from an intensity she couldn't quite fathom.

I'd given her a key to my apartment. On school days I'd come home and often she'd be at work at my kitchen table, books piled high around her or pages spread out filled with her loping script. For hours sometimes then we'd go about our separate tasks, she in the kitchen and I at my desk in the bedroom. From a certain angle of doorways and passages I could catch glimpses of her from my room as she worked, the hunch of her shoulders, the sweep of a hand as it came up to brush back her hair. While I'd been in Africa we'd written letters to each other, full of tentative self-revelations; and yet all that I'd gleaned of her then seemed nothing next to these glimpses I stole, to the sense of her presence there in my kitchen working unawares while I watched.

She had befriended the building's black superintendent, Eddy. Eddy was known in the building mainly for his frequent late-night arguments with the white boyfriend he lived with, arguments that seemed intended both to announce and deny what the relationship between them was. There was an evasiveness to him that made him appear almost simple at times, a tendency to stare off, to avoid the commitment of eyes; but he kept a close tally of the building's comings and goings. In the warmer weather he'd kept vigil from across the street, or from an old lawn chair he would set outside the window of his ground-floor apartment under a leaning sumac tree; and then when the cold had come on he'd taken up a post just inside the front entrance. I'd hear his voice filtering up from there whenever Rita came by, laconic and flip, conceding nothing, a cross between aging drag and Southern drawl.

"You again."

"That's right. You can't seem to get rid of me."

"Well someone should tell Victor up there to watch the company he keeps."

Since Rita had started coming around, Eddy had begun to perform little favours for me, clandestinely though, as if to avoid the humiliation of being seen to be kind. He'd clear the snow from my fire escape when I was out; he'd bring my mail up from downstairs and slip it under my door. There was something so intimate in these gestures that I saw them at first almost as overtures, even if Rita was somehow the permission for them. But there was more to them than that, some subtle enfolding of Rita and me that was Eddy's necessary type of affection at a distance, his way of watching over whatever fragile thing he imagined Rita and I formed.

At some point I came around to discussing with Rita the codicil to my father's will. I thought her knowledge of it would somehow bind us more intricately, but the subject seemed to make her uneasy.

"It was just his way of admitting that you were my sister," I said. "It's not as if you owe him anything for it."

"It's not that. It makes me feel strange, that's all. I never told you this but I saw him on the street once in Mersea not long before he died. The way he looked at me, you know that way he had, like a cloud had just crossed his face – when I was a kid I used to think he was angry but that wasn't it at all. He was ashamed. For the first time I could see that. It was as if he'd spent all his life trying to forget what had happened and then there I was to bring it back again. When I found out how he'd died all I could think of was that look in his eyes when he saw me."

I knew from my father's letters to me in Africa the volatile state he'd been in during that time, how little it might have taken to break him.

"There were lots of things going on then," I said. "It wasn't anyone's fault, what happened."

We never mentioned the codicil again after that. But our awareness of it had its effect: it was as if a space had opened up between us where we were free again to be family, to count on each other in that way. An old protectiveness was rekindled in me, what I'd felt toward Rita years before when she'd been simply the unwanted child in our house; only now there was no other side of things to feel guilty about, no troubled father looming in the background except in this sanction he'd given me to fulfil an obligation that he could not.

In December, Rita and Elena decided to move out of residence. For several days the three of us trekked through the cold and slush in the neighbourhoods surrounding the campus searching out FOR RENT signs in windows and tracking down listings from the classifieds.

"I suppose having you along will give us a little credibility," Elena said.

But her resistance to me seemed to be losing its edge, as if she'd expected some betrayal that hadn't come.

The places we saw that fell within their budget turned out mainly to be rooming houses. There was a whole string of them along Spadina Road north of Bloor Street, run-down places with shared kitchen and bath where roaches scurried for cover when lights were turned on, or shoddy renos parcelled into tiny "self-contained" bachelors with two-burner hotplates and beds that folded into the wall. There was a smell in these places of transience, of decaying humanity, though some of the residents, the old men who stared out from doorways, the women who came in dressed in tight skirts and stiletto heels, looked as if they had never known any other idea of home.

We saw a promising place on St. George, a one-bedroom on the tenth floor of a highrise with a view of the city skyline and beyond it of a shimmering sliver of lake.

"I keep a clean building," the superintendent said. "No niggers. No Pakis."

"Thanks, asshole," Elena said, and turned and walked out.

On our fourth day out we looked at a place on Robert Street not far from my own. The house was a pretty Victorian painted in deep and pastel blues. But the apartment, which had been advertised as airy and bright, turned out to be in the basement, the ceilings so low I had to hunch to move beneath them.

"I've got something open on the ground floor as well," the landlord said. He was a man in his early thirties perhaps, slick, well-dressed. When we'd arrived for our appointment his eyes had gone immediately to Elena. "It's a little pricier than this one but very nice."

The apartment took up the whole of the main floor, living room, dining room and kitchen and then a small, carpeted bedroom in an addition at the back. The previous tenants appeared to have left in a hurry – there were still odd bits of furniture and debris strewn about, a tattered armchair, an old rug, a few blackened pots and pans in the kitchen cupboards.

"All it needs," the landlord said, "is a coat of paint."

"Will you be doing that?" I said.

"Well, I suppose I could. For the right tenants."

The living room had a fireplace in bare brick, and a semi-circle of stained glass above the window; the kitchen was slightly run-down but had space enough for a table. Off the back bedroom was a walk-out to a large and secluded garden, a few evergreen shrubs pushing up through the blanket of snow there.

"There's been quite a bit of work put into the garden," the landlord said. "Very nice in the spring."

Rita and Elena and I conferred out back.

"It's more than we can afford," Rita said.

But she and Elena had clearly been taken with the place after some of the other ones we'd seen.

"I could help out," I said. "You might as well have a place that's decent."

The two of them exchanged a look.

"The landlord seems like a bit of a scumbag," Elena said.

"You don't have to live with him, just pay him your rent."

"I dunno," Rita said. "Maybe we should keep looking."

But when we did a second run-through, I could see the two of them already picturing themselves living here, figuring the placement of things, the little order they could establish. Before we'd gone I'd made out cheques for first and last months' rent.

"We'll pay you back when we get our refund from residence," Rita said.

"Don't worry about it."

They were to take possession at the end of the month. Coming back from Centennial the next day I went out of my way to drive past the house – it didn't look quite as pretty, as trim, as when I'd first seen it, simply one of a long line of narrow semi-detached Victorians of which it was perhaps the least graced, for better or worse, by renovation. But still it had an air of welcome about it, of long-lived-in solidity. Perhaps some tradesman or clerk had first owned it, before the immigrants had come and then the speculators, buying up his tiny plot to build what would have been back then a shady suburban retreat.

On a whim one day, shortly after we'd taken the place on Robert, we followed up a listing we'd seen earlier for a place on Toronto Island. A ferry took us out across a steely stretch of lake to where the island's houses were clustered at its far eastern point. There were no cars here, no sounds of the city, only small, placid streets and little houses in clapboard or painted cedar shingles like cottages in a fishing village. There had been a snowfall the previous evening and a blanket of white lay over everything like sugar coating in a fairy tale, drip-dripping from eaves and gurgling in hidden runnels as it melted in the morning sun. It turned out that the place we were looking for had been rented that very morning; but the owner, white-haired and bearded and burly, invited us in for coffee nonetheless. His house was only a tiny place after all, with just a living room and kitchen and then a glassed-in loft up above. But he had set it up so cosily, with knitted rugs all around and bits of bric-a-brac in every cranny, that it seemed as much as a person could ever need in the world.

Walking back to the ferry in the sunlight and snow we began to wonder aloud what it would be like actually to live in this place.

"I could buy a place from my inheritance," I said. "Just the three of us."

I had put the thing as a joke but for an instant we seemed silenced by the idea's suddenly taking on this reality. I had an image of us gathered around a fireplace in our house with a view of the lake while outside the city, the winter, the world, were made distant and small by the surety we formed against them.

"You could afford that?" Elena said.

"I don't know. Maybe."

But then in a few minutes we were already back on the

water and the island was just a thin strip of white against the water's grey.

We drove home together to Mersea at Christmas. Only a few months had passed since I'd last been there and yet in the interim I seemed to have crossed some absolute divide, the point where going back was impossible. I stayed with my Aunt Teresa – she had finished building a scaled-down version of the house my father had started before his death and had established herself there like a matriarch, the farm stretching away behind her and her brother Umberto and his sons spread out in their various houses on either side of her like her minions. Nothing in her house had any associations for me, any history, the new furniture she'd bought, the unpainted walls, the ceramic and marble. It was as if with my father's death my own past on the farm, whatever place I might have once had there, had been erased.

My aunt belonged to a church now that didn't recognize Christmas, some sort of evangelical sect whose services she attended across the border, in Detroit. What little Christmas I had consisted of a lunch at Uncle Umberto's and then a few afternoon visits to cousins for liqueurs and sweets. By Boxing Day the time had already begun to hang heavy on me. Then in the evening, Rita called from the Amhersts'.

"We thought we could leave tomorrow, if you wanted. To get a head start on moving and all that."

I came by for them in the morning. There was a load of things waiting piled in the front hall, towels and bedclothes, old pots, a toaster-oven, an old beanbag chair from the rec room, an old black-and-white television. Mrs. Amherst, in a floral pantsuit of Christmasy reds and greens, greeted me at the door.

"They might as well have a few things if they're going to start out on their own."

But there was a tentativeness in her as if she realized that she was losing them now, that they had never been hers. What had once seemed such a solid thing, the household the Amhersts had formed, now appeared merely provisional, come down to these two young strangers taking their leave, to this heap of borrowed possessions on the hallway floor.

Mr. Amherst had come up from the basement. He looked aged, at once boyish and frail, hovering timidly by while Rita and Elena and I made trips out to the car.

"Let me give you a hand with that stuff."

"It's all right, I think we can manage."

And then we were off, the back seat piled high with Rita's and Elena's things and the three of us sharing the front. As we pulled out of town there seemed a tangible sense of relief among us.

"No place like home," I said, though no longer certain whether we were moving toward it, or away.

V

We moved Rita's and Elena's things into their apartment on the last day of December, along with two mattresses and a kitchen set we'd picked up at the Sally Ann. The landlord had had the whole place repainted in white; in the blaze of snow-reflected light coming in through the windows the apartment looked charmed, incandescent. We made tentative order and then shared a bottle of cheap sparkling wine on the living-room floor, our New Year's Eve.

"You did all right for yourselves," I said.

"Yeah," Rita said. "Thanks."

Within a few days the apartment had taken on the rough shape of home. Elena had claimed the front room as her bedroom, Rita the one at the back. It was the first time since they'd lived together that they'd had separate rooms. With the split, their tastes seemed to have veered from one another's as if the collective aesthetic bred of their years of closeness had suddenly broken down, Elena's room spare and obsessively ordered, Rita's girlish and cluttered. Rita's room had the air of a cottage, with its low ceiling and panelled walls, its windowed view of the still snow-filled back garden.

We stood a moment staring out her window at the snow.

"So how do you like being on your own?"

"I dunno. I keep expecting Mom to come in and make me clean my room."

The middle room, closed off from the front one by pocket doors, had been arranged as the living room, the television in a corner on top of a plastic milk crate, and a large corduroy sofa, apparently new, positioned to face it.

"Nice sofa."

"We thought we'd splurge a little from our residence refund," Elena said.

She seemed to be making a pointed reference to the money that Rita had offered to use to repay what I'd fronted them. It was as if she were marking off territory, downplaying the help I had given.

"It wasn't very expensive," Rita said. "There was a sale."

"Anyway it really sets the room off," I said, and let the matter drop.

I got into the habit of coming by on weekends or on my way home from classes, to help with little jobs around the apartment at first but then staying on for meals and maybe a couple of hours of TV. There was no explicit invitation for these visits, more an understanding, an instinctive accommodation even on Elena's part to the notion that we formed a sort of household, one that stood like the inevitable coalescing of the shadowy alliance that had existed among us in childhood. The days, with their cold and snow, their after-Christmas somnolence, gave their apartment the feel of a winter retreat. The heat there was a bone-soothing radiator heat that left a throb in the air like after music had played; when it came on, the rads clicked and clanged the way the steam pipes had in the greenhouses on my father's farm.

Rita and Elena had worked out a schedule of TV shows they allowed themselves, trashy sitcoms mainly or bad detective dramas like "Charlie's Angels." The shows seemed to function like a common language or code between them from the years they'd spent watching them together. Elena would install herself in the old beanbag chair from their childhood with her cigarettes and a can of Coke at her side and a bowl of popcorn or chips in her lap and focus in on these shows like someone in the thrall of a hated rival, looking never more vulnerable than she did then, sitting there in her scruffy house clothes and stockinged feet so obviously at war with herself, so taken in.

"I can't believe this crap," she'd say, but there was always the same wordless single-mindedness in her whenever one of the shows from their schedule was coming on.

Sometimes when I came by, Elena would have friends over. These were women she'd apparently met in her classes or in a discussion group she was part of, a few who came by fairly regularly and then a changing roster of others. Some were prankish and loud, full of bravado, punked up in leather and spiky hair or wearing oversized Arrow shirts or rolled-cuffed blazers obviously culled from the Goodwill; others had the same terse, sardonic air as Elena herself, which when joined with hers made everything they said seem part of some on-going inside joke. Toward me, these women tended to show not so much hostility as a kind of willed indifference, the making a point of excluding me from their conversation. Elena would neither support them in this nor discourage them, allowing me a place of sorts as if I were a roommate passing through but in the same way suggesting I was extraneous, not a part of them.

These women would change the mood of the apartment like some fleeting shift of light, leaving afterwards always the small, not unpleasant bruise of their presence, the dim, background sense of something known and not, never quite put into words. You could almost smell them in the place, their particular energy, the almost cultish air of agreement that bound them in their little circle like a haze of cigarette smoke. I was always aware of their bodies, not so much as sexual things, but more like phrases or words in some unknown language; the word "maternal" kept urging itself on me but it wasn't right, was perhaps just a way of explaining a physicality that had none of the usual messages or points of reference. I kept wanting to please them in some way, as if in so doing I could gain access to this secret energy, get in on their joke, but it didn't take long before I'd been put off by the little pools of silence that tended to stretch out around any comment from me.

Rita and I didn't talk much about these friends, even though their import began to grow less and less mistakable.

"They're quite the troupe," I said. "A little forbidding."

But Rita wouldn't engage.

"I don't know. They're all right."

"Do you get along with them?"

"Sort of. They're Elena's friends, I don't really know them very well. And then they're pretty political and all that."

"So that kind of thing doesn't interest you?"

"It's not that. It's just – they make it seem like I'm a part of them somehow, like I'll just go along with them. It can get a bit weird sometimes."

Then one day I came by to find that Elena had had her hair cut, short, her long feminine tresses and curls given way to a kind of homely featurelessness. The change was so dramatic that it seemed she'd switched personalities overnight.

"It's a pretty big difference," I said.

"Maybe that's the point."

It was as if a whole layer of her had been stripped away to reveal this stranger beneath. Only now did it occur to me that this thing, this difference in her, might have to be dealt with in some way. In Rita, too, there had been a shift: she kept the slightest distance between herself and Elena now as if Elena were charged, electrostatic. I'd make joking references to her about Elena's "political" friends, trying to break the ice, but always the same screen would get thrown up, the same clouded look would come into her eyes. She had grown up with this woman, traded make-up and clothes, been a sister to her. Perhaps there were things about their relationship she preferred not to know, entanglements she didn't want to look into. Or perhaps the thing was simpler than that, for her as for all of us, just a matter of what was easiest, safe, what would least disturb the comfortable calm we'd settled into.

Toward the end of February we got the news that Mr. Amherst was ill. Everything happened very fast: the word came that he'd gone into hospital and then a few days later that he'd been transferred up to special care in London.

"The Big C," Elena said. "Not that Mom would ever come out and say it."

There was a bitterness in her I couldn't place, whose object I couldn't decipher. As a child she'd always been the good one, the well-behaved one, Rita's foil. But now she never spoke of the Amhersts without this undertone, this air of dismissal.

I drove them down to London. Stretched out in his bed Mr. Amherst looked small as a child, his body just a frugal hieroglyph against the bedsheets. His skin was so jaundiced it looked as if it had been painted up for a gag.

"You cut your hair," he said to Elena.

"Yeah. For a change."

"Well I always wanted a boy," he said.

He had pancreatic cancer. Elena learned this not from Mrs. Amherst but by making enquiries at the nurses' station, passing the information on to Rita and me when we went down to the cafeteria for a smoke.

"That's why he's yellow like that," she said. "The bile or something."

But back in his room, where Mrs. Amherst sat in grim, smiling guardianship next to his bed, no one made any reference to his condition.

Rita and Elena stayed on in London through the weekend. But then they'd been back at school only a matter of days before Mr. Amherst died. His death had come so quickly it seemed unreal. It was hard to gauge what it meant to Rita and Elena, who Mr. Amherst had been to them.

"It was stupid of her to send us back to school," Elena said. "We should have been there."

"Maybe she thought he was getting better," Rita said.

"Right. She could have looked it up in a medical book, for Christ's sake. He was lucky he lasted as long as he did."

We drove back to Mersea for the funeral. There was a viewing the night before at the funeral home, Mrs. Amherst sitting in stony composure between Rita and Elena in the receiving line yet seeming afflicted beyond words. The casket was open but they'd been unable to hide the jaundice in Mr. Amherst's skin. It felt indiscreet somehow to see him like that, shrivelled and yellowed like a dried reed, so much slighter in death than he'd been even in life.

When I went by the house after the funeral the next day, Mrs. Amherst's breath reeked of liquor.

"It was very kind of you to come," she said, her face drawn up in false self-control like a mask.

When other visitors came it was Rita who covered for her, taking coats and offering coffee, Elena meanwhile hovering gloomily in the background seeming at once angered and humiliated, not only by her mother's drunkenness but by her father's death, by the sordidness of it, the intractability. In the small-town domesticity of the Amhersts' house she looked like a foreign species, someone who'd walked in by mistake. For a while she stood pretending to look through a bookshelf against one wall of the living room. I could see some of the guests smiling nervously in her direction, trying to work up the resolve to approach her, then finally turning away.

Rita was wearing the same dark dress suit she had worn to my own father's funeral less than a year before.

"You don't have to stay," she said. "It must be awkward for you."

"It's all right."

Coming out of the bathroom upstairs I slipped into a little room whose shelves and glass-coloured cabinets held

Mr. Amherst's collection of toys. Things his great-grandfather had made, mainly, a wooden train set, a tiny village complete with people and houses and trees, but also others, old jack-in-the-boxes, yellowing painted-cheeked dolls, that had obviously been bought. I had seen the collection only once before, when I'd stumbled on it by chance during one of my Sunday visits years earlier. It struck me as odd suddenly how it had been sequestered away here all these years like some shameful secret. It looked even more forlorn now than it had when I'd first seen it, as if something in Mr. Amherst, some passion or sense of wonder, had remained forever closed up here, had never found any expression outside this roomful of yellowing, unused toys.

The day after the funeral Rita called me at my aunt's to say she and Elena would be ready to leave the following morning.

"I thought you'd stay on a while," I said.

"I don't know. Mom thinks it's best."

Mrs. Amherst came to the door when I arrived for them. She seemed to have managed to pull herself together: there was a sense in the house of some gargantuan effort made, of everything drawn up around her like a cloak.

"There's no point in their missing any more school than they have to," she said.

She was wearing rouge on her cheeks, just slightly over-applied. Around her the house sat in calm, quiet orderliness like an extension of her: this was what she had always been to me, these varnished tabletops, these lace doilies, this cut glass; these were the things that had always seemed to hold her in place.

But once we were on the road it came out that she was thinking of selling up and returning to England. There seemed something unconscionable in this, preposterous, that these solidities she had ruled over could be allowed to vanish without a trace.

"But she's been here for years," I said.

Rita was staring out through the side window.

"I guess she never really felt she fit in," she said. "She doesn't have much to keep her here now."

There was an emotion in the air I couldn't place, a sort of inchoate churning of things, the inexpressibility of loss. In a matter of days, the very foundations of Rita's and Elena's lives, their whole idea of home, had shifted, fallen away.

"There's you two," I said.

"Yeah." But there wasn't any anger in this. "Though maybe it's a question of who's leaving who."

It sounded like a confession, the acknowledgement of the need to run, to get past, to start again. No looking back. In the rear seat Elena had stretched out and closed her eyes as if nursing a headache.

"Thank god it's over," she said, and then we were on the highway again, counting the miles across a desolate February landscape.

VI

Not long after we'd returned to the city Rita showed up at my apartment one afternoon, unannounced, a stack of library books cradled in one arm.

"I was wondering if I could work here for a while," she said, not quite looking me in the eye.

The books' grey, generic covers gave them the look of props, imitations of books. At the top of them, incongruously, was a tattered paperback.

"Everything okay at your place?"

"Yeah. I just needed to get out for a bit, that's all."

She set herself up at the kitchen table as she used to do in the fall, spreading her books around her, setting a writing pad out for notes. But when I came to look in on her, she had the paperback propped open inside one of the library books.

"You want a coffee or something?"

"Sure. Great."

I hadn't really talked to her much about Mr. Amherst's death – it seemed like something that had lodged in her throat,

36

some word, some tail-end of a thought, that she couldn't get out. But I couldn't find the right way to bring the matter up.

"I was meaning to ask you if you're going to be all right for money now," I said. "If it's going to be a problem."

"I don't know. Mom didn't really talk about it. I could always get a part-time job or something."

"I should give you something to tide you over."

"You don't have to do that."

But I went into my room then and there and made out a cheque to her. I wavered a moment over the amount, then settled on a thousand dollars. That was less than half of what I received every month from my cousins from the sort of mortgage they paid me to buy out my father's share of the farm. But when I handed the cheque over to Rita I felt embarrassed at its apparent excess.

"I can't accept this," she said.

I felt like my father: emotion in him had always been translated across gifts, sums of money, sudden acts of excessive generosity.

"You don't want to be working while you're in school," I said.

She eyed the cheque uncomfortably.

"I'll work it off in the summer."

"That's fine."

Evening came on. I invited Rita to stay for supper, pouring us wine from a gallon I'd brought from home. While I busied myself with pots and pans she sat chopping vegetables at the kitchen table with a careful, small-handed deliberateness. Between her and Elena, it was Elena, oddly, who was the more domestic one, who seemed more at home in a kitchen, who in their apartment would instinctively clear away glasses and ashtrays, re-establish order; whereas in Rita there was always a tentativeness about such things as if she had never quite grasped the essence of them.

"I was thinking about something you wrote in one of your letters from Africa," she said. "About the first time we'd seen each other again after I'd gone to live with the Amhersts."

I could still remember that reunion: it had been a year or more after she'd gone, and the Amhersts had come in their car to St. Mike's to invite me to lunch after mass. In my memory of the event it had the feel of a scene from a movie, my father turning away from me at the church steps and then the waiting car, the shadow of Rita in back.

"You said you felt like you couldn't reach me. That I was like a picture, that's how you put it. That you knew there was something behind it but you couldn't get at it."

I was surprised I'd been as open as that, had always thought of our letters as more careful, more oblique.

"That more or less says it, I guess."

"It was just – I don't know. When I thought about all the things I didn't understand back then, how stupid everything was."

"You were only a kid," I said.

"I know. It's just sad, that's all."

We had our dinner in the living room, Rita taking her place at the end of the couch. We had got into the habit of eating there in the fall whenever she'd stayed for meals, to avoid the knocking together of elbows and knees at the cramped kitchen table.

"Sometimes I think how strange it is that I spent the first six years of my life on your father's farm and then never saw it again," Rita said. "Not once. I've even never gone past it. It's like some fairy-tale place that stopped existing once I was gone, even though the whole time I was growing up it was there, just a couple of miles away. I have this picture of it in my head, how it was then, and it's never changed. But it's probably completely different now."

"I could take you there one day, if you want."

"Do you remember your neighbours from across the road? What was their name? They were so blond, almost white. I guess they were Mennonites."

"The Dycks. We never had that much to do with them."

"I went over there once, on my own. I remember it so clearly. I must have been about five – I just crossed the road like that, as if it had only just occurred to me that it was possible to do that, that there wasn't some invisible wall holding me in. And then there I was in this completely new place, with that little red house they had, and the barn across from it, and the trees, those huge trees. A man came out from the house, this big, blond man with boots on – I knew I should have been afraid but he was smiling, and he came over and just picked me up as if I hadn't done anything wrong at all, as if this was exactly where I was supposed to be. We went into a room in the barn that was full of pigeons – there must have been a hundred of them, it seemed like, up along the rafters and then in some nests that were built along the walls. He took me to one of the nests and there was a pigeon inside, and he moved her a bit to show me the eggs she was sitting on. He never said a word, at least that's how I remember it. He just showed me these eggs as if he was sharing a secret with me."

Outside, it had begun to snow. Great, fat flakes were falling against the windows and into the street, muffling the sound of traffic and the whirr of the streetcars as they passed.

"It's funny how people remember things," Rita said. "Like Elena. Some of the things she comes out with."

"Such as?"

"I don't know. Some of the things she says about Dad, for instance."

She had barely touched her food. She stared down at it now, moving it around on her plate with her fork.

"What kinds of things?"

"Just something she said. Not to me, to one of her friends. About our being adopted and all that."

"That seems pretty indisputable."

"It's not that. It's just how she put it."

She was still staring down at her plate.

"It's bothering you," I said.

"It's just – she made it seem like he was some kind of weirdo or something. Because we were girls and all that. The way he used to watch us sometimes."

None of this accorded with what I knew of Mr. Amherst. He'd been such a harmless man, with his timid anecdotes and jokes, his boyish deference to his wife. Toward Rita and Elena he'd always seemed to maintain a sort of self-deprecatory pride as if they were special things he couldn't quite account for, didn't quite understand.

"Did he ever do anything to you?" I said. "I mean, touch you or anything."

"No. That's just it. It wasn't anything like that."

She still wouldn't look at me.

"It was like she was taking him away from me," she said. "It was like he was all I had but she was taking that too."

She had started to cry. I went over and took her plate from her, and because she crumpled a bit then, because I could feel her body giving in to me, I sat down beside her and put an arm around her.

"She's just angry at him, that's all," I said. "She's angry at him for dying."

We sat for a few minutes without speaking while she cried. She had turned in to me slightly so her head was resting against my shoulder. At some point, without even quite being aware what I was doing, I leaned in and kissed her lightly on the forehead.

"Are you going to be all right?" I said finally.

"Yeah." She wiped her eyes. "Sorry about that."

"There's nothing to be sorry about."

The snow was still falling when she left. I watched from the corner window as she made fresh tracks in it on the sidewalk before disappearing in its swirl toward home. For the longest time after she'd gone I could still feel the impress of her body against mine, the heat of her skin against my lips.

I dreamt that night, for the first time in months, of my father. He appeared rising out of the pond in which he had drowned himself, dripping algae and weeds like some underworld god, at once himself and not, at once the particular gloom he had been in my life and something more elemental, more general, the force of all fathers in their haunting, larger-than-life peculiarness. Afterwards, awake in the night, I thought of Rita cradled against me and it broke my heart to think of this need in us, this endless procession of fathers we turned ourselves over to as if we huddled still in some primal dark, guided only by the animal sense of what could protect us, and what could hurt.

Once as children, Rita and I had crouched in silence behind a row of packing crates in the barn to hide from my father. We'd heard his footsteps coming up while we were playing, and had hid, with no other motive than the fear that he should find us there, being children. Rita couldn't have been much more than three at the time and yet she had crouched beside me in perfect, almost unbreathing stillness, so feral had been the awareness of danger in her. We could see my father like an enemy through the slits in the packing crates, could feel the barest tremble of earth as his steps moved near, then away; and then he was gone. Afterwards, I'd wanted to hold Rita in my arms and take her fear from her, make it small. But instead with a ten-year-old's diffidence I'd simply helped her up roughly from her place, and sent her home.

VII

The next morning, a Saturday, she came by my apartment again, simply there against a blaze of frigid, snow-reflected light at the fire-escape door, hunched and shivering from the cold.

"I was on my way to the market. I didn't mean to bother you."

She was wearing an old oversized blue parka I remembered from her high-school days, gone a bit ragged now.

"Not at all. Really. Come in."

We stood shyly at the door while she took off her things.

"Have you had any breakfast?"

"Actually, no."

"I'll make you some."

She settled herself at the kitchen table near the rad while I started breakfast, huddling up against the heat. The sun coming in through the window there lit bits of orange and red in her hair.

"I wanted to say I was sorry again. About last night. I didn't mean to break down like that."

"Don't mention it."

She had pulled her legs up on the chair, had pulled her hands up into the floppy sleeves of her sweater. I had the sense I could have whisked her up from where she sat, this economical package she'd hunched down to, and hardly felt the weight of her. I remembered her as a baby, how hopelessly tiny her limbs had been then, how soft the underside of her head, how I'd been afraid of breaking her each time I'd held her.

"I hope you and Elena can work this thing out," I said. "Maybe if you talked to her about it."

"She's not that easy to talk to these days."

"I guess you're right."

We ate in the kitchen. The heat from the stove and the rad had made the room steamy.

"Do you have any plans for the day? I mean, apart from the market."

"Oh. That wasn't anything important."

From the moment she'd arrived it had seemed that there was some tone between us that would have been the right one, but we hadn't found it yet.

"We could go for a drive if you wanted."

I had tried to put this offhandedly but still felt infected by the intimacy of the previous evening, the memory of holding her in my arms.

"Actually," she said, "that would be very nice."

We set out early in the afternoon. Almost as a kind of joke, we'd settled on driving down to Niagara Falls – Rita had never been there before, though it had been a regular destination for people from Mersea.

44

"I remember that film," she said. "With Marilyn Monroe. The one where her boat is drifting toward the edge of the falls."

The weather had turned overnight to a brittle cold, the city streets skinned over with an unmelting slick of icy wet from the previous evening's snow. But out on the outskirts, the cold seemed to have sucked the roads dry. We followed the expressway through the built-up outer suburbs – they stretched unbroken for miles, a string of quaint-sounding older communities, Streetsville, Port Credit, Lorne Park, that had slowly been swallowed up by the city, their sea of snow-covered roofs just visible above the sound walls that lined the expressway. Further out, the houses gave way to warehouses, silver-glassed office buildings, the occasional factory sitting desolate amid fields of asphalt or snowy rubble. Watching the landscape fly by us from the warmth of the car put me in mind of the Sunday afternoons that Rita and I used to spend alone watching TV when we were small, Rita cradled against me in my father's armchair in the living room's sheltering warmth while outside it was winter and cold.

Past Hamilton I veered off onto a secondary highway. We were in open country now, the road flanked by grey-limbed orchards and by the orderly rows of a crop I couldn't place at first: vineyards. It was strange to see grapevines in that flat, snowbound countryside, frozen there in their rows by the bright cold like startled pilgrims.

"Almost like home," I said, but then, seeing that Rita hadn't understood, added, "The vineyards. Like Italy."

"Oh." We seldom spoke about Italy. Sometimes it would come to me to share some memory with her, but then the instant I'd try to put it into words it would seem false. "I

45

guess you made your own wine and all that, when you were there."

"To tell you the truth I can't remember," I said, and laughed.

"When I was in England, I kept imagining that that was what Italy might look like. Those rolling hills and little villages."

She had been to England a few years before, to see Mrs. Amherst's family.

"I wouldn't have thought England, exactly. But I suppose from here it might look that way. All those old buildings and things."

Mrs. Amherst was travelling to England for Easter, with the thought of looking into her possible return there. Rita hadn't spoken much about the trip; there had been some talk of her and Elena going along, but more, it seemed, as a matter of form than as a real possibility. The few times Rita had spoken about her previous trip, it had always been in a forced positive tone that had suggested its opposite.

"Elena was thinking of having a party at our apartment on Good Friday," she said. "Since Mom won't be around for us to go home. But I guess you'll be going back to Mersea then."

"I don't know. Maybe not."

"It'll be her friends, mainly. Though I think she wants it to be a sort of birthday party for me."

"That's right. I forgot."

There had never been any sort of protocol for us around Rita's birthday. Every year it came around less as a day I remembered than as one I passed through: it seemed too intimate, somehow, to commemorate a birth which I'd seen the blood of, which our mother had died from.

"There's someone I want you to meet," Rita said. "Maybe he'll be there."

So she'd met a boy, then. I was surprised how casually she'd brought him up, how much her casualness hurt me.

"Is it someone you're seeing?" I said, though in a tone gentler than I'd intended.

But she blushed.

"It's nothing like that. He's just a friend."

There was an instant's awkward silence.

"I've told him about you," she said.

"What's there to tell?"

"Oh. Stuff."

It was already late afternoon by the time we arrived at Niagara Falls. The town looked smaller and meaner than I remembered it from when I'd come with my family as a teen, although then, too, we had come in the off-season, half the sights closed down and the town giving off an air of desolation like after the departure of a circus or fair. I remembered my father on that trip being in unusually good spirits, pulling wads of tens and twenties from his wallet to get us into museums and laughing with Uncle Alfredo over the exhibits in Ripley's and Madame Tussaud's. But it had already been years by then since Rita had left us.

There was a huge parking lot, nearly deserted, across the road from the falls. We pulled up there and stepped out from the comfort of the car into a bitter, mist-soaked wind. Even at this distance the spray from the falls fanned out in great, gusting sheets, rainbowing in the setting sun before falling frozen to the pavement. The path down to the observation lounge and shops at the edge of the falls was a treachery of ice despite the heaps of salt that had been sprinkled there. In one of the thicker patches Rita instinctively hooked her arm in mine for support, but then let go apologetically when the pavement cleared.

"I suppose it's not the best time of year to have come," I said.

"I don't know. You could write something about it. The power of nature and that. Like the letters you used to write me from Africa."

"You're making fun of me."

"No I'm not. I thought your letters were beautiful. Really. Sometimes they were the only things I had to look forward to."

We had come to the falls. Out in the islanded shallows upstream, the river was covered with ice and snow. But here at the brink the water coursed freely. It was such a relentless thing, this surge and surge and surge, this aeons-ancient heaving forward like the bloodrush of a continent.

The spray had built up massive pillars of ice, great phantom shapes that loomed up from the folds of rock at the falls' edges like rising spirits.

"It's pretty amazing," Rita said.

We stood a few moments without speaking. A sudden gust of wind sent a shower of spray against us, and Rita sank deeper into her coat. I stood behind her and instinctively opened my own coat to enfold her within it, holding her to me; and then for several minutes we stood like that without tension, staring into the falls, though it was clear in the way I held her, in the way she leaned in against me, that some line had been stepped over, that some emotion that had been hovering between us barely acknowledged had grown suddenly real. I remembered a picture in my grade-one reader of a young boy and girl, brother and sister, making their way along a rotting footbridge over a rocky chasm, and had the same sense of beginning a dangerous crossing. In the picture, a guardian angel had hovered over the two; but still the outcome had seemed uncertain, a matter of one careful step after another.

The sun had almost set.

"I guess we'll freeze if we stand here much longer," I said.

We walked back to the car in silence. For a few minutes the sense of our closeness lingered between us like a note struck in a bell; but then the strangeness began to settle in.

"Are you okay?" I said.

"Yeah. I guess so."

We drove back through town toward the expressway. With nightfall, the town had taken on an eerie, dream-like quality. A few marquees had come on in neon blues and reds above some of the restaurants and museums; on the sidewalks a few straggling shoppers were making their way through the bitter cold toward home. At a traffic light an ancient big-finned Chevrolet crammed with teenagers wheeled out in front of us from the lot of a corner take-out, then rounded a corner and disappeared down a darkened sidestreet.

Out on the expressway there was nothing for us to focus on in the growing dark but the stream of tail-lights racing ahead of us. I caught a glimpse of Rita hugging her window, staring out into nothing.

"We could stop somewhere to eat, if you want."

"It's all right. I'm not that hungry."

The wind had picked up. On the Burlington Skyway, a gust of it caught the car broadside and seemed ready to heave it over the rails. Then toward Toronto it began to snow, in small, blizzardy flakes that formed shifting patterns on the surface of the highway. For some reason the sight of the city's skyline through the snow, something distantly hopeful in it, brought a lump to my throat.

The silence between us had begun to grow oppressive.

"Maybe we could catch a film or something," I said.

But if was as if our parts were interchangeable, as if we were both merely trying to find the way to say no.

"I don't know. There's some work I should probably do."

When I pulled up to her house, Elena was standing at the front window like a waiting parent. She stared out expressionless toward the car, arms folded over her chest.

"I'll call you," I said, and though conscious of Elena watching, still I leaned over and brushed my lips against Rita's, the barest flicker of a kiss.

My heart was pounding.

"I'd better go," Rita said, and then without looking back she was out in the cold, and home.

VIII

Sunday morning, early, there was a knock at my door. I hurried up out of bed expecting Rita again, but it was Sid Roscoe from upstairs.

"Sorry, man. I didn't mean to get you out of bed."

Sid had moved in above me in January. In his first few weeks he had come by to borrow things – tools, some paper, a bread knife, the knife coming back flecked with small, greenish bits of what I took to be hash. Then at some point I'd made the mistake of lending him a bit of money, and afterwards he had more or less dropped out of sight.

"I just wanted to leave that cash off," he said now, and my first irritation at seeing him abated.

"Sure, sure. Come on in." He was dressed in his usual street clothes, boots, jeans, leather jacket, but I couldn't have said if he was just rising or just coming in. "You want a coffee or something?"

"Don't mind if I do."

He took a seat in the kitchen and went into a long explanation about why he was late with the money, something to do with a deal that hadn't gone through and a late paycheque from the bar on Queen Street where he worked as a bouncer. I had developed a habit of only half-listening to him when he talked, to save the trouble of sorting truth from fabrication. Even this money he'd borrowed: when I'd first met him he had dropped comments about the large sums that passed through his hands from his dealing, and yet he had had to come to me for the piddling amount he was repaying now.

"Don't worry about it," I said when he'd finished, neutrally, not wanting to sound either encouraging or reprimanding. It was hard to tell with Sid when he might suddenly call up short my low expectations of him. Once, for instance, he'd mentioned that he did some writing, and then had actually shown up the following day with a sheaf of stories in hand, neatly typed with uniform margins and carefully whited-out corrections. The stories had surprised me, a bit crude in execution but with a real power to them. In one, a man went out on a weekend drinking binge that ended with his picking a woman up in a bar and then seriously beating her. What was chilling in the story was how it was presented utterly without judgement or excuse, stuck simply to the plainest telling of what had happened. Sometimes Sid would bring women home with him from work and I would think of the story when I heard their laughter on the stairwell, the thud of Sid's fire-escape door.

"So I saw that woman you drove off with yesterday," he said. "Pretty classy."

It took me an instant to realize he was talking about Rita.

"That's my sister."

"Victor, my boy, you've been holding out on me."

I felt the anger rise in me.

"She's out of your league."

He covered his hurt with a smile.

"I'm sure you're right," he said, his voice dripping false magnanimity.

The incident soured what little good feeling remained in me from my day with Rita. In my memory of it, the day had the dreamy ambiguity of something utterly hermetic and private, that had happened outside of time and space; it seemed a violation that there had been this witness to it. I felt like a criminal at the instant of a first crucial misstep; from this, all the rest would unravel.

It was afternoon before I'd gathered the courage to call Rita's.

"Gone to the library," Elena said. "At least that's what she said."

"What's that supposed to mean?"

"She said the same thing yesterday."

"We decided to take a drive."

"So I hear."

I felt a throb of paranoia.

"Just tell her I called," I said.

By evening she hadn't called back. I went out and in a few minutes found myself at the head of her street, then just across the way from her house. Through the front window I could see Elena seated at her desk silhouetted by the glow of her desk lamp; as I watched, Rita came to her doorway and stood leaning against the door frame in conversation. From where I stood I could just make out the movements of her face as she spoke. It was like reading directly through to a subtext: she was talking, smiling, responding, and yet beneath was this complex, subtle shifting of emotion as if I were seeing through to some darkness in her, some side of her where forces I knew nothing of contended.

I went home and phoned her.

"I tried to call," she said. There was still a note of timid intimacy in her voice. "I guess you were out."

"I went for a walk."

Now that I had her on the line I had no idea what to say to her.

"I thought maybe we ought to talk," I said.

I asked her to come by the following evening. But already we were getting too far away from whatever it was that had happened at the Falls, whatever the feeling had been between us then. It was the sort of feeling, it seemed now, that could only have been right for those few minutes it lasted, that had to have come out of nothing and then had to return there.

From the moment she arrived at my apartment, the two of us awkwardly sidestepping and shifting at the door as she took off her coat, everything seemed wrong. She had dressed as she might have for a first date, in nylons and a cream-coloured skirt and a silky white blouse. We both seemed aware at once how inappropriate this was.

"I shouldn't stay long," she said. "End of term and all that."

I went into the kitchen to make coffee. I caught a glimpse from there of Rita sitting stiffly in the living-room armchair like someone awaiting a reprimand.

"There's wine, if you want," I said stupidly.

"Sure. I mean, if that's what you're having."

I was stuck then not knowing whether to bring coffee or wine and ended up bringing out both, in an awkward flurry of glasses and cups that then sat incongruous and untouched on the coffee table.

"How are things with Elena?" I said.

"They're all right." The way her eyes avoided me reminded me of my visits to her at the Amhersts' when she was a child. "I was probably just overreacting before. I mean, she's always been really supportive and everything."

There was a knock at the fire-escape door. Rita's eye went to it with what looked like a mix of panic and relief.

"I guess you should get that," she said.

It was Sid.

"Hey, Vic." He was dressed in an elegant black overcoat I'd never seen him in before. "Just wondering if you wanted to grab a drink."

But his gaze went immediately to Rita. It was as if he had been watching for her from upstairs, ready to pounce.

"So this must be your sister," he said, flashing me a mock-innocent grin.

Before I could find a way to deflect him he was inside introducing himself.

"Wine. Very romantic. Mind if I stay for some?"

He had directed the question not at me but at Rita.

"I guess not," Rita said, looking toward me uncertainly. "I'll get you a glass."

"It's all right, I'll find one."

He put on a gallantry around Rita I'd never witnessed in him, pouring wine for her, asking her questions about herself. Rita seemed baffled by him at first, warily putting him off;

55

but then slowly he managed to draw her in. He had a way of disarming people with the impression he gave that he needn't quite be taken seriously, that he was someone you simply observed; and then suddenly he was the one in control.

"So I suppose you're a brain like your brother here."

"I dunno. Something like that."

"I'm going back to school in the fall, eh. I've just got a few courses left for my degree. What I really want to get into though is film."

He had never mentioned to me having been to university. But when he quizzed Rita on her courses he seemed to know the terminology well enough. It turned out – or so he said – that he'd actually done one of the courses that Rita was currently enrolled in.

"I've still got all the old exams and things, if you want to come up and have a look at them. It'll just take a minute to dig them out."

Rita's eye went to me again.

"I guess that's all right," she said. But we both seemed merely at the whim of Sid's momentum now. "I mean, if Vic doesn't mind."

"No, no. That's fine."

She was gone for more than half an hour. I heard the creak of their footsteps on the hardwood above, then the low reverberation of Sid's stereo. When she came back down it was clear from her distracted air that she was stoned.

"I guess I better get going," she said.

"Did you get those exams?"

"Uh, no, he couldn't find them." A pause. "He asked me out."

"Oh." It only occurred to me now, from the dead note in

her voice, that she was probably thinking I'd planned all this, that I'd set her up. That that was my way of dealing with things. "What did you say?"

"I said yes." She wouldn't look at me. "I thought it'd be fun."

We'd remained standing at the fire-escape door. She had gone up without her coat and now she removed it from the rack near the door and stood staring at it in her arms.

"So when are you seeing him?"

"Thursday, I guess. He's off work then."

"Just before your party."

"Yeah."

The stupidest, the easiest thing seemed to be to let things stand as they were.

"So I guess I'll see you at the party then," I said.

"Sure."

I stood watching from the living-room window as she walked along College through the pools of light the street-lamps cast. At Spadina she paused, looked around and behind as if searching for something; and then instead of continuing westward and home, she turned south on Spadina and dropped out of view. It struck me that I had no idea where she was going. There seemed something vaguely encouraging in that, reassuring, as if she were a character in a book who had suddenly veered off the page, stepped into some secret life where there were other ways of working things, other possibilities. Without quite knowing what I intended, I grabbed my coat and hurried out after her – I could run into her, on neutral ground there on a night-time city street, and something would be different. But by the time I'd got to the corner she was nowhere in sight.

IX

I ran into Sid the following morning at the convenience store in our building. He was buying groceries – bread, tins of soup, canned salmon – though he could have got the same things for half the price at the market five minutes away.

"So you're seeing Rita," I said.

But he wasn't playing the matter at all as I'd expected.

"It's no big deal," he said, almost peevish. "I'm just going to show her around a bit, that's all."

He seemed almost surprised now at his own good fortune, as if he thought of himself after all, despite his talk, his hopes, as simply what he appeared to be, a two-bit drifter trying to make his way. I thought of how his apartment had looked the few times I'd been up to it, how it had reeked of transience: dirty dishes piled up, dirty clothes strewn about, the furnishings mainly milk crates and planks and the windows tacked over with yellowing newsprint that let in a weird, sallow light.

"Anyway it's none of my business," I said.

I had papers due for my courses at Centennial but couldn't put my hand to any work. Everything seemed askew, as if a story had been proceeding in some normal way and then an error, a shift, had sent it off into strangeness. Even the weather, which almost overnight had turned spring-like and warm, seemed a kind of senseless reversion, the melting snow, the patches of greenish lawn re-emerging here and there littered with the debris that had collected over the winter. In the lot of the service station which my apartment looked onto across Huron, a great mound of snow that had been built up by progressive ploughings during the winter was slowly melting down through its layers as if time were moving backwards; in a matter of days only bits of gravel and grime would remain like the insoluble residue of all the past weeks and months.

I called my Aunt Teresa to let her know I wasn't returning home for Easter.

"Oh, it's you," she said, as if she'd had to fight to dredge my image up from her memory. It seemed like years since we had spoken, like we'd never been part of a family.

"Say hello to everyone," I said.

"Well. We can't force you to come home if you don't want to."

Thursday I skipped my classes and spent the whole day searching for a birthday gift for Rita. I was in and out of gift shops, jewellers, antique stores; every item seemed wrong, seemed infected with our strangeness, open to misinterpretation. The shopkeepers offered up their suggestions, laid trinkets out on their counters; all wrong. It was a kind of obsession, finding the proper thing, what would hit the right note, would say, this is where we stand, just here. Then, impulsively, I bought a watch, too elegant, too expensive, already chiding myself as the saleslady wrapped it for me, already knowing it was excessive, that that was the message of it. I couldn't possibly give it to her; at home, I simply stuffed it away still in its plastic bag at the top of my closet.

It was getting toward evening; I didn't want to be in if Rita came by the building to meet up with Sid. I got in the car and drove. The streets were clogged with rush-hour traffic; at one point, going down toward the lakeshore thinking to stop in a little park there, I missed a lane change and was forced out onto the expressway. At the end of the on ramp I had a moment of panic as the ramp narrowed and nearly pulled into the path of an oncoming truck. Its lights flashed, its horn sounded, and then somehow I ended up squeezed onto the shoulder, fighting the slide of the wheels against the gravel until I was able to bring the car to a stop.

Another car had already pulled up behind me. A bearded man in a parka got out and came to my window.

My heart was still pounding.

"Is everything all right?" he said.

"I think so."

"You came pretty close to that truck."

He eyed my car uneasily, its luxurious bulk. Perhaps he was afraid that I'd stolen it, that I was on the run. I saw myself for an instant as he might, through a veil of fear and good intentions: I could be anyone, capable of anything.

"You sure you're going to be okay?"

"Yes. Thanks."

More than my near accident, the look in the man's eyes left me unnerved. It was as if I had suddenly lost any internal sense of what I was: for that instant I was only what he reflected me back as, an unknown quantity, a threat.

I took the first exit and headed north. I had got it into my head to visit my friend Michael, though I hadn't seen him since the fall. It took half an hour of driving, past older stretches of city and then up through the slow deterioration into discount furniture shops and strip malls, to get out to his suburb. From a distance the little island of tidy bungalows his subdivision formed cast up a halo of collective light like some protective dome that enclosed it.

Michael came to the door looking dishevelled and tired as if he'd just risen from a sleep.

"I was on my way home from Centennial," I lied.

The television was on the living room, but the rest of the house was dark. There were no toys in the hall, no baby sounds in the background.

"Come on in. It's good to see you."

He offered me a beer. I followed him into the kitchen expecting it, for some reason, to be in shambles. But everything was in purest, pristine order, as if in waiting.

"Suzie left me," Michael said, before I asked. "A couple of months ago."

"Oh."

There was an awkward silence. We sat nursing our beers at the kitchen table like two interlopers, out of place there.

"What happened exactly?" I said.

"You know how it is. You don't notice the signs at the time, and then it's too late. She was pretty young when we got married and all that. I guess she felt she'd never had much of a life. It's just hard with the kid and everything."

He set about to make us some supper, setting out food-stuffs and pots with an instinctive carefulness and frugality as if not to disturb the kitchen's ordered calm. I thought of the three of us having supper there the fall before, drunk on homemade wine.

"I'm thinking of moving back to the city," he said. "There's no point keeping a house like this. My father jacked the rent up just after Suzie left, that's how he thinks about these things."

He talked a bit about the things he would do, his new freedom, but it was clear that Suzie's departure had broken him. The baby would be about a year old now – he said the silence was the hardest thing, coming home every day and instinctively waiting to hear a child's sounds that didn't come.

"They're back with her mother now, she looks after the kid when Suzie's at work. But it's not as if her mother and I ever got along. I get it coming and going, from her family and mine. You just become this pariah or something."

His father, though he'd never approved of the marriage, had hardly spoken to him since the split. He was like that, Michael said. Twenty years before, he had disowned Michael's oldest sister when she had got pregnant out of wedlock. She had eventually married, got a good job, had more children. But in all those years their father had never spoken to her again.

"You have to understand what that's like. What kind of a mind it takes to cut off one of your children like that. But here's the thing: a couple of years ago Suzie and I went to Italy and I got talking to this old woman in the village who told me my mother was already pregnant with my sister when she got married. There was even some talk that my dad wasn't the father. It all made sense then, in a kind of crazy way. But to think we went all our lives without understanding that. Even my sister didn't know."

I could picture Michael's village, its stony houses and mountain solitude, and his father there a gloomy young man like my own, hemmed in by his limited possibilities.

"To tell you the truth," Michael said, "I think that's why Suzie left me. She started to see my father in me. She could never forgive him for what he did to my sister. But the funny thing is, I could. Even after I found out, or maybe because of that. You'd think it would have the opposite effect, but all I could see then was the pain this guy had gone through. It's like something that's blinded him."

We were not so different, then, Michael and I, though I hadn't known this, had the same family entanglements, the same receding into darkness and sin. Perhaps all families were like this, were hard exactly because of their failings, were then fated through that hardness to repeat the very things they sought to avert.

"How are things with your sister?" Michael said.

"Oh. All right."

"You're still getting along?"

"Off and on. It's a bit complicated."

"It always is."

It grew late. Michael offered to drive me to the subway.

"I have a car," I said. "My father's old car."

"A sort of hand-me-down?"

I had never told him about my father's death. It seemed ungenerous not to do so now, but it was too much to cram into a moment at the door.

"Something like that."

We stood an instant on his front steps. There would be time, I thought, time to tell him things; and yet somehow I had the sense also that time was running out, that soon I'd be past the point of telling.

"If you ever need anything," I said.

"Thanks."

I drove home. It was warm out, almost balmy, the air laden with smells that the winter had held in check. In the damp warmth, the lingering piles of dirty snow in parking lots and at the edges of driveways looked alien, anachronistic. As a child in Italy, at this time of year, I would wander sometimes above our village with my friend Fabrizio to search out the snowfields still nestled among the higher slopes, playing with him there as if in full winter while below us the valley lay stretched out already coloured over by the wheat- and olive-greens of spring. It had given me a peculiar sense of disorientation, the unnaturalness of that like some secret transgression, some line between absolutes that we had blurred.

The lights were still on in Sid's apartment when I arrived home. For a long time I stood across the street in the darkness of a burnt-out streetlight, watching. There was movement across the newsprint over his windows, vague shapes I couldn't decipher. Then one by one the lights began to go out until only the small, flickering glow of what must have been a candle remained, casting a long shadow onto one of the windows before finally receding from view, as if someone had picked it up and carried it into a far room.

Sid's bedroom was directly above my own. When he had women home, the floorboards would send messages like code – not even quite so much noise as small, telltale reverberations, what fell between sound and simple tremor, like the groan that went through the building when a streetcar went by. Eventually my body had begun to register these cues almost instinctively, with a strange combination of repulsion and arousal; and sometimes I would awake to them in the middle of the night and fall back into troubled, sexual dreams, dreams of watching, dreams of being exposed.

I waited outside ten minutes, fifteen, then longer, sitting smoking in the car with the window down and the radio on the way I'd sometimes snuck cigarettes at home as a teen. Then finally I made my way up the fire escape to my apartment, and to bed.

X

I awoke, to a commotion, in darkness: there was a pounding somewhere, frenzied or soft, imagined or real, I wasn't sure which. For a moment I felt the panic I'd felt sometimes as a child, waking up in the dark and not remembering where I was.

The sound again: a knock at the fire-escape door.

It was Rita.

"I'm sorry about this."

She had been crying. Her eyes were puffy; her make-up was smudged like runny watercolour.

"What happened?"

"I don't know. I'm sort of messed up."

She broke into sobs.

"Are you coming from Sid's?"

"Yeah."

"He didn't hurt you?"

"No. It's nothing like that. It's just – I don't know."

"It's okay. Everything's going to be all right."

I got her onto the living-room couch. She was wearing the same skirt and blouse she'd had on when she'd come by earlier in the week. The blouse was untucked a bit at the back like a sloppy child's.

"I'll make you some coffee," I said.

"Thanks."

I took a seat across from her while the coffee brewed, self-conscious suddenly at being only in my bathrobe.

"So I guess you had a bit of a rough night."

"Yeah. I'm really sorry about this."

"There's nothing to be sorry about."

She took a Kleenex from her purse and wiped at her tears.

"I should probably just go," she said.

"You don't have to do that."

I brought the coffee in. She had pulled herself together a bit, had tucked in her blouse, had dabbed some of the mascara from her eyes.

She was sitting at the very edge of the couch as if ready for flight.

"We could talk about this, if you want," I said. "We don't have to."

"There's nothing to say, really. It's just stupid."

"Yeah. Maybe not so stupid."

I watched her hands as she picked up her cup. There was the barest tremor in them, an infinitesimal lack of control.

"This is my fault," I said. "Not just you and Sid. The whole situation."

"It's no one's fault. It's my fault. I guess I was trying to prove something to you."

"What?"

"I don't know. I don't know."

Outside, it had started to rain. A streetcar passed by, a low, rumbling churn of metal against metal. In the corner window I saw it float like a phantom through the misted night-time desertion of College Street.

"It's raining," I said. "Maybe you should just stay here for the night."

"I've already bothered you enough as it is."

"You haven't bothered me. I'm glad you came here."

"Are you?"

"Yes."

She was still perched on the edge of the couch.

"I suppose Elena would be worried," I said.

"I called her from Sid's before. She's not really expecting me."

"Oh." We both seemed to feel the same shame and relief at this. "Then I'll fix the bed for you. I can take the couch."

"You don't have to do that."

"It's nothing."

I changed the bedsheets with an old linen set I had from home and put out a bathrobe. The robe, in a fusty blue check, was one my father had worn when he was in hospital years before. I'd been surprised when I took it over from him at how small it fit on me.

Rita came to the door. She had washed her make-up away to leave just a puffy tiredness around her eyes, as if she'd just risen from sleep.

"I'm not sure I have any pyjamas for you."

"Maybe just an old T-shirt or something."

She changed for bed while I fixed up the couch.

"Can I get you anything?"

"No. Maybe a glass of water."

"I'll bring it in."

68

She was sitting on the edge of the bed in my father's robe when I went in. She had draped her clothes over the bedside chair, the strap of a bra dangling from them.

I sat down beside her.

"Are you feeling any better?"

"Yes. Thanks. You've been great."

The tension of the previous days seemed forgotten, as if we'd somehow circled back to the moment that had preceded it, before the confusion had set in.

"I guess things have been a little strange between us lately," I said.

"Yeah. It's been hard."

"That day at the Falls. I didn't mean – I'm not sure what I meant."

"It didn't feel wrong, if that's what you're saying. It's just afterwards –"

"Yes."

The only light was the dim glow of the bedside lamp. The particular angle it caught Rita at made her look changed, softer but also more sage, more sad, as if some hidden side of her had been revealed.

"Maybe we're not normal," she said. "I just think – how things worked out between us. How mixed up it's been."

"Maybe you're right."

She had half-turned her face from me so that her hair, slightly tangled and still damp either from her tears or from when she'd washed, cut off my view of her.

"Sometimes I feel like I've never had anything," she said. "Anything that was really mine."

"I know what that's like. I suppose I always thought that *you* were what was mine."

"How do you mean?"

"I don't know. Just that. That I wasn't anything, really, except for you. I guess I hated you for that in some ways."

"And now?"

"Not now."

She was still half-turned from me.

"Would it be all right if you held me for a bit?" she said.

"I think so."

I put my arms around her. She had started crying again.

"I'm sorry," she said. "I just feel – I don't know. There's no way to put it."

"It's all right."

I held her. There was a moment then that was like falling into a kind of darkness, like the two of us opening a door in a dream and stepping out; and then we were kissing. There seemed no decision in this, just a giving-in to the darkness, to the falling. The darkness was like a tangible thing, what the world had been stripped down to; only our lips had vision within it, probing along the contours of skin and bone until they met with an instant's small, delicious cushioning of padded flesh on padded flesh.

We were still falling. There seemed no distance between us now, just this awful relinquishing as if everything were unfolding at once unreal and yet inevitable, having nothing to do with us and yet what our lives had always been moving toward. I slipped her robe from her shoulders, pulled her T-shirt up so that finally she lay before me with her breasts, her belly exposed like the pale underside of some infinitely fragile thing; and then I was lying beside her, kissing her, running my hands against her skin, doing these things and being inside the doing of them and yet seeing them as if their reality were merely a mirroring of something already lived through, that had already long ago been done and atoned for.

I entered her. For an instant then when we were looking directly into each other's eyes, when what was going on with our bodies seemed merely the adjunct to this moment of unblinking sight. There was something almost ruthless in us then, hopeless, the instantaneous mutual admission of wrong and its flouting. There would be this one time, we seemed to say, when the world would split open and every unspeakable hope, every desire, every fear, would be permitted. Then I came and it was as if we had suddenly dropped to earth again.

We lay several minutes without speaking. Rita had wrapped herself in her robe again.

"Are you all right?" I said.

"Yes."

In the dim light our voices seemed disembodied. There was a mood between us of blank calm like the unrippled surface of a pool; but it seemed the slightest word, the slightest thought, might disturb it.

"Maybe we should get under the covers," I said.

We fell asleep cradled against one another like children. In the first haze of sleepfulness what I felt to be holding her, to have her there in my bed and be able to run a hand if I wished along the whole, smooth plane of her body, was the sort of matter-of-fact elation I felt on first waking from dreams of flying: there was always a moment then when the thing seemed truly possible, because of the way in the dream it had come about not like some miracle but like the slow working out of mathematical law, something that had had to be worked toward, tested, refined, till at last my heaviness gave way to willed, precarious flight.

But then as I fell deeper into sleep, further and further away from the place where we'd been together, where things had made sense, the horror began to take shape. It began with just a gnawing at the back of my mind like the onset of a fever dream, the scrambling search for a solution to a question that refused to take solid form; and then gradually it grew into a kind of panic. I was running, running, through deserted night-time streets, down subway stairwells, through dim, blue-lit passageways only just wide enough to slip through; and there was something I was moving toward or away from, it was never clear which, something inevitable and large, unnameable, but also, in a way, banal, all the more horrible for that.

I awoke, with a start, toward dawn. Rita was still beside me, turned away now and sprawled face-down like someone who had fallen from a building. Her breathing was rhythmic but shallow; once she sucked in her breath as if at some sudden fright, then resumed her regular rhythm again. I could smell her there beside me, a complex mixture of sweat and sex and a soapy, milky scent that made me think of how her pillow had smelled when we'd slept together as children years before.

I slipped out of bed to the bathroom. There was blood on me from her, I saw now. There were smears of it on my fingers, on my thighs; in the morning there would be dried stains on the covers and sheets. I tried not to think of what this meant, how dire, perhaps, this made things. I remembered the wedding jokes about bedsheets when I was a child in Italy, how strange they had struck me then, how brutal a thing they had made marriage seem.

I went back to bed, my hand going out instinctively to test the sheets, expecting wetness; but they were dry. Rita shifted as I settled myself, pulled herself in, away. She had turned again, so that her face was etched out in greys and whites against her pillow; what I saw there for an instant were my own features, the set of her jaw, of her cheeks, could read in the placement of muscle and bone my own genetic code.

For a long time I lay awake turned away from her toward the window, staring into the brightening dawn. A few scudding clouds left behind from the night's rain gradually dispersed, leaving behind a clear, northern sky that held the intimation of sunrise like a great blue-dipped bowl. For a while, before the traffic increased, I could make out a sound of birds, tiny, industrious whistles and chirps like the coming to life of some vast, miniature household.

At some point I felt Rita stirring beside me and instinctively closed my eyes to feign sleep. The bed creaked, then the floor, and then I could feel her weight rising up from the mattress, hear the rustle of clothing as she went through the clothes on the bedside chair. She went into the living room to dress: I could picture with each sound, each hiss and whoosh of cloth, as she slipped on skirt, stockings, blouse. There were a few minutes of silence then, the moments when I should have gone to her; and then finally the sound of motion again, of furtive footsteps across creaking hardwood, of a closing door.

XI

When she'd gone I fell into fitful sleep, fighting consciousness like a swimmer refusing to surface. My dreams were the shattered remnants of dreams, without centre: images flashed, took on portent, but resisted coalescing into meaning. There was no question now of solutions, only this frenzied rushing-by like the brain short-circuiting, sending out random impulses that the unconscious still tried to arrange into a whole.

When I awoke, finally, to a haze of spring light through the window, it was only eleven. I felt a despair at how little time had passed while I'd slept. For a long time I lay in bed in a kind of paralysis – there seemed no possible next action in my life, no gesture that could move me forward. It was as if I'd come to the point in a story where it retreated back to the unwritten void: this was the end, everything had already happened, there was nothing left to be done.

Through the window I could hear the traffic on College, the dull roar of engines, the clack, clack of streetcars as they crossed over the switches at Spadina. Every few minutes the clacks repeated themselves as another car passed, giving a rhythm to the traffic like the relentless thump of a heart beneath a roar of blood. I had an image of my body laid out like the roads, the tracks, of the endless network of things stretching away from me and which I formed the meaningless centre of, the streets leading to highways, the highways to other cities, on and on to take in the whole wearying edifice of the world.

There was a single stain of blood on the bedcovers, and then a smaller one on the sheets. They were tiny, really, not much bigger than coins. Somewhere, in my dreams, I had imagined awaking in gore as if after a murder; but instead there were only these pinpricks of purple-red.

From the bedroom doorway came a beckoning of late-morning light. It was the light that I moved toward, finally: it seemed to bathe everything in a quality of remembrance, to say, these were the rooms I once lived in, this was the life that I led. It was possible to reconstruct things in that way, to quell the panic, to touch my hands to coffee cups, kitchen faucets, cupboard doors, as if they were real, to reassert an order over things. I poured coffee into a cup as I once had; I tasted the bitterness of it on my tongue. Everything could unfold in the usual way; there was just this gap to account for, this doubling over, the sense that every feeling, every act, was itself and only the memory of itself.

I sat at the kitchen window, staring out. Eddy the super-intendent was patrolling the sidewalk along Huron, prowl-ing outside again, in his furtive, casual way, now that the weather had changed. As I watched, he ambled to the corner of College, hands in the back pockets of his denim overalls, and gazed for a long moment in each direction; and then apparently satisfied that nothing threatened there, he turned into the sun and raised his arms in a lazy, feline stretch. He seemed to take the sun in like some liquid on him, some tangible balm, for an instant alive only to that sensation, to the sun shining warm on his skin while his muscles stretched.

Coming back toward the building, he looked up at my window. For an instant he seemed to stare right at me, right through me. There was no greeting, just that hard, assessing stare. Perhaps in the glare of the sun he hadn't seen me, had seen only the mirrored dark that daytime windows gave back. But there had seemed to be knowledge in his look, some kind of message that had passed. I had a sudden sense of being monitored, under surveillance, not anonymous here as I'd imagined but the focus of a careful, calculated attention.

The panic had started again. I felt the need to do something, act, to get away from the apartment. I tried to slip out via the fire escape, but Eddy caught sight of me from his lawn chair outside the front entrance.

"Hey, Vic," he said, cool, as if nothing had happened.

There was something wrong in the quality of the day, a strange conjunction of the sultry, springtime warmth, the bitter sun, and an uncertain slowness to things. I wandered into the market and instead of the usual Friday bustle the streets were deserted; it was as if the apocalypse had come, as if time had ended after all, and the slowness I'd felt was the world's mechanism winding unnaturally down to a stop. There were packing crates piled at the curbside, green garbage bags, heaps of rotting vegetables, and then just the desolation of empty sidewalks and closed shops. Up ahead a door shot open at a café, a hole in the wall where the market's derelicts and dealers collected; for an instant laughter rang out into the street, but then a hand pulled the door closed again before anyone had emerged.

At Bathurst Street, I came on the straggling fringes of a crowd that seemed to be converging on Little Italy. A police cruiser was angled across College, two burly officers in sunglasses and shirtsleeves lazily redirecting traffic. In the cleared street beyond, people were moving in twos and threes toward some kind of gathering further up. Past Manning, barricades had been set out along the curbsides, people lined up behind them apparently awaiting a procession or parade. From a distance came the deep, mournful sound of a brass band, a sound of singing; but the procession itself hadn't appeared yet. I moved into the crowd, seeking a vantage point, open space. But the further in I moved, the more the crowd thickened, until the passageway through it had narrowed down to a single person-wide corridor.

I stopped, finally, near the steps of a church. People were tiered up behind me on the steps, craning to watch as the head of the procession rounded onto College from a side-street. The procession was led by four men on horseback dressed in the armour of Roman soldiers; behind them came a line of men in ragged robes, their hands bound and their waists linked by rope. For an instant I thought I'd stumbled onto a film set, so incongruous did this vision seem amidst the shops and coffee bars of Little Italy. One of the horses balked at the sight of the crowd as he rounded the corner, whinnied, took a step back; a suited man came in from the sidelines to calm him, and the procession continued.

It was Good Friday, I remembered now; this was a Passion play. I had seen them in Italy as a child, had a sudden vivid recollection of the smell of horses on the air, of the clatter of hooves against cobblestone. In my father's town the procession had ended on a windswept hill above the cemetery – I had an image of a half-naked Jesus actually roped to a cross and raised up there. That couldn't be right, the barbarism of that. But still the image persisted, the grunting heave of men as they lifted the cross into its hole and Jesus splayed and sweating against a background of graves.

The first grouping of prisoners had passed. Behind them came a small brass band and a choir of mainly older women in widow's black, an island of village anachronism within the greater anachronism of the Roman procession; and then children dressed as angels, parish groups, floats, more choirs and bands. The floats formed representations of the Stations of the Cross – the condemnation to death, the meeting with the Virgin, Veronica wipes the sacred face.

Two more prisoners came into view, these bearing crosses, their robes torn to leave exposed patches of shoulder and thigh; and then Jesus. Three soldiers preceded him bearing lances and three trailed him with whips, holding back an entourage of wailing women and children in peasant's kerchiefs and robes. He seemed an unlikely Christ, slightly balding beneath his crown of plaited twigs, his features the plain, grizzled ones of some local factory worker or mason; but an odd intensity radiated from him. His cross was two planks of rough wood crudely bound together with rope; he looked genuinely strained beneath the burden of it, his muscles taut, his face beaded with sweat. Next to me I saw a girl of sixteen or so make a sign of the cross as he approached, and was moved by this depth of belief in someone so young.

Coming to the intersection of Grace Street, Jesus fell. An audible gasp rose up from the crowd. Some of the women following behind had rushed forward to help him, but the soldiers held them back; and as the crowd looked on Jesus struggled slowly upright again beneath his cross. The hem of his robe was dirtied where he'd fallen – there was a stain of asphalt there and then what seemed a stipple of blood at one knee. He continued on several more paces and then fell again, fully this time. Once more the women rushed forward, keening; once more the guards held them back. The crowd craned to see what had happened, pressing up against the barricades, and for an instant then it all seemed real, the keening women, the crush of the crowd, and Christ lying prone on the asphalt among the streetcar tracks of College.

The crowd had pushed in. I felt elbows, limbs, pressing against me, but there seemed no individual they were attached to, only this shapeless mass that stretched unbroken now for several blocks in either direction. People closed in in front of me, cutting off my view of the procession, and then something happened up ahead – perhaps he'd fallen again – and the whole crowd surged forward an instant and then back like a wave, a single entity. A panic took hold of me again, a nausea like a forced submersion under water.

"You okay?"

It was a woman in front of me; I had stumbled against her. I must have blacked out for an instant.

"A little dizzy."

"You need some air." Focused, no-nonsense. "Maybe the church is open. You should sit down."

She led me up through the crowd on the church steps, keeping a distance between us but with one hand in the crook of my arm to guide me. A few heads turned toward us as we passed, then away. I had the sense that we were invisible somehow, that this was a thing that concerned only the two of us.

She tried the church door. It opened.

"I guess they wouldn't lock up a church on Good Friday," she said.

She was in her thirties perhaps, a bit matronly, with short-cropped blonde hair, blue eyes, dressed in jeans and a bright purple windbreaker. The windbreaker seemed like a marker, something setting her apart.

"I really appreciate this," I said.

The noise and glare of outside had given way to dim stillness. Dots of colour swam before my eyes in the sudden shift from brightness to dark.

She led me to a back pew.

"Are you feeling any better?"

"Yeah. Thanks."

The church was deserted. She seemed uneasy now at the sudden intimacy we found ourselves in.

"You should just sit for a while."

"I'll be okay."

"You sure?"

"Yes. Thanks again."

I was left alone. The dizziness had passed, leaving only a faint taste of bile in my throat like the metallic aftertaste of fear. There had been something about the crowd, about being caught like that in its collective energy. In Nigeria, once, when I was teaching there, I'd seen a thief chased down by a crowd in one of the markets – they had beaten him until his clothes had been reduced to bloody rags, overtaken by a kind of frenzy, an impersonal rage that was like a contagion the air had bred.

The church was a cavernous place in Gothic style, though overlaid with ill-considered renovations – dull grey carpeting on the floor, acoustic ceiling tiles above the entrance hall and side aisles – as if someone had tried to scale down its largeness to the proportions of a suburban rec room. But up around the chancel, an older dignity remained, the curving back wall ringed with tall, traceried windows made up of little circles of swirling, blue-tinted glass. The light through the glass bathed the altar beneath in an eerie bluish glow. It was the colour I would have imagined that God would take, not the God of my childhood, the smiling old man in the sky, but the one who knew the crooked byways of things, the back alleys and half-open doors, the mix of darkness and light. I had a sudden sharp pang of regret for the loss of that older God, the simpler one, for my stories of sinners and saints, the hope of some sudden flash that could cleanse things, make them right again. At bottom I had never quite ceased to believe in these things, had only grown distant from them like some subtle turning I'd missed, the point on a path between wandering lost and going home.

Somehow the sun had arched northwards to come to shine directly through the western curve of the chancel's windows, minute by minute the light increasing there to cast a silvered radiance of direct and reflected light all along the deep well of the nave. Then, as I watched, because of some passing cloud or of some particular angle the sun had reached, there was an instant when the church seemed to take all this silvered light back into itself like a breath, then exhale again. The thing happened so quickly that I wasn't sure afterwards if I'd only imagined it.

"*È venuto per confessarsi?*"

Someone had come up silently behind me: a priest.

"I'm sorry?"

"Ah. I thought you were Italian."

"Yes. I mean, I don't speak it much now."

"I see."

He was an older man, watery-eyed and grey-haired and spry, dressed in a simple black soutane and clerical collar.

"So you came to watch the procession," he said.

"Yes. It was very beautiful."

"I suppose. If you like that sort of thing." He gave an odd smile. "*Da dove?* Which part of Italy?"

"Molise."

"*Molisano*, that's good. I'm from around those parts myself. What was the town, exactly?"

"It was just a small place. Valle del Sole. Near Rocca Secca."

"Yes, yes, I know it! Just a little hole in the wall, isn't that it? You must have known the priest there, old *Zappa-la-vigna*, what was his name?"

"Father Nicola?"

"Yes, that's it! The times we used to have together in the seminary!"

For a moment time seemed to shift: I was back in a class-room, watching Father Nicola roam the rows of desks as he tested us on our catechism.

"He used to tell us stories about that," I said. "About the seminary."

"What, did he tell you about Dompietro?"

"Yes, that was one of them. About the shoe under the bed."

"Ha, the rascal! That was *my* story, he stole it from me! 'Ho, Dompietro, what are you doing under the bed?' 'I'm looking for my shoe!'"

He was laughing, his eyes bright with tears.

"It wasn't true, then?" I said.

"Oh, no, Dompietro was just someone we made up like that. Then every little thing that happened, who'd done it? Dompietro had done it."

I felt a knot of emotion in my chest like a fist that had lodged there. All that past, irretrievable and mysterious and grand. For an instant it seemed that we had unfurled it before us almost tangible, almost real, that it had brought us to the brink of some wonderful revelation.

"Ah, well," he said finally. "All that was so long ago now."

He stood a moment in silence. I wanted to hold him there but couldn't think what more to say.

"You're sure you don't want to go to confession, then?"

"I don't know. Maybe not this time."

"Well, it's up to you."

He gave me a final, scrutinizing look.

"If you want," he said, "you should come by some time. I'm here. We can have a little glass together."

"That would be nice."

He moved off toward the front of the church. At the foot of the altar he went down on one knee and made a slow sign of the cross, then made his way up the steps of the chancel and disappeared through a side doorway.

People had begun to filter into the church, old women who came in alone, a few families with children. Two altar boys emerged from the chancel door to light the candles at the altar: apparently a service was about to begin. As more people arrived and the pews started to fill, the church took on an air of waiting. Outside the sun was just setting, darkness coming on like a hush; someone switched on the church lights, but their dim glow seemed only to round out the coming dark.

The old priest emerged and began to go about his preparations. He was dressed in his robes now and looked more sombre than before, more estimable, weighted with the gravity of his office. There were a dozen careful arrangements to be made, the missal to be turned to its page, the chalice to be checked, the water and wine to be set out. All the years, all the centuries, these little rituals had been gone through, back to primitive midnight rites whispered fearfully around a fire – they seemed poignant now, though I'd long ceased to connect to them, seemed like the feeble attempt to reduce the vastness of things, the darkness, to a small, domestic order. The priest went about them with an air of pleased, solitary attentiveness; in a moment everything would be in its place, and his work could begin.

From somewhere above us the initial tentative notes of the introit sounded, and we rose. This had always been the moment for me, because of that first communion of voices, that rising up, when faith had felt truly possible, when it had seemed to hover before me almost graspable, almost mine. I was singing now, the words came: I was a child again in a small village church in Italy; I was a child at St. Michael's in Mersea. What had I wanted then, what would the boy that I was have seen in the man I'd become? All that longing and hope, what had it come to? My head was filled with a rush of images, my whole past seeming to tumble through me like something being taken away, that there was no going back to; and then I was crying.

My god, I thought, my god, what have I done?

XII

The traffic was flowing again along College when I came out, the barricades removed and aftermath debris from the procession littering the sidewalk and curb like washed-up flotsam. In the doorways of the coffee bars, middle-aged men in suit coats stood smoking and talking, feet planted solid and broad as if they'd come out to survey their dominions after a storm. All along the street these clusters were repeated at intervals like an endless proliferation of village squares, the tiny bars with their counters and stools, their dim, bluish light, the men outside. The bars were like factories the men spilled out of, were made by, like secret societies where they practised or learned a certain laugh or shrug, a certain movement of hands, the way smoke curled away from the end of a cigarette.

I caught a snippet of Italian outside one of them, my own dialect.

"I never cared for that sort of thing, back then. You only know afterwards."

I walked back to my apartment. For a long time I sat in my darkened living room staring out the corner window onto College. I hadn't eaten all day, but by now was well past the point of hunger: it was as if my body had ceased sending messages to my brain, was only this shell I carried with me, without desires or rights. I imagined going on like that till I had slowly stripped myself of every physical need, had become simply a point of undesiring awareness. All day, every day, a hundred petty wants formed the substance of my life: I wondered what blank space lay beyond them, what clarity things would have there.

The streetlights from College cast strange shadows in the room, gave objects a protean look. I had the sense that someone had been here in my absence; but everything was in its place, nothing had been disturbed.

There was a knock at the door. It was Sid.

"Going over to Rita's?"

I had forgotten: it was Rita's birthday.

"I don't know. I'm not feeling great."

"She'll be pissed if you don't show up."

He gave no sign that anything was out of the ordinary. There was something at once reassuring and chilling in this, as if he were presenting like a trick mirror the false reflection of a world still in place.

"It's probably early," I said.

"I thought we could grab a bite."

He had a bottle of wine tucked under one arm. It was the wine, somehow, that seemed to make my going inevitable, the simple covenant it represented, that Sid had chosen it, planned his evening, that he'd been able to do these things as if they mattered.

"Just let me change," I said, though in my bedroom I simply sat several minutes on the edge of the bed, then got down the bag that held Rita's watch. It didn't seem right to arrive empty-handed – it was just a watch, after all, just a gift, a box wrapped in gold foil. I had the sense that Sid knew I had it there in my closet, that he was waiting to see if I would leave it behind, if I'd so clearly incriminate myself.

It was only when we were outside that I noticed a strange, subtle energy coming off Sid.

"I dropped some acid," he told me, and flashed me his exaggerated, happy-face smile.

We ate at one of the more expensive Chinese places on Spadina. Sid had a metal flask in the inside pocket of his leather jacket from which he kept pouring small shots of whiskey into our tea. He ordered three dishes to start, sent one back because it was cold, ordered two more but then hardly touched a thing, sampling a bite or two and finally pushing the dishes aside with a satisfied air as if he'd in fact cleared them down to their final scraps. From the back room the waiter and the manager looked on, but Sid ignored them.

The whole time he kept up a steady stream of talk.

"On me," he said, when we got up to pay, pulling a crisp hundred from his wallet.

We walked up through the market to Rita's street. I had an image of her house dark as if in mourning, the party cancelled, the door locked to bar us entry; but already from down the street I could see the lights, hear the thump of music. The front door was open, a handful of women I didn't recognize clustered around the stoop there. The women looked like replicas of one another, loose-jeaned and mannish, conspiratorial. They made just the slightest accommodation to let us by, a sort of bristling as if we were a gust of wind blowing through.

"Evening, ladies," Sid said.

Inside, laughter, music, smoky heat. The pocket doors into Elena's bedroom had been opened to join it to the centre room: women and more women, some of whom I'd seen at the house before but a host of others as well, among them a scattering of older women with a professorial look. A few heads turned as we came in, someone smiled, wryly; and then just the same indifference that had greeted us on the stoop, that air of charged exclusivity that I recognized from Elena's kitchen gatherings.

Sid looked completely unfazed.

"Let's grab a drink," he said, and began to make his way to the kitchen.

I hadn't spotted Rita. But then suddenly Sid was veering off toward the corner of the living room: we were at her back.

"Hey, birthday girl," he said.

She turned.

"Oh." Her eyes had the panic of a trapped animal's. "I didn't see you."

"I had to drag your brother over."

"Oh."

She looked wrong, completely wrong. She was stoned, it seemed, her pupils had the telltale dilation; and then her make-up was overdone, her clothes were out of character. She was wearing high heels and a sleeveless black dress with a slit up one side – it was as if she had wilfully, self-punishingly, set out to stand apart from the rest of the crowd.

"Hello, Rita," I said.

"Yeah. Great. It's great you could come."

Her eyes refused to focus on me. It was only now that I understood what I'd hoped for, that a message would pass between us, that we would say, yes, this thing is possible, we have chosen it.

She was standing beside a tall, older-looking man, as far as I could see the only other male in the place.

"This is John," she said.

"Oh."

"I think I'm going to the washroom."

We were left standing with John. Sid still had his wine tucked under his arm.

"I guess we men should stick together," he said.

"Ha, yes," John said, a little awkwardly.

"I'm Sid. And this is Victor, Rita's brother."

"Yes. I gathered that. She's spoken about you."

So he was the one Rita had talked about on our trip to the Falls. But this was a man old enough to be her father, in his late fifties perhaps, or early sixties. His speech had the slightest accent, a small stumbling over like a lisp.

"Are you one of her professors?" I said.

"No, no, we did a class together, that's all."

Someone turned the music up. Sid leaned in to John's ear and shouted some comment at him, to which John responded with a nod and what might have been a smile or a grimace; and then Sid launched into a long monologue I couldn't follow, talking, gesticulating, John bending his ear to listen with the same nods and uncertain half-smiles. He looked entirely out of place here, uncomfortable, embattled, but also resigned, as if some complex sense of duty obliged him to remain. There was something about him that seemed not quite right – his clothes, perhaps. They were normal enough, even stylish – beige chinos, an off-white cotton blazer – but looked just slightly overly rumpled, overly worn.

Sid had stopped talking.

"Ah," John said. "Yes."

We stood a moment in silence.

"How about we get that drink?" Sid said.

I followed him to the kitchen. Elena was standing outside the kitchen doorway in conversation. Her eye caught mine and she nodded, just that small condescension of greeting.

"Must be the famous lesbian sister," Sid said.

So Rita had told him things.

"Yeah."

"Are you feeling all right, buddy? You look a little pale."

"It's just a flu or something."

He had opened his bottle of wine.

"Down this," he said, pouring me a glass. "It's good for the soul."

We stood at the edge of the living room. Rita was at the far end of the space now, near the front window, in conversation with a largish woman in a bulky sweater who looked like her glaring opposite. She was not pulling her look off at all, visibly self-conscious, unnerved, her whole body drawn into itself as if she felt every eye in the place was on her. Her dress was cut low in the back to reveal a half-moon of pallid skin spotted with acne. I wanted to go up and drape a jacket around her, lead her away.

"I have to use the can," I said to Sid.

In the bathroom I sat for a long time on the edge of the tub. I had made a mistake in coming; everything had been a mistake. Our trip to the Falls, my coming here to this city, back to the remote, barely accessible confusions and half-formed emotions of childhood – it was all like some endless equation I strained to find the answer to, whose variables I was forever hammering into place only to find that the whole had reverted again to chaos. It was madness, what had happened; and the only way forward was through further madness.

The bathroom was littered with evidences of Rita and Elena, plastic shower caps on a hook, rows of mascara and lipstick, perfumed soap, bath oils, a few hairs on the floor. It had an air at once intimate, private, yet neutral, the one room in the apartment where Rita's and Elena's shared life seemed still compatible, where they might have been children again. I thought of Rita taking her bath here with her oils and soaps, stretched out naked in the tub, possessing her body yet taking it utterly for granted.

There was a knock at the door, then a woman's voice.

"Hey, what's going on in there, your thing get caught?"

Then laughter.

"Maybe he's playing with it."

"Who is he, anyway?"

"I think it's Rita's brother."

"Hey, Rita's brother. Cute sister you've got."

When I came out, a group of them was clustered outside the door.

"He must feel like he's in Holland," one of them said, though not unkindly. "Lots of dykes."

I looked for Sid. Somehow he'd managed to insinuate himself into a group of four or five women in the living room.

"I'm not telling you I'd do it," he was saying. "But maybe that's more a social thing because of the way I was raised."

"Whoa. Mr. Philosophical."

And yet it was clear he'd won them over, the group of them focused on him as on some mascot or prize.

Rita passed around us making her way to the kitchen. Then for a moment she was alone there. I came up to her as she was bending into the fridge and instinctively reached out to touch her. She flinched.

"Oh. It's you."

"Look, Rita –"

But the thing seemed impossible. She stood at the fridge door, inert, half-turned from me, and for an instant the same repulsion, the same spasm of loathing, seemed to pass through us, the kind of loathing only siblings could feel, intimate and humiliated and searing.

Sid came into the room.

"Hey, guys, what's up?"

For the first time he was showing an edge beneath his casualness, the need to know what his status was.

"I've got to bring these drinks out," Rita said, and was gone.

"Everything okay with her?" Sid said.

"I don't know. Yeah."

"A little heavy on the make-up, I'd say. It's not her style."

I noticed now the cake that had been set out on the kitchen counter. HAPPY 20TH, it read.

"I have to go," I said.

"It's up to you. I think I'll stick around a bit."

I passed John on the way out. I had the sense suddenly that he'd been keeping an eye on me the whole time I'd been there.

"You're not feeling any better?" he said.

"Sorry?"

"Your friend. He said you weren't feeling well."

"Yes. No. It's just a cold or something."

"Ah." He seemed to want to hold me there, to impart something to me. "Well. Perhaps we'll see each other again."

Outside, I realized my head was spinning. I was dimly aware of feeling feverish and sore, but still with the sense that my body had nothing to do with me any longer, was just a burden, something I might slough off at any moment if I could only find the way to unshackle myself from it. It was like reaching a point just beyond pain, just beyond the bearable. In Africa, once, I'd walked for miles in sub-Saharan heat stupidly trying to make my way to a remote Dogon village; and at some point the weight of my pack, my aching muscles, the desperation in me at having gone wrong, had given way to this same dizzy feeling of detachment, the sense of floating in the present moment without recourse.

Along the street, the windows of the houses shone with curtained light. Each window was like an eye I passed by: this was where I was not, each seemed to say, curled in front of a television or fire with children, a lover, a wife, my life staid or nearly over or still all quivering possibility.

One of the neighbourhood's regular street people had come out to squat in the doorway of a College Street bank, the mysterious burgeonings of great stuffed garbage bags and burlap bundles tied with twine heaped up behind him. He was one of the crazy ones, a regular at the psychiatric institute across from my building, moving in and out of it like the cats we'd had on the farm who'd hole up a few weeks in the warmth of our boiler room, then run wild again. Eddy called him José, which simply might have been some private joke of his since the man didn't look especially Latino, didn't look like anything at all except a street person, with that generic look street people had, the acned skin, the clotted hair. Sometimes he would spread out bits of paraphernalia on the sidewalk before him like fetishes, a broken picture frame, a candle stub, a chipped statuette of the Virgin.

He was rocking on the balls of his feet, rocking and rocking.

"Spare any change?"

No eye contact, no sense of connection, the words coming out like a sort of tic. He pocketed the coins I handed him without looking at them.

"Thank you."

In my apartment, the feeling again of intrusion, of a presence. I checked every room: nothing. I was dreamy now with fever, truly ill. I was vaguely aware that the bed was contaminated in some way but wasn't sure how to deal with it; in the end I spread my sleeping bag over top and crawled inside. It was only as I was turning out the light that I noticed the parcel on my desk, what I must have been clutching the whole evening like a talisman to bring it back to where it sat now, Rita's gift.

XIII

I threw up several times in the night, stumbling from my bed each time the churning began in my stomach to kneel half-dazed at the toilet while I retched. In the end I was reduced to dry heaves mainly, though they seemed to still for a few minutes the world's mad reeling; but back in bed it would start again. In my confusion I imagined I was in a storm at sea, that I was back on the ship that had brought me to Canada, crawling up to my bunk while beneath me my mother sighed and slept slowly bleeding to death.

At some point in the night, a real storm started up. Rain, wind, through the slit I'd left open in the bedroom window; I had the presence of mind to pull the window shut but the room seemed to have ingested the storm by then, seemed filled with an incessant rustling of paper and a mad ringing like the clashing of a thousand glass pendants. Outside, blue light flashed against a wash of black, light and then thunder, a great gnashing and scraping of fissured sky. I was a boy again, thinking the world a tiny ball and the sky a vast firmament that enclosed it: with each flash, each peal, the firmament cracked and for an instant heaven's forbidden light blazed through.

Around dawn I fell into fitful sleep. There was a period of dreams then, though more like half-waking memories that had somehow got tangled up in the logic of dreams: I was en route to the Dogon village again only now it was raining, in the distance great monoliths of smoothed rock, four-square and vast, towering up from the landscape like stones the gods had dropped; and there was a mystery to solve, and a ritual whose end was the expiation of some ancient crime. When I arrived at the village – had this happened? had I ever arrived there in real life? – the villagers were all in their separate homes in the cliff face, caves really but also a sort of hotel. I went from home to home, conducting my interviews; but in each place it was the same, the same indifferent, evasive shrug, the claim that there was no ritual, no culprit, no crime.

Rain and more rain: it continued on through the day and into the evening. I got up briefly to make food, my stomach like a pit that had been scoured, then dug deeper. Outside, the rain formed a continuous sheet on the roads, rivering into the sewage drains and sloshing up over the curbs as cars passed. José was holed up in an open shed at the back of the service station across Huron; he was in his usual stance, squatting, rocking, his eyes doing reconnaissance along the street while his bundles and bags sat heaped around him like precious spoils.

I called Rita's.

"She's out." Elena's inscrutable tone, and at once the paranoia in me: she knew or would know, was like a time bomb from which, in moments or weeks or years, all the outrage at what had happened would be unleashed.

"Do you know where she went?"

"Dunno. I thought she might be at your place."

A pause.

"You sound sick or something," she said.

"Yeah. Just a flu."

I slept. The racing of my mind had eased: it seemed to have worn itself out, to have entered some new, limbo-ish place where there was only fatigue, only the dreamy relinquishing of no way out. I had a vision that Rita had come and was tending to me, that she was there on the bed wiping fever sweat from my neck, my brow, with a heated cloth. There was a chipped enamel basin on the night table, a crucifix on the wall. At the door, a sound of hooves against cobblestones, the grind and complaint of cartwheels: someone was coming for us, in an instant we'd rise and ride off together into golden afternoon light.

When I awoke, Easter Sunday, the fever had dimmed. The apartment looked as if the storm of the previous day had ripped through it: there were clothes strewn about in the bedroom, a couple of vomit-flecked towels on the floor, a heap of bedsheets, the ones Rita had bloodied, bundled in a corner; in the kitchen, pots of half-eaten food on the table and dishes I couldn't remember having dirtied piled up in the sink.

I couldn't form my thoughts around any plan. On my desk were spread the pages of a paper I hadn't finished, more than a week overdue now, then beside them a stack of library books, also overdue. My mind was fixed somehow on that overdueness, the nickels and dimes of it, the vague forces lined up to punish me. I stood staring at the pages I'd written out, with their slanting blue scrawl, the evidence that I'd formed thoughts, made decisions, considered one thing more important than another; and then at the books with their arcane titles, their careful systems of words. I had the sense I'd been tricked in some way: none of this mattered, there was nothing holding the systems in place.

I went out. The streets looked scrubbed, hosed down, from the previous day's rain. It was still overcast, the air liquidy and thick, wisps of fog rising up from the pools that had formed in parking lots and on front lawns.

At the back of my mind was the thought that Rita hadn't returned my call; and then I was ringing her doorbell.

Elena came to the door.

"Hey, Vic." She gave me her sardonic smile. "Happy Easter."

There were footsteps in the background, then a woman's voice.

"Who is it?"

"Rita's brother."

She was coming toward us down the hall, an older woman, hair wiry and streaked grey, who I recognized from the party.

"Suzanne," Elena said, by way of introduction. This was probably as far as she'd ever gone in allowing me into this side of her life.

"Hello, Rita's brother," Suzanne said, but didn't extend her hand.

They were both dressed in sloppy house clothes, jeans, tattered sweats.

"Rita's out," Elena said. "She went for a walk."

"Did you say I phoned?"

"To tell you the truth, she got in pretty late last night."

"Where did she go?"

"I dunno," Elena said. "Maybe she had a date."

Suzanne laughed.

"You know, boy meets girl," she said.

I couldn't get my mind around any of this. The thought that kept forming in my head was that it was Easter Sunday. But none of this was like Easter, everything was out of whack.

"You should ask him in for a coffee," Suzanne said. "He looks a little beat up."

"No. Thanks. I should get going."

When I got home my shoes and socks were completely soaked, though I couldn't remember stepping in any water. The fever began to come on again, a dark glow at the back of my brain.

The phone rang. It was Elena.

"Just thought you might want to know that she's back."

"Is she there?"

"She's in the shower. I'll tell her to phone you."

But no call. They were playing a game: Elena was in on it, Suzanne, perhaps even Sid. At some point I had the impression again of an urgent ringing and clanging, the jangling pouring-forth of a million nickels and dimes. But by then I was back in the fever's darkness, burrowing through its conduits and tangled paths trying to trace there the connections, the careful, deliberate scheme being laid out for my downfall.

It was Tuesday morning before I surfaced again, the apartment filled when I awoke with a glare of morning light like at the instant of a bomb blast. The only sign that I'd lived through the previous day was the apartment's increased ruin, more half-eaten food, more clutter. At some point I'd moved my sleeping bag from the bed to the couch and set up a sort of encampment there; there was dirty cutlery on the coffee table, and a blackened pot with some sort of noodles and sauce congealed at the bottom. In my mind, the residue of dreams: backwoods and marshy, ramshackle settlements, dark dirty rooms, half-naked children streaked with grime. A sense of the thin line between human and beast, of order broken down, of being pushed back to the outer rim of the known world.

Then, in the half clarity of wakefulness, a sort of revelation came, the understanding that there was no way to think this thing through. I could only act, headlong, could only push forward bloody-mindedly until something had come together or been smashed.

I went out again. This time I came at Rita's house by circling around to the cross-street just beyond it. I hadn't showered or shaved, must have been in a state by then but was aware of my body only as a kind of machine, something to move me from place to place and be forgotten.

I waited at the corner. I knew Elena had a class at ten, Rita not till mid-afternoon. The minutes ticked by, nine-forty-five, nine-fifty; then finally Elena emerged from the door, a book bag on one arm. Seeing her secretly like that, as she swung her bag up, as she pulled the door shut to lock it, still her staunch, unswerving self though she was alone, I had an insight: that Elena was what she was right down to her sinew and bone, while Rita was changeable, shifting, someone who blended into things like camouflage. For an instant I couldn't even call up an image of her: there was a blank in my mind like a photo that had failed, that showed a background, a setting, but where her likeness should have been only empty space.

I waited till Elena had disappeared down the street, then rang the bell. Footsteps, then Rita's voice, tentative, wary.

"Who is it?"

"It's me."

Her eyes flashed fear when she opened the door: I must have looked crazed.

"Are you all right?"

For a moment, face to face like that, all our defences seemed down.

"Yeah. I dunno. I've been sick."

"I tried to call," she said.

"Oh."

We stood not looking at each other. What the matter came down to was this: we were the same, were both frightened and ashamed, were both alone.

There was a sound of movement in the background. Rita's eyes met mine for an instant like a curtain rising and falling.

"John's here," she said.

He was in the kitchen, sitting with his awkward bulk in one of the rickety vinyl chairs there. He smiled his pained smile when I came in and rose to shake my hand. The smile gave him the look of someone who'd borne all his life some small, unremitting affliction.

"So we meet so soon again after all," he said. "I hope you're better now."

He was a bit formal and stiff, uneasy perhaps at being

found here or simply sensing, if only from the look of me, the charged atmosphere that my arrival had ushered in.

"Yes. Better. Thanks."

There was a moment's strained silence. Something in the chemistry of the three of us alone in Rita's kitchen seemed to have set up a hum of weird, not-quite-readable tensions.

"Please, sit down," John said.

We sat. Rita had already melted into the background, collecting a few dirty dishes off the table and then turning her back to us and busying herself at the kitchen counter. All of this seemed to have come about as if by arrangement, John and I at the table, Rita safely away. I had a flash again of the fevered paranoia of the past few days.

"So you must be busy now with the end of term," John said.

"Yes," I said. "Yes."

"Ah."

There was a sort of stumbling forward into conversation. Rita was making coffee, using the conversation like a shield. Every time there was a lapse, her movements would quicken slightly as if to push us on.

"You were saying you and Rita met in a class or something."

"Yes. In the fall."

I still couldn't place his accent: Scandinavian, perhaps, or German or Dutch.

"You're doing a degree?"

He looked a little embarrassed.

"Well, perhaps. Mainly I just do courses. What I like."

His embarrassment made me uneasy about asking him any more questions. He was this big lump of a man, all gangly limbs and bulk, his skin ruddy and pink as if someone had over-scrubbed it. What was he doing here, at ten on a weekday morning? It went through my mind that he was Rita's "date" of Saturday night. But it was somehow clear that there was nothing sexual between the two of them, not merely from the few things Rita had said about him but from the plainly paternal air he had around her.

"I was wondering," he said. "We were thinking of taking a little excursion. Because of the weather. Maybe you'd like to join us."

An excursion. The word sounded absurd, as if we were leisured aristocrats arranging some parasolled outing to the country. Here we sat, at the frayed edge of sanity, and we were planning an excursion.

"I don't know. There's things I should do."

"Yes, of course."

I couldn't catch Rita's eye.

"Rita has a class at three," I said.

John's gaze went to Rita uncomfortably, as if this contradicted something she'd told him.

"I didn't realize. Anyway it's probably just review now and that sort of thing."

I was still awaiting some sign from Rita. They would go off together and another day would pass with nothing resolved.

"Are you going far?"

"We were thinking of the zoo, actually," John said. He looked embarrassed again. "It's a bit of a journey to get there by transit, of course."

"You don't have a car?"

"No. Actually, no."

The whole idea was crazy. It seemed there was no way to get to Rita except through this chaperon.

"We could take mine," I said.

"Ah. Well. Yes. That's much quicker."

Rita was still standing at the kitchen counter.

"Is that all right with you?" I said.

"It sounds great." Her voice was toneless, perfectly neutral.

"I'll get my car, then."

The zoo lay to the northeast of the city. We drove out on the Gardiner Expressway and then up the Don Valley, John in back and Rita and me together in the front. Beside me Rita sat eyes forward, in another world but also stilled somehow, as if she had moved into a new territory where anger, shame, were irrelevant, where there was only the brute fact of what had happened.

"You're very quiet this morning," John said.

"I'm just a little under the weather."

"Perhaps you've caught something from your brother."

The traffic moved swiftly. In the bright spring sun the speeding cars looked like night things scurrying for cover.

"So Rita tells me you grew up on a farm," John said.

I wondered what she'd told him of the entanglements of our childhood. There was that forced quality in his question of not being certain where to begin, how much foreknowledge it was proper to reveal.

"Yes. A small one."

"You like nature, then. Or perhaps you've had enough of it."

Somehow I couldn't connect our farm with what he seemed to mean by nature.

"Yes, I suppose," I said.

The zoo was set out on a great sprawl of rolling woodland. Several large pavilions were clustered near the gates; beyond them, a maze of trails led past large outdoor animal runs. Despite the weather the place was almost deserted. There were a few mothers here and there pushing carriages or trailing toddlers, a few school groups that would appear from time to time, all frenzied energy and noise, then vanish again. John had put on a pair of sunglasses that gave him a slightly sinister look: I had an instant's sense that if he removed them, some secret about him would be revealed, but when he did, to rub the bridge of his nose, they uncovered only eyes of a kind of silvery-blue indeterminateness like the colour of a river under cloud.

The trails that wound through the grounds were laid out by region, African, Eurasian, North American. We followed the African route, past a group of elephants in repose on the hard, barren earth around a scratching post, past a pair of giraffes just ducking out from a huge hangar-like shed. The giraffes moved like dream things, with their slow motion, larger-than-life unwieldiness and grace.

"You were in Africa for a while, I understand," John said.

"Yes. In Nigeria."

"You must have seen some game."

"No. No. Not where I was. I saw some in the east, when I was there. In Kenya."

"Ah. So you were in Kenya." He seemed to register this as if it were the first piece of new information about me he'd garnered.

"You've been there?" I said.

"Yes. Many years ago now."

Something in this intersection between our lives had touched a chord in him. He seemed to want to go on, but held back.

"What brought you there?" I said.

"Just travelling like that."

"You travel quite a bit?"

"Here and there. It's my hobby, I suppose."

Rita had wandered ahead to the next enclosure. Despite the warmth she held the lapels of her sweater clutched tight against her as if warding off a bitter wind. She seemed hardly aware of me and John now, withdrawn into the far remoteness she would go into sometimes as a child.

"She seems very preoccupied," John said. "Perhaps it has to do with her mother."

"Sorry?"

"With her plans to move back to England. I think it's very upsetting for Rita."

At the big indoor chimp cage, she left us to use the washroom. John and I waited on a bench that faced toward the cage. A commotion of some sort, a fight, sent one of the smaller chimps scurrying toward where we were sitting. When he was safely away from danger he stopped, sat, licked at some hurt on his arm, looked furtively about. He caught sight of us watching him from our bench and stared an instant, then turned away; and then with a kind of evasive, meandering gait, as if to hide his curiosity, he began to come toward us. At the fence he stopped and gazed at us with his old man's eyes, then stretched his fingers through the fencing's narrow mesh as if in pleading.

John was still watching. In the absence of Rita he seemed older, diminished.

"Who was that writer, I can't remember now. The one who talked about the first drawing by an ape and what it showed was the bars of his cage."

Five minutes passed, then ten, and still Rita had not returned.

"Do you think we should check on her?" John said.

"I don't know. Maybe."

I stood at the washroom door and called out to her. She appeared a moment later; I had expected tears or some outburst but she was perfectly, chillingly composed.

"Is everything okay?"

"Just feeling a little sick, that's all. Anyway I was thinking that maybe I should try to get to that class after all. With exams coming up and everything."

"Sure."

We were mostly silent on the trip home. Rita had asked to be in the back so she could stretch out there. I wanted to drop John off first to get Rita alone, but he had left his bicycle at Rita's.

"It's getting kind of late," Rita said. "You can just leave me at the university on your way."

"You sure you don't want to go home first?"

"It's okay. I'll be all right."

We left her at the corner of College and St. George.

"I'll call you," she said. On the sidewalk, bookless and purseless, still clutching the lapels of her sweater, she looked abandoned, cut adrift. But by the time I pulled away from the curb she had already disappeared in the crowd of passersby.

I left John at Rita's door. A few minutes later, while I was waiting for a break in traffic at the head of the street, he pulled up next to me on his bicycle and smiled, waved. He dismounted and walked the bike onto the sidewalk to cross over at the light further up, then started east along College.

I pulled out. John was already a couple of blocks ahead of me, more or less keeping pace with the traffic. I crossed Spadina, but then instead of turning in at my street I continued on, not certain why. John had stopped for a light at St. George; it only occurred to me now, as I slowed, afraid he would turn and see me, that I was following him. The light changed and John moved on. He kept up a steady clip, his legs moving regular and precise, the tail of his windbreaker flapping behind him. His bicycle was an old red C.C.M., anachronistic next to the sleeker ten-speeds people rode now; it held him dignified and straight-backed as if he were some old-world gentleman out on a Sunday tour.

Further on he turned up a sidestreet. I got held up at a light, turned, thought I had lost him, but then caught sight of him at the head of a cross-street just turning onto Yonge. When I made the corner I saw his bike, put up on its kickstand, parked near the door of a variety store. I pulled over to wait.

It was one of the seedier stretches of Yonge Street, mainly discount stores and porn shops, army surplus, the occasional head shop or bar. When I'd first come to Toronto several years before, the long central artery Yonge Street formed had seemed the essence of what the city was, even then when it was just an endless strip of arcades and second-storey massage parlours. But now whenever I crossed it it felt like some ravine that the city's detritus collected in, the bored suburban kids in from the malls and the addicts and drunks in search of a fix.

Today, in the spring sun, the street looked slightly redeemed. The sidewalks were thick with pedestrians, shoppers with their parcels, young men idling outside doorways, young women in sweaters and skirts. Across the way, a moustached older man with the magisterial air of some gold-rich desert merchant had come to stand in the sun at the doorway of his shop. He took me in watching from my car and stared an instant, arms folded over his chest, then finally retreated back into the darkness of his shop.

Through the open doorway of the variety store I saw John go up to the counter, place some items there, smile at the cashier though in a tired, distracted way. The doorway I saw him through was like a frame: it held him a moment anonymous and alone, out of context, so that it seemed I was seeing him – the cut of his limbs, his simple animal presence – for the first time. Some energy seemed to pass between us as he stood there, a deep, wordless line of force as if for an instant the world had been whittled down to just the two of us: he was predator or ally or prey and I was brute instinct in the shadows, watching.

He came out of the store. I thought the intensity of my attention on him must draw his gaze in my direction. But he simply pushed his bicycle off its stand unawares, his bag of purchases balanced off its handle, and walked it up a bit to an unmarked door wedged between two storefronts. Leaning the bicycle against his hip, he pulled a set of keys from his pocket and opened the door. So he lived here, then, in one of the second-storey flats that rose up above the shops. With a single deft movement, he swung his bike over his shoulder and disappeared with it through the doorway. I waited, staring up at the curtained windows of the second floor. Sure enough, after several minutes, one of the curtains opened and John appeared at the window there, still in his windbreaker. For a moment he stood staring down into the street like some sea captain gauging the threat of a coming storm; and then the curtain closed.

XIV

Two days went by before I saw Rita again, from the car as I was driving westward past the university buildings on College. I recognized her from behind: she was dressed in the same sweater and jeans she'd worn to the zoo, as if she'd simply been wandering this stretch of sidewalk since I'd dropped her here two days earlier.

I pulled up beside her.

"Would you like a ride?"

For a moment, she seemed truly not to recognize me.

"Oh." She stared up the street an instant as if to gauge the distance home. "Sure."

In the car, a silence. I had waited for her call after our day with John, but it hadn't come.

"Coming from school?" I said.

"Yeah. The library."

But she wasn't carrying any books.

It was a grey early evening. All day, rain had been threatening and now it began, a fine drizzle that hit the car with a sound like needles spilling. On the sidewalks, people ducked into doorways or raised newspapers above their heads to shield themselves.

"Are you better now?" Rita said.

"Sorry?"

"I mean, you were sick."

"Oh, that. Yes."

We were already at her street; in a minute more, at her house. I pulled over to the curb. A car wheeled around us with the slick, wet sound of tires against rain, then another.

"John said you were upset about your mother. About her moving away."

"Yeah. Well. It's no big deal."

"Is it set then?"

"Sort of."

"You know you can still count on me for help. You know that."

"I know."

In the tiny front lawns lining the street, clusters of old leaves preserved through the winter sat glistening in the rain. The weather, the leaves, the barren trees stretching out their grey limbs made it seem as if we had skipped through the seasons to autumn again. I had an image of making wine in the fall back in Mersea in this same drizzly wet under a lean-to my father had built against the kiln, cooking the pressings over a fire that we huddled around against the cold.

"I guess we made a bit of a mess of things," I said.

"I guess."

"I don't know what to do."

"I don't know. There's nothing to do."

Twilight was coming on. In the car, darkness had settled like silt, Rita just a wash of shadow across from me.

"I don't want you to think it's your fault," she said.

"It's hard not to think that."

"I'm not a kid. We both did what we wanted. We could look at it that way."

"Yes."

"Except that it was a mistake."

We were coming to an agreement, how to see things, how to live with them. That wasn't the difficult part after all. What was harder was the sane reasonableness of letting go, of being on the verge of grasping an unutterable thing, and passing it by.

"I was thinking of that tree near the barn at your father's farm," Rita said. "The mulberry tree. Is it still there?"

"I don't know. We cut some of them down."

"It was the one you built the treehouse in."

"Oh. Yes. I'm not sure."

The house had been just a crude platform of old planks where the trunk branched. On the far side of the trunk, where my father wouldn't see them, I'd nailed a few two-by-fours as steps to allow Rita to climb up.

"We used to go up there together," she said.

"I remember."

"You used to tell me not to go up alone, but I did. It was so quiet there, with the leaves and that smell. That mulberry smell. I'd sit up there for hours sometimes."

The rain was still falling. For some reason the streetlights had not yet come on; with the growing dark, it seemed the world was dissolving, slowly washing away. There was no traffic now, just the hush of early evening with its eerie expectancy, the tiny hammering of rain.

"What made you think of that?" I said.

"I'm not sure. The rain, maybe. We sat up there when it was raining, once, the two of us. The leaves were so thick we didn't get wet. I thought then that that was what made it a house. That we could stay dry in the rain."

It hurt me to remember her as a child, in my charge, the ways I had held her life in my hands then, the ways I had failed her. All the things that had brought us here to where we were now, and that made being here impossible.

"I'm thinking of going away," she said.

"Going where?"

"I don't know. Away. For a while."

"Because of what happened."

"Maybe. Because of everything."

"If you need money –"

"I can get by."

I couldn't read her expression in the dark.

"We could go together," I said.

The smallest pause.

"You know we can't do that."

We had reached a point of stillness. Everything had been acknowledged, every possibility veered toward and passed over.

"I'm probably going with John," she said. "Just so you know."

"I see."

"It's easier that way. He was planning a trip. He asked me."

"I suppose it's none of my business."

"You think it's strange, his friendship with me."

"I'm not one to talk," I said.

"It's just easier, that's all."

"Sure. Anyway, thanks for telling me."

The streetlights came on. A moment later a light went on in the front room of Rita's apartment: Elena was there, moving through the room, arranging things on her desk. In a minute she'd turn and see us sitting in my car at the front of the house, and begin to wonder.

"So is it set?" I said. "Your going away?"

"More or less."

"When?"

"In a few weeks. After exams."

"Does Elena know?"

"I'll tell her. Maybe she'll have to move to a smaller place until I get back."

"Which is when?"

"The end of the summer, I guess."

"It's okay. I'll cover the rent."

"You don't have to do that."

"It's okay."

"Maybe she could get a roommate or something."

"Sure."

But we were just spinning words out now. In a moment she would have to get out of the car and there would be nothing more to say.

"It might be better if we didn't see each other before I left," she said.

"If that's what you think."

"I don't know what I think."

Her hand was on the seat between us, a delicate tracery of shadow and bone.

"I should probably go," she said.

We didn't look at each other.

"All right."

And then she'd stepped out into the rain, crumpling slightly beneath it before disappearing through her door, no looking back.

The weather continued cold and wet. April weather, not quite free of the shackles of winter. It put me in mind of my first month in Canada, closed off in the house with Rita, just a baby then, and the cousin who'd come to look after her. At times when my father was working night shifts and slept in the day, we'd take Rita out to the porch to keep her from waking him, though the wind rattled the windows there and the cold seeped in at every crevice.

My classes had ended by now but I still had final papers to write. I kept to my apartment, trying to work though my mind was like an alien substance no longer matched to the world, that no new thought could take shape in. I'd picked up a small black-and-white TV at a yard sale down the street, and for days sat watching reruns on UHF of shows I'd seen as a child. There was an innocence in them that was like a balm, the television world they presented of hopeful suburban domesticity as if they'd preceded some global loss of faith, a great falling away that had somehow broken us.

Then one day, I got a call from Elena.

"I'd like to know what's going on," she said.

My heart was pounding.

"I don't know what you mean."

"Bullshit. You knew Rita was going away."

"She mentioned it."

"Was it supposed to be some kind of secret?"

"No."

A pause.

"Look. I'm not sure what's going on with you two. It's probably none of my business. But I think I'm entitled to some information. Getting anything out of Rita these days is like pulling teeth."

"She's just going travelling for a while. With John."

"And you don't think that's a little weird?"

"It's what she wants to do."

"Okay. Fine. But in the meantime, I'm a little involved in all this. Like this apartment, for one thing."

"I told Rita I would pay her rent while she's gone."

"That's not exactly how she put things to me."

"What did she say?"

"Something about not taking money from you any more. That I should look at getting a place on my own. If that's what you want, fine. It's just that I'd like to know."

"That's not what I said. I told her I'd pay."

"You're sure about that?"

"Yes."

Another pause.

"Jesus. All of a sudden everything feels so fucked up. I don't get it. Maybe it's just this whole thing with Mom."

"I thought you guys were all right about that."

"Yeah, well, think about it for a minute. How would you feel if you were suddenly homeless?"

"Is she leaving you any money?"

"Yes. No. I don't know. Maybe after she sells the house. Meanwhile, Rita decides this is when she has to go off and find herself."

I was left feeling that Rita was much more concerned about her financial situation than she'd let on. The question of money seemed to put what had happened in an entirely different light: I had abused a trust. She was my ward, I was her family; there couldn't be any emotion between us that wasn't tinged with these half-shades of dependence and power. It had been a life's work just to reach a point of sanity between us, of normality, and now in a matter of weeks, of days, an hour, all that had been wrecked.

I decided to send her a cheque to help tide her over, finally making it out for just over half what I had in my account. I tried to write her a letter to accompany it, but was at a loss what to say. I thought of the letters I used to write her from Africa, with their careful weighting of implication like a balance set to tip – the tension between us then, the very possibility of expression, had been all in that balancing, the constant featherweight of difference between what we said and what we held back. With that gone, there seemed no place to speak from any more except to descend into ravings, apologies, pathetic pleas. I ended by attaching only a short note:

This isn't a gift or a loan, just part of your due. I hope it saves you from being dependent on me or anyone for a while.

I put the cheque in the mail and waited. The days went by and still the money sat in my account; but just after a week had passed it was gone. I had expected some relief at this, but instead it was like having something cut out of me, a splitting down the middle of what was hers, what was mine. Another, perhaps a final link had been severed: she was on her own.

One afternoon toward the end of April I saw her from across the street at Spadina and College. We had hit another day of cold after some warmer ones, and she was dressed in her old blue parka again. When I spotted her she was just coming out of a bank at the corner; at the threshold, she looked both ways like someone in flight from a pursuer, then started south down Spadina. I followed from across the street. At Baldwin she turned into the market and I had to run to make the light. I caught sight of her turning down Kensington, then reached the corner in time to see her entering a coffee shop at the market's edge.

It was one of the cleaner places in the market, a sort of European-style café with a large front window that allowed a clear view inside. I watched her from the vegetable store across the way. She had taken a window seat at a table for two; from her shoulder bag she pulled out a paperback, then a pack of cigarettes, something that surprised me, since I had never known her to smoke more than the occasional one she cadged from me or Elena. A waiter came for her order and returned a moment later with a coffee; and then for several minutes she sat smoking and reading. A vase on her table held a single yellow tulip that made her look as if she'd been posed for a painting: woman reading in café window.

A man in a dirty overcoat went into the café and up to Rita's table. She smiled at him as if she knew him, exchanged a few words, handed him a cigarette from her pack. She watched as he brought a match tremblingly to the cigarette to light it, then reached into her bag and took out some coins from a change purse to put them discreetly in his hand.

She finished her coffee and came out. At the street entrance of a second-storey pool hall on the corner, she looked nervously in each direction again, then went inside. It was another of the places where dealers hung out; sometimes acned acid-heads or dreadlocked Rastas stood at the door whispering to passersby as if not to wake some sleeping infant inside. I waited a little way down from the entrance. When Rita emerged several minutes later, her hands fisted down in the pockets of her coat, she did so swiftly and eyes forward, disappearing almost at once around the corner back in the direction of Spadina.

I followed again. It was utterly different, seeing her this way, not only because of her secrets, her delinquencies, but because I was glimpsing the space that I was not in, what in the usual course of things was always kept from me. I had the sense I was invisible, that if she turned now, as this different person she was, she'd see only a stranger's face amongst others, and walk on. Or else being here among strangers, outside other people's ideas of us, or our own, it would be possible for a smile to form, for a complicity to make itself manifest: something had happened between us, a devious, hoped-for, unexpected thing, we were large enough to let that be part of us. I'd go up and silently take her arm, and we'd walk on together, into the anonymous world; and we would not stop.

She returned to College Street. An eastbound streetcar was just coming along and she boarded it. I followed behind in a taxi, the driver not understanding at first but then taking on an air of pleased collusion, as if we were playing a game. At Yonge, Rita emerged from the streetcar amidst a throng of other passengers – I thought she'd turn up the street toward John's place, but she went into an office tower on the far corner. I followed her inside to check the building's directory. The automobile association had its offices here, an architectural firm, several lawyers, a medical clinic. The thought formed that she might be pregnant: there would be doctors then, procedures, lies, some monstrous thing taking shape inside her. I didn't know what would be worse for her, carrying that alone or sharing it with me, admitting the sordidness of it, the horror.

I waited. Everything had to be lived through now, every consequence. Even standing here outside this building in the cold, this crazy shadowing: it seemed part of a story already fixed, where every turning had been laid out in advance to lead exactly here, to this moment. In a minute or ten Rita would emerge and I would confront her or not, we would come to some new understanding or stay imprisoned in inchoate emotion; and at each instant it would be the story deciding, propelling us forward. Perhaps there was only this tyranny, with nothing to choose, no moment to say, We will do things differently.

Across the street, a vendor was selling roasted chestnuts from a trolley, a grizzled man in an apron and cap with a disconcerted look as if he'd been tricked by the sudden cold into appearing here out of season. I had an image of a chestnut vendor I'd seen in Italy once, of his own grizzled face and crooked teeth. It might have been at the harbour in Naples, when my mother and I had caught the boat for Canada. All the years since then that image had lain in my memory like a photograph growing yellow in a drawer. What could it mean to have called it up now, what use could I have for it? Long ago the instant it referred to had vanished utterly from the earth, and yet this record of it had stuck in my mind as if at some moment it might be of worth to me.

She came out. I wasn't making any effort to conceal myself any more, and if she had turned the slightest bit, she would have seen me. But she made a direct line for the stairs that led down to the subway. A streetcar was just unloading at the corner, and she disappeared in the crush of other bodies descending the stairwell. I paid and hurried down to one of the platforms – two trains were just pulling out, one in either direction. It took a few minutes for the exiting passengers to clear, and to see that I'd lost her.

XV

A few days later I learned from Elena that John and Rita had gone. Elena's voice on the phone was dry, outraged, controlled.

"I guess she must have talked to you," she said.

"No." There was a part of her that wanted me to be on top of all this, to make it seem normal. "Did they say where they were going?"

"You tell me. All I know is they got on a bus to New York to catch some cheapo flight. Frankly the whole thing gives me the creeps."

"It's not such a strange thing to do."

"With a guy who's forty years older than her?"

"They're just friends."

"Yeah. Well. How much do you actually know about him?"

"Why? Was there something specific?"

"It's not that." She relented a bit. "He seemed fine, I suppose. You know, very paternal and all that. I'm just a little freaked out is all."

She was turning to me, in her way, but somehow what seemed most clear in this was the tenuousness of the link between us. It occurred to me that with Rita gone, she and I might go months now without seeing one another.

"I should come by with the rent cheque," I said.

"Don't bother. She left enough to cover it. I guess she came into a bit of money."

"Oh."

"Don't be an asshole. I know you gave it to her."

I didn't know how to respond to this.

"I guess I did."

A pause.

"Look, sorry, that was out of line," she said. "Maybe you should come by here when I'm not being such a harpy. Anyway, there's probably a few other things we ought to talk about."

She invited me to come by the following evening. Her friend Suzanne was there when I arrived, at the kitchen table, an empty coffee cup in front of her and an ashtray filled to overflowing.

"So I hear your sister's flown the coop," she said.

"It looks that way."

She gave me a tight, mirthless smile.

"I wouldn't worry about her. She's a big girl, from what I could see."

She got up to leave. At the door, she and Elena stood a few moments in low conversation. I expected them to hug or kiss, but Suzanne merely reached a hand out to squeeze Elena's shoulder.

"I'll call you," she said.

The apartment had already taken on an air of absence. I didn't remember the walls looking so bare, the furnishings so rickety and provisional. It seemed now that it had never quite been a home after all, just a space to fill, four walls and a roof.

Elena suggested we go out back to the patio. To get to it we had to pass through Rita's bedroom, which lay in a kind of tidy, sterile expectancy like a guest room, all the comfortable dishevelment of before given way to crisp corners and cleared surfaces. A single poster, from the *Rocky Horror Picture Show*, was taped to one wall, a bottom edge curling up where the tape had come loose.

"You haven't heard from her yet?" I said.

"No. Not yet. I've been out a lot."

"You'd think she would call."

But Elena was more detached now than she'd been on the phone.

"Maybe she figures she's not being much of a rebel if she has to call home every night."

The patio was just an arrangement of cheap concrete paving stones heaved up from winter freezes into rolling instability. Elena had set out a few old lawn chairs that she must have picked up at a yard sale, and a small end table whose top was stained with cigarette burns. With the warmer weather that was finally settling in, the garden had begun to show some of the promise that the landlord had spoken of when Rita and Elena had rented the place. A few rows of tulips had sprung up in beds along the side fences, and at the back a forsythia bush was just coming into bloom.

Elena had taken a seat on the steps that led down from the patio door.

"So I got a job today," she said. "Waitressing, if you can believe it."

"Are you all right with that?"

"Why?" She laughed. "Don't tell me you're going to support me too now."

She took out her cigarettes and offered me one, which I declined, then lit one for herself.

"I guess the whole money issue is none of my business," she said. "But you have to admit it's a little strange. I mean, you must have given her quite a chunk."

"I'm not sure what you're saying."

"It's a pattern, that's all."

"She needed money. I was just helping out."

"She could have gotten a job. Or a student loan. Whatever. I don't notice you taking the summer off to see the world."

"There are other factors."

"You mean your father's will."

I was surprised that Rita had told her about that.

"That's part of it."

She seemed to be taunting me, prodding me, as if the money I'd given Rita were some sort of payoff I'd made.

"Well, like I say, it's none of my business. It's just always pissed me off a bit the way you used the whole thing with the will as if you were suddenly her sugar daddy or something."

I was angry now. She was distorting everything, making what had felt genuine seem selfish and twisted.

"I don't remember you ever objecting when it worked to your benefit."

"True enough." There was an undertone of conciliation in her voice that I hadn't expected. "Maybe I'm the one who has a problem. Except, I dunno, you go for years just being this kind of ghost in her life, and then suddenly you want to make it seem like you're indispensable. I'll tell you what it was that set me off – it was the day we went out to the island to look at that place for rent, you telling us you could buy us a house there. It was as if you were saying, you guys don't have anything but I've got the power to give you what you want."

I thought of that day on the island, of the sun and the snow, the cosy cottage we'd seen with its fireplace and bric-a-brac. Our versions of the day seemed so different now, and yet at bottom the same instinct had joined us then, the same longing.

"It wasn't like that," I said.

"Maybe not. Maybe I'm just a bitch." She took a last puff off her cigarette and dropped it, slowly grinding it out with her heel. "Like buying that couch after to piss you off. Rita could have killed me."

It was hard not to feel admiration for her consistency. Even her spite had always this moral contour, this larger principle it arose from like some natural counterbalancing of anything that hinted at falseness.

"Anyway," she said, not looking at me, "I doubt it helped much for her to be dependent on you like that. For one thing, it was probably kind of hard for her to be honest with you."

"Honest about what?"

"The fact that she was flunking out, for instance. That she dropped half her courses months ago and will be lucky if she passed the half that she kept."

My heart sank. It was the feeling of having a not-quite-articulated fear confirmed, of knowing the clues had been there before me, and I had ignored them.

"I didn't know that," I said.

"Well, I hate to be the one to break it to you."

"She always seemed to work hard enough."

"Right. Like all those nights she was supposedly at the library."

"Where did she go?"

"You tell me. Out. Around."

"Maybe she was spending time at John's," I said.

"I doubt it. I remember asking her once where he lived and she didn't know."

It was strange now to be seeing Rita as merely this absence, this darkness, to think of all the questions I'd never asked, how I'd let the little I had known of her stand in for all I had not. I thought of my following her that day into the market, how different she had appeared then, how her aloneness had seemed like a hard, sad kernel of her that everything else merely served to obscure.

"When did all this start?" I said. "The problems in school and so on."

"I can't say things were ever great. But they definitely got worse when Dad died. She started getting a little weird then."

"She told me you said something about him that upset her."

"What?"

"That you made it sound like he was some sort of pervert."

"What are you talking about?"

"Something you said to one of your friends. About his adopting you only because you were girls. The way he used to watch you sometimes."

"She told you I said that?"

"Didn't you?"

"No. Of course not."

There was an edge in her voice, but I couldn't tell if it was anger or defence.

"Why would she lie about something like that?" I said.

"I have no idea."

"So you're saying she made the whole thing up."

"I don't know. Maybe it was just creative listening. It wouldn't be the first time."

"It doesn't sound like her."

"If you want the truth, I think she was the one who always wondered about him. I mean, she never really understood why either of them would bother taking someone like her in."

The possibility that Rita had twisted things, that there was this underside of obscure intention, seemed to call everything else into question. Her coming to me that day after Mr. Amherst's death, her ending up crying in my arms: all the rest, in a way, had followed from that, hinged on there having been something, some honest moment, that had set in motion what came after.

"You make it sound like she's disturbed," I said.

"Wouldn't you be? Look at the life she's had. All in all, it wasn't exactly like growing up with the Waltons."

"She always made it seem as if she was over all that."

"Yeah, well, some people just hide things better than others."

We sat silent. Elena lit another cigarette, tense and quick. It had put her out, being pitted against Rita in this way.

"Look," she said. "It was probably just a misunderstanding, that's all. She's not a nut case or anything, if that's what you're thinking. Or malicious. She's just, I don't know, different. You must remember those moods she'd get into when she was a kid, when she was just gone somewhere. It's like she's always fighting that. It's like she's afraid the world won't hold on to her or something."

Evening had come on, settling over us a darkness made grainy and soft by light from a streetlamp in the back lane. The lamp rose up almost directly above the forsythia bush at the back of the yard, making it seem, with its yellow blooms, like some rare, radiant thing that had briefly touched down from another realm to grace us with its presence.

"Let me know if you hear from her," I said.

But already Rita's absence had a quality of inviolability to it, as if it were not something she could be reached in or called back from. At home, I took out the letters she'd sent me while I was in Africa – they put me in mind now of the rotting bundle of letters I'd discovered by chance in the remnants of my father's desk after the fire we'd had on the farm had wrecked it, letters my mother had sent him from Italy during the years when he'd been in Canada alone. They were more or less unreadable by the time I found them, reduced to simple artefacts, bits of crumbling paper and faded ink that attested to the existence of certain things without, however, offering up their essence. Rita's letters I had kept bundled and bottom-drawered much as my father had kept my mother's. Perhaps the same impulse had guided us in this, the hope of thus holding onto some indefinable thing, whatever had been over-looked or not quite understood but that could continue to be held weighted down by this accumulation of paper and ink rather than being forever lost.

Among Rita's letters was a photograph she had sent me, early on, a wallet-sized school portrait showing her acned and adolescent and inscribed "Hot Stuff!" on the back. It had obviously been cut from one of those sheets of multiples that school pictures came in so they could be distributed to family and friends, one of its sides angled a bit crookedly so that it caught a sliver of colour from the photo adjacent. I wondered what might have become of the other photos in the sheet, who in the world now had one lost in the folds of a school album or tacked to a diary page or piled with others in a drawer. Or perhaps Rita herself had a sheet somewhere with only this one photograph removed – that was what the sliver of extra colour seemed to imply, that she hadn't cared enough about the next photo to keep it intact, had thought of only this single connection to make, this single use for her likeness. To my brother in Africa, she might have thought, turning the phrase around in her mind, feeling the weight that the word *brother* took on, the word *family*, and then finally slipping the photo into an envelope and mailing it on like a rope sent out, an anchor, to hold her to the earth.

XVI

With Rita's departure I fell briefly into a kind of a fog, unable for a while to muster the energy to perform anything more than the simplest daily tasks. I would rise and for a few hours feign the semblance of intention before ending up huddled in front of the television again or drifting back into sleep; and eventually the days began to merge one into the other, the separate islands they formed eroding into this general wash of decaying awareness. It was like the body's slow shutting down for the half-deadness of some long, long-awaited animal sleep: one day my heart would slow to nearly stopping, and I wouldn't rise at all.

At school, deadlines had come and gone, then extension dates as well. I risked the loss of my scholarship, failing grades, an expulsion, but couldn't muster the sense of urgency required to avert these things. At the prodding of one of my professors, I finally went into the university's counselling centre one day to get a letter of excuse that would allow incompletes to be registered on my file rather than failures.

The centre was the same one where I'd attended sessions several years before with a young graduate student who wore muslin blouses and did body work with me in a mat-lined room. It looked unchanged now except for the strangeness of remembering myself within it, the same narrow, labyrinthine halls, the same reception area hidden away at their core like the prize or trap at the heart of a maze. The receptionist smiled as one had back then, handed me a form to complete with that air of not wanting to let it be seen how she thought herself different from me. It occurred to me as it had then – and it was reassuring, in a way, to feel this thought repeat itself across the years, to feel there was still a link between who I'd been then and who I was now, as if I had not, after all, become a monster – that it was exactly in a place such as this, a place of cure, that you felt most ill.

I was assigned to an older woman who had the trace of an accent, with that attractive, well-groomed look professional women often had that always touched a particular chord of longing in me. Her office was cramped but had none of the usual institutional air of a university office – there were a few plants in the window, a hand-knitted rug on the floor. She asked me questions and gave me small, encouraging smiles. There was a certain shyness in her manner that somehow put me at ease, perhaps simply because it was the normal thing to expect in a stranger rather than the false intimacy I associated with this setting.

I told her about my father's suicide a year before and my mother's death when I was small. I had thought these things could somehow stand in for the rest, but it was surprising how small a space they seemed to occupy in the bald relating of them, how much they didn't account for.

"And the baby," the counsellor said. "The girl. After your mother died. You didn't say what happened to her."

"Oh. She was all right. She came to live with us."

"Your father accepted her?"

"Yes. Not really."

I found myself telling her about Rita, how we had treated her, how she had ended up leaving us. There was that one incident that had started things, when my father had beaten her while my aunt and I stood by.

"It seems stupid now," I said. "It was over a dog we'd taken in. My father wanted to kill it because it got into the chickens, and Rita tried to stop him."

"Kill it how?"

"With a shotgun."

"He was holding a gun the whole time?"

"Yes. I mean, he dropped it or something when he took off his belt. I don't remember exactly."

"And then he hit her."

"Yes."

"And what were you thinking?"

"I don't know. We were all thinking it. That he was going to kill her."

"Would he have done that?"

"I don't think so."

"But you didn't know that then."

"No. But that wasn't even the point. It wasn't even that he was actually angry at her. It's just that she was always *there*. That she didn't just disappear or something. I thought then, we all must have thought it, that if he just killed her it would be easier."

"Oh."

We both seemed a bit taken aback to have arrived at this admission. There was an instant's awkward silence.

"Anyway it's normal," the counsellor said. "You were only a child then."

"Yes."

At the end of the session, she made a few quick notations on a writing pad and said I could pick up the letter I needed the following day.

"And your sister?" she said. "Do you still see her?"

"Yes. She lives in the city now. She goes to school here."

"And you get along?"

"Yes."

She gave me a sort of timid look, as if embarrassed for me at all I'd been forced to reveal.

"You can come back again if you want to. I'm here the whole summer."

"Thank you."

I went back to my days of television and sleep. They were growing almost comfortable now, like time taken out from the ordained order of things that was only for me, that didn't connect to any future or past. It occurred to me, in this state, that there could be a dissolution point in a life where the logic of cause and effect suddenly ceased to apply, where there was not enough sense in things for any forward line to present itself. Perhaps that was how people came to kill themselves: they simply reached this blankness they disappeared in, this moment when the story of their lives no longer cohered.

To get out of the apartment I'd sometimes stop in at the café on College where Elena waited tables, sitting with her in a back booth during her breaks while she drank coffee and chain-smoked cigarettes. She was letting herself turn pretty again, had let her hair grow and had revived some dresses and skirts from her old wardrobe as if she was reverting through a sort of negligence to her former self. She had taken to her work with what looked liked a dogged commitment to getting it right, quick and civil and precise in everything she did as if waitressing were a science she was mastering. But it was clear from the quiet energy that came off her as she worked that she relished being out in the world like this, having a job, being on her own. It was a kind of respite for me to watch her, to see this little piece of the world that was still functioning and sound, hadn't lost its way.

She'd finally had a call from Rita, from London, about a week after her departure.

"How did she seem?" I said.

"I dunno. Just fine, I suppose. We didn't really get into details."

She'd had a call from Mrs. Amherst as well, who was back in Mersea finalizing the details of her move. Apparently Rita had phoned her and given her some story about travelling through Europe with a tour group.

"Did you tell her the truth?" I said.

"Which is what, exactly?"

"She must have wondered. Where she got the money, for instance."

"It's not the kind of thing Mom would ask about. She doesn't really like to know any more than she has to."

"Maybe it's because you don't tell her things," I said.

"Tell her what? That Rita's run off with a sixty-year-old man? That I'm a lesbian?"

A couple of heads turned at the booth across from us, but Elena ignored them.

"I know you think I'm hard on her," she said. "But we're the kids, remember? She's the parent. When Dad died she was basically drunk the whole time we were home. We could have used a little support then too. Just a word. Anything. Rita especially. She's pretty messed up where Mom's concerned. When she was a kid Mom used to make her feel she was defective or something because of where she came from. It was like she was hedging her bets in case she didn't turn out right."

But beneath the bitterness in her voice there was a lingering note of question, of doubt, as if she were inviting someone to contradict her.

"Will you see her before she goes back to England?" I said.

"Yeah. I don't know. We'll see."

Since the night of Rita's party, Sid seemed to have gone back into whatever hole it was he occasionally disappeared into; I'd sometimes see his lights on in the night or hear his steps on the fire escape, but then days would pass and there'd be no sign of him. Finally one day I ran into him outside our building. Somehow he'd managed to find out that Rita had gone.

"So I guess she's doing the whole sixties trip," he said. "On the road and all that."

"I guess."

He was his usual blithe, unreadable self, with that disarming smile he would put on like a reflex to hide the wheels turning beneath.

"Anyway, I just wanted to say that nothing happened between us," he said. "I mean, she's a nice kid."

I had no word from Rita directly until nearly a month after her departure, when I got a postcard from her, from Paris. It showed a reproduction of a Degas, a pastel sketch of a dancer done against a wash of pale, almost unearthly green. The note on the back had no salutation, only a single floating phrase, "Just to let you know I'm okay," and her initial. At the bottom, John had included a note: "Sorry to have missed you when we left. I hope your work goes well."

I took heart from the simplicity of her note, had been imagining her completely changed, inaccessible, and yet there was still this core of her that I knew that for all the questions and revelations was still something I was connected to. The thought of her in Europe, in a specific, locatable place there, conjured up less a sense of distance than of proximity: it was the continent that had conceived us both even if we had never shared it. If things had been different I would have liked to have returned there one day with her, into the mountains that were perhaps encoded in her cells, into the winding streets of our village. We'd go along and I'd point out this street, this house, her own womb-dark history, what she perhaps had taken in back then through some dim, deeper-than-thought awareness.

There was something about her card, though, that left a niggling residue: the note from John, its simple presence or just the look of its tight, careful script that wasn't right somehow. I was reminded again that I knew next to nothing about him; and yet the strange thing was exactly that I'd never had the least doubt that Rita was safe with him, had known from the outset, in some animal way, that he wouldn't harm her. I thought back to the day that I'd followed him home, the sight of him in the shop doorway, the weird, almost preternatural energy that had seemed to come off him then but which I'd never quite been able to give a shape to or trace to an origin.

One night when I was out in my car I drove by John's apartment. I thought I noticed a light on in his front room, and drove back around to the sidestreet nearby to make sure I'd seen correctly. Yes, it was his place: I remembered the shop below, the pale yellow brick of the façade. Perhaps he had a timer on; but then I saw a figure move across the light, in one direction and back again. I had an instant's throb of suspicion, a sense of duplicity like a tiny alarm in some not-quite-accessible chamber of the brain, before realizing there was probably a simple explanation, that he'd sublet the place or that a friend had come by to look after things. My first thought then was that it would be possible, therefore, to get inside; and it was in having the thought, in seeing, in my mind's eye, John's apartment laid out before me as if it were the inside of his head, that something shifted in me like a tumbler falling into place, and some new understanding of him seemed to shimmer briefly before me. For an instant that sudden sense of him played in my mind like the barely held fragment of a dream, never quite coalescing into solid shape; and then it was gone. I sat watching his window for several minutes more, hoping it might help dredge up what that instant's certainty had been, what it had been trying to tell me. But finally the window went black, showing only the mirrored reflection of neon and of other blank windows across the street.

XVII

I went by John's apartment again the following morning, watching it from the window of a coffee shop across the street. It was a Saturday, and the sidewalks were thick with shoppers, in shorts and halters and flimsy summerwear because of a sudden heatwave. The heat gave a slow, shimmery unreality to things as if some conspiracy were unfolding, as if every movement, the passersby peering in windows, the customers emerging from shops, had been carefully choreographed to present the bland, false face of normality.

Around eleven o'clock a woman emerged from the door that led up to John's apartment, wearing sunglasses and jeans and an untucked Indian blouse. She fumbled with her keys a moment as she went to lock the door, dropped them, bent to collect them. Her hair was a dark, wavy mass that shifted and swayed like a separate entity when she moved, with that permanent windblown look as if she'd been standing for hours in a stiff ocean breeze.

She went down the street and into the variety store I'd seen John use. A few minutes later, a bag of groceries in hand, she emerged and returned to the apartment. It was unclear to me now what my plan had been, how I'd thought that just the evidence that someone was actually inside John's apartment could be enough to gain me entry into it. I watched the people going in and out of shops along the street and it seemed strange that one floor above there were these other spaces that were completely inviolable.

I crossed the street. There was a single buzzer at John's door; I pressed it.

She was at the door in an instant, swinging it open with a guilelessness that made my heart sink. Her hair had got tousled in her descent and she reached up to pull it back from her shoulders, her blouse hiking up a split second to reveal a thin rim of naked waist.

"Hi," she said, a little breathless. Behind her, a narrow staircase led up through semi-darkness.

"I'm sorry to bother you. I'm a friend of John's."

"You mean Mr. Keller?"

I realized I didn't know John's surname. It crossed my mind that this whole thing might be a mistake, that I'd got the apartment wrong or that John had moved, had never existed.

"Yes," I said.

"He's away in Europe. I'm just subletting."

"Oh. I wasn't sure if he'd gone yet."

"Yeah. About a month ago."

I was losing heart. She looked younger than she had from a distance, in her early twenties perhaps; without sunglasses, her face radiated a pale, freckled innocence.

"There were some books that I lent him. They were kind of important. For my thesis. I'd replace them but they're sort of hard to get a hold of."

A barest flicker of hesitation: there was this problem to solve, but no clear solution.

"I could look for them, if you want. I don't think he'd mind that."

At some point soon, she would begin to see through me and the whole thing would turn ugly.

"I'd have to write out the titles, they're a bit complicated. If you've got a pen and paper –"

The hesitation again. Her eyes flitted to the stairs and then to the street as if she were seeking permission from someone.

"I guess maybe it would be easier if you just came up and looked for them yourself."

"I don't want to bother you. It would just take a minute."

"Just don't look at the mess, that's all."

I was in. I felt a kind of horror at the ease of the thing: it would be this simple to plot a con or a murder or rape, I had it in me to deceive like that. I watched myself go inside, follow her up the stairs, as if I were watching a stranger, not sure what he was capable of.

"So you're a friend of Mr. Keller's?" she said.

"More an acquaintance, really." I couldn't see her face in the narrow stairwell, to judge if there was any suspicion in it. "And yourself? I mean, do you know him at all?"

"I was in a class of his at the institute this spring. You know, one of those crash courses for beginners. I thought it would be faster than doing it at university."

So he was a teacher of some sort.

"I see," I said.

We had come to the landing. There was no separate entrance, just an arched passage that opened directly into the apartment.

"I'm Ieva, by the way." There was an overly cheerful tone in her voice that made me think she was lonely. "It's Latvian for some kind of tree that doesn't grow here, if you're interested. People usually ask."

"Oh. I'm Victor. Vittorio really. It's Italian."

I had started to incriminate myself. At some point John would return, and all this would have to be accounted for.

"Italy," she said. "I've always wanted to go there."

The apartment had a long, open-concept living and dining area and kitchen on the street side, and then a hallway at the back that led past a series of closed doors. At first glance there seemed an odd disjunction in the place, a combination of the already dated earth-and-smoky-grey-toned modernity of the seventies with an older, fustier, more cluttered sensibility as if some graft of different species hadn't taken. The furniture had that look of having been culled over many years from second-hand shops, a little frayed and not quite matching, and arranged with a haphazardness that didn't give much definition to the openness of the front space; the one exception was an arrangement of bookshelves and a worn, maroon-coloured leather armchair and matching ottoman near the window that formed a sort of reading area. The walls throughout were covered in prints and old photographs of various sorts, though with that same, slightly cluttered look as if part of a life never quite under control, never quite cared about enough for its minutiae to be put in proper order.

"It's not exactly the sort of place I thought he would live in," Ieva said. The bit of unease she'd shown at the door was gone now, as though the simple fact that I was here, that she'd allowed me entry, was somehow proof that I wasn't dangerous.

"How's that?" I said.

"I don't know. Him being German and all that. I thought it would be more Bauhaus or something. Not that I know a lot of Germans."

My mind registered the fact that he was German without any sense of revelation, though I wasn't sure if he or Rita had ever said as much.

"Help yourself looking around," Ieva said. "I'll check the bedroom to spare you having to look at my dirty laundry."

Now that I was here, I had no idea what I was looking for. I'd somehow expected that all the secrets of John's life would be set out for me in plain view; instead there were only these bits of things like some archaeologist's half-hearted reconstruction of a life. There was something sad in this gloomy half-completeness the place had, though perhaps it was just the sadness of how little of ourselves we actually surrounded ourselves with, how much was just the generic debris that accumulated against us like litter against fences.

I went to the bookshelves near the window. They held a host of texts in what I took to be German, most by authors I didn't know, and an eclectic assortment of novels, philosophy, poetry, in English. On a bottom shelf was what looked like a collection of Holocaust literature – Primo Levi, Elie Wiesel, Jerzy Kosinski. It was the only shelf on which the books weren't arranged in alphabetical order. I wondered if there was a meaning to this, if some special code was being revealed to me.

145

Ieva had emerged from one of the doors along the back hallway.

"Nothing in the bedroom. Any luck?"

"Not yet."

"You'd think he'd have set the books aside in a special pile or something."

She led me to a small office toward the back of the apartment. There were no windows in the room, only the deep shaft of a skylight sending a rectangle of honeyed light onto the parquet floor. Two walls were covered with bookshelves, more untidy than the ones in the living room, many of the shelves double-stacked.

"I forgot how many books there were in here," Ieva said. "I can give you a hand if you want."

"I'll be all right."

"I'll leave you to it, then. I'm making some tea, if you'd like some."

"Sure." But I never drank tea. "That would be great."

There was an old oak desk in the room with some bulging manila files and dog-eared notebooks stacked precariously to one side of its surface as if someone had tried to make quick order; next to it was a two-drawered filing cabinet, with more files on top and a framed Kandinsky print, floating circles and squares in purples and oranges and blues, on the wall above it. There were a few reference books lined up against the wall on the desktop: a German-English dictionary; Fowler's *Modern English Usage*; a *German for Beginners* teacher's guide. The desk was like the one my father had had where I'd found my mother's letters, with a big double drawer on one side and those pull-out side counters like breadboards whose uses, as a child, I had never been able to fathom.

I scanned the bookshelves. The books here were mainly German as well. There was a yellowing paperback copy of *Mein Kampf*, with notes scribbled in the margins; there were what looked like complete editions of Goethe, of Hölderlin, of Kant. John's Germanness seemed the single message that I had so far gleaned about him, and even that less as some essence than as just a label affixed to things, an abstraction. It felt important suddenly to be clear whether I'd known he was German before this, whether I'd attached any significance to that fact. But somehow my sense of him had got skewed, as if every discovery, even the look of this place, the disjunction and the unfamiliarity, were after all just the remembrance of something I'd already known. I imagined him moving around this room, amidst these books, and could feel an almost corporeal identification with him, a feeling of being inside his skin, being able to take for granted things about him I couldn't possibly know.

From the kitchen came a steady bustle and clink of movement. I tried the top drawer of the filing cabinet; it opened. There was a fairly orderly arrangement of files inside containing what seemed to be notes from courses he had taken, labelled by number rather than title, Hum 304, His 413, Psy 211. From the look of things, he'd taken courses over the years in practically every major department. Each file held a thick sheaf of notes, all in his tight, careful script, and all in English. In some of the files, though, two- or three-inch margins that held sporadic scribbled comments in German had been ruled off to the right of each page. Some of the comments were in a different-coloured ink, red or blue instead of black; almost all of them ended in question marks. There was something slightly eerie in the look of them, ruled off like that with their little question marks to the side of the page, in the running commentary they formed like the inscrutable underside to the plain certainties and facts that flanked them.

In the bottom drawer, the files were labelled in German. There was one that held a certificate of citizenship, issued in 1966: he had likely come to the country in the early sixties, then, the same time as I had. The certificate was issued in the name "Johannes Elias Keller," written out in large, florid calligraphy. It was strange how the name, set out in full like that, seemed to open up some new side of him, as if names had the power to create our different selves. To Ieva, he was Mr. Keller the teacher; to Rita, John the student. Now there was this third person, this Johannes Elias; he was the one who lived in this slightly run-down flat, who read books and made margin notes, who in some way I was connected to.

Toward the back of the drawer was a file that was unlabelled. It held a single old and tattered five-by-eight photograph in black and white, deep creases dividing it in four as if it had been carried for a long time folded in a pocket. The picture showed a man in a uniform standing next to a young woman holding a sort of hamper in which a frilled-bonneted baby lay swaddled. But the photo was so faded and cracked, the surface come away entirely where the creases were, that many of its details were unclear. Where the man's face should have been there was only a frayed blot of browning paper; and it was hard to say what sort of uniform he was wearing or what the baby's gender was or even in what era the picture had been taken. The one thing that was clear was the woman's face, which had a sort of haunted look, as if she was staring past the photographer to some point far beyond him.

"Tea's up."

Ieva was at the doorway. She saw me kneeling over the open file drawer and a look passed through her eyes that seemed both the sudden understanding that something was amiss and the quick suppression of the thought.

"Great," I said, quickly replacing the photo and closing the drawer.

She served the tea at the kitchen table. Neither of us had mentioned the books again.

"So you're a student?" I said.

"Yes." But she had grown circumspect. "History. That's why I was doing the German course at the institute. To help with some research I wanted to do."

I hadn't noticed the sticky heat in the room before. There was the barest patina of sweat on Ieva's upper lip.

"Why history?"

"I don't know. To get into law, mainly. Though also a roots thing, I guess. Latvia and all that."

"Has your family been here long? In Canada, I mean?"

"Since just after the war."

Something in the finality with which she said that seemed to cut off further enquiry. She didn't look quite as innocent now as when she'd first come to the door. There was also something else, a vaguely Semitic look I hadn't noticed before, that was there in a certain angle of her profile like a clue I'd missed, the little detail around which a hundred others might coalesce.

"So maybe he left those books at work or something," I said.

"Yeah. It's too bad."

"Well, I should probably be going."

She followed me down the stairs. At the exit, I had a sharp pang of regret at how I'd handled things, at being this stranger she was hurrying out the door after the openness she had greeted me with.

"Sorry to have bothered you."

"It's all right."

I could feel the lingering sense of question in her, of betrayal. Perhaps if I had been honest with her; but I couldn't shape my mind around what I would have said then.

"Anyway, thanks again."

And I could feel her eyes on me as I turned, and the beat, then two, before the door closed and the lock clicked into place.

XVIII

The following day I dropped by Elena's place, after looking for her at work and being told she was off. There was a letter from Rita on the kitchen table, a slim blue *aérogramme* from France.

"You can read it if you want," Elena said. "Not that it says much."

The letter read like the shorthand of journal entries, just the barest details of how they'd travelled, where they'd been – London, Paris, now a small tourist town in Lorraine. Everything was put in the plural, "we," though she never referred to John by name. Toward the end she mentioned a monastery they'd been to, where, from a clifftop terrace, they'd had a view of the Black Forest across the border. The detail seemed an odd one to throw in after the preceding wash of bald fact; or perhaps it was simply that the nagging sense of strangeness from my visit to John's had made things seemed skewed, meaning more than they said.

Elena was sitting across from me at the kitchen table with that inviolable air she had that always gave her a hint of threat.

"I was wondering about John," I said.

"Wondering what?"

"I don't know. Just wondering."

"Like I said, he seemed normal enough, if that's what you're worried about. Better than that guy Sid."

"You knew about him?"

"It was hard to miss him. He kept coming by here after our party. Rita wouldn't see him."

"I didn't know that." This put my encounter with him on the street in a different light. "Why wouldn't she?"

"I didn't ask."

"So he'd come and you'd just send him away."

"Oh, he'd hang around a bit. You know, talk me up, try to seem cool. But it started getting a little weird after a while."

"It doesn't sound like him."

"Yeah, well, she has that effect on guys. They all want to take care of her. It's the whole father thing again."

"Whose father thing? Hers or theirs?"

"You have to admit she attracts it. Which is only logical given that she never had one."

She always made these pronouncements about Rita that made my own knowledge of her seem so amorphous. I was never able to separate out the bits of her in this way, as if she were just an accumulation of small inevitabilities, the adding up of everything she'd suffered or lacked.

"Did the two of you ever talk about her father?" I said. "Her real one?"

"It's not like we had much to go on. I mean, if anyone was likely to know anything, it would be you."

She might have asked me at this point what I did know about him but that wasn't the way with us. Instead she left openings like challenges that I might take up or not and that then set the rules between us, how close we would come to each other. I was on the verge of saying something to her now but was afraid that even the small bit of certainty I had would slip from me then – it had all been so long ago, from another life, set out in the approximations and half-phrases of memory like lists of contents written out on boxes that could never be opened. I thought of witnesses to a crime, who even moments after the event couldn't agree on the simplest details of what had happened, how tall the man was, what he wore, the colour of his skin. But still across the years, an impression had persisted: I remembered the flies, the heat, the rustle of leaves, two eyes staring out from a stable door. I had a relationship to the eyes like one might have to some crucial, irretrievably lost object – I'd never expected to see them again, had long ago consigned them to the unexplainable, the out-of-reach, and yet in some under-narrative of the mind there had always been the point where they recurred, like in some final meeting place, the denouement of a story or life, where every loose end was tied and every lost thing restored.

In the days after my visit to John's, my dreams began to take on a sudden vividness. A few times I dreamt I was in his apartment again, moving through the rooms, trying to elude some threat; but mainly the dreams seemed simply a hodgepodge of scattered images whose links were never quite clear, like bits of a story that had somehow got jumbled. Real memories were mixed in, or they seemed real enough, though sometimes on waking, or in the hazy middle of a morning when an image would suddenly surface out of nothing, it was difficult to sort out the real from the merely imagined. I felt I was losing myself, that the walls that kept truth from fabrication were slowly decaying; one day I might wake and be just the stranger that my dreams had conjured up, like some character in a science-fiction story whose memory had been subtly altered while he slept.

Sometimes I dreamt I was redreaming the dreams I had had as a child. That was the worst, because in daylight then I couldn't piece together what was the dream and what the dream's dreaming, back and back like the infinite regression of mirrors mirroring back your mirrored reflection. The dreams churned up memories, associations, that floated in the grey of almost-possibility like sea things briefly darkening the sea's rippled surface: this might have happened, or this might have been what the dream's dream had made me dream might have happened. There was a recurring dream that I'd had as a child in Italy that returned to me in this way: in it, two soldiers, Germans, came in the night to my mother's room to lead her away. As I remembered things now, through this double scrim of shadow seen through shadow, the soldiers had had to do with the stories I'd been told of the Germans who had been billeted in our house during the war. That would have been a decade before my birth, when my mother would not have been much more than a girl. *One of them wanted to be your father*, my mother had said of them: that was what I remembered. It was the fact that I couldn't have understood what she'd meant then, the joke she was making, that seemed to make this train of memories real, something I couldn't have invented. The soldiers had come; my mother had spoken to them. Or else this version of events, along with all the bits and shreds of quarter-remembered things that my mind offered up now in relation to it, was just a story I'd dreamed up based on some lost, mistaken assumption or logic of childhood.

It seemed almost impossible now that any of these things could have happened at all, that my mother had been a girl, that she had existed, that soldiers had come to a place in the past whose rocks and stones had been solid and real; and impossible too that out in the world there still remained the residue of these things, that the mountainside where I'd grown up, the village, the church on a hill, hadn't simply vanished with my leaving them. At any moment I could return to them, simply, in the time it took for a night's sleep: close my eyes, and I would be there. There would be a house that I had lived in, perhaps crumbling now, the roof fallen in and lizards making their nests among the rotting floorboards; there would be a stable door at the back, leaning on its rusted hinges, and inside, a hovel of dirt and stone much smaller, much meaner, than I remembered it, with an ancient pig's trough and the rough-hewn boards and posts of a sheep stall. It hurt my mind to think of these things still waiting abandoned there like injuries that had never been tended to. I remembered a man who had come once to sit cap in hand in my father's kitchen in Mersea to tell me that back in the village, my grandfather had died: he had seemed like a messenger from the void then, from a world that could not possibly, in my absence from it, have continued to exist. He'd mentioned some property that had been bequeathed to me, some land, my grandfather's house; and yet in all the years since then I'd never been able to trace a line between my existence here in this other country, this other present, and the stones and beams of an actual physical place that could be travelled to and walked around in.

Some time in June, after the postcard and the letter, after my visit to John's, I had a phone call, in the middle of the night. Dead air; and then a transatlantic blip.

"It's me."

It was Rita.

"Where are you?"

"It doesn't matter. Switzerland."

There was a delay in the line, a split-second lag, and an echo like a voice reverberating through empty space.

"Are you okay?"

"I'm all right. I'm fine. I just wanted you to know that."

Another blip.

"Is John with you?"

"Yes. Not right this minute. I'm at a phone booth."

The crackly hollowness of the line gave me the sense that she was receding from me, that time was running out.

"I'm thinking of coming to Italy," I said, forming the thought as I spoke it. "To our village."

"Oh."

"You could meet me there."

A pause.

"I don't know."

Her voice sounded hopelessly frail and thin, as if the buzzing wires it travelled across could barely sustain it.

"Please," I said.

"I don't know. I'll see."

"Just go there. I'll wait for you."

"I'll see."

In the morning, I had a instant's unsureness as to whether the call had been real. I had an image of a voice tunnelling through an impossibly long, hollow tube, and Rita at the end of it a tiny shadow against a pinprick of light. It took a moment for me to pull from the dimness of sleep the memory that we'd made an arrangement of sorts: I'd left no question that I would go, that I would wait for her. That had been how I had wanted to put things, as if there were no option involved, as if I were a place on a map that would be there whether she came or not.

I had tried to show her once in an atlas where the village was. But even in the big reference atlas in the university library it hadn't been listed by name, so that it had seemed she had had to take it on faith that the place existed at all, wasn't a figment of my imagination, that somewhere in the criss-crossing of tiny highways and relief lines the map showed was this unnamed cluster of real houses you could go to, with real people walking the streets. If she went now she would have to grope her way there with only this spectre to go by, this possibility. In my mind, I traced the line she would follow, the small dip down through a mountain pass out of Switzerland to the plains of the Po, the ride south into history and heat. The country would hold her; it was half hers, after all, the hills were in her blood and the sky, the crumbled ruins, the cooked earth. Even for her it wasn't a place to visit but to go back to, like somewhere a road led after years of wandering; and slowly she'd drift down into the dream of it and the village would call to her like home, and she would go.

XIX

I began to prepare for my departure, dismantling my life as if it were a tent I'd briefly pitched. It seemed necessary to divest myself of things: I gave up my apartment, sold off most of my furnishings, took boxes of clothing – ancient things, things I had owned since high school, that still had the smell in them of my life then – to the Goodwill. The ticket I bought was a one-year open return: it had the sound of a different order of travel, an open return, something that airlines, travel agents, slipped in amidst their usual fares to allow for those whose lives were unfixed, who might suffer catastrophe or a change of heart or find waiting for them at their destination the thing that put going back out of the question.

It was surprising how little my possessions – what was really mine, what had meaning, wasn't just the detritus of being alive – actually amounted to when I gathered them up. There were Rita's letters; there was a book I'd had as a child, *The Guiding Light*, that told the story of the Bible in pictures.

I remembered how I had gone through the house after my father's death collecting his belongings and had come up with only a few trinkets, a watch, a razor, his old wedding band, which I'd worn for a few weeks like a piece of string tied to my finger to remind me of some important errand, then removed. In the end, his things had come to no more than what fit in the old Crown Royal bag I kept them in now, that bulged it like so much ash or dust. I came from a line, it seemed, that did not hold on to things, that had no heirlooms to pass on, no signet rings, that didn't think itself a weighty enough presence in the world to leave some record of its having passed through. I thought of the gifts I'd brought with me from Italy, a jack-knife, a *Lives of the Saints*, my grandfather's war medals, things that I might have passed on to a daughter or son along with their stories but all scattered now, lost like memories I could not quite recall. It wasn't so much that these things hadn't mattered to me as that my life had not seemed receptable enough to hold them, to keep them from slipping away from me.

I had a coin that I'd got a few years before from an old man in Mersea, a pre-war one *lire*, the exact duplicate, down to a flaw on one side from the minting, of one I'd been given as a child by a friend of my mother's and had lost. The coin seemed now the symbol of everything that had vanished from my life, in every respect the same as the first except in the important one of being the actual physical thing, what had passed from hand to hand, what could have proved the reality of a certain moment or person or place. It hardly seemed possible sometimes that a life could go on at all with only such phantoms of phantoms to lend it credence, with almost nothing that could ever be nailed down for certain. Yet that was what matters always came down to, to faulty recreations of things that had themselves perhaps only been tokens, that hadn't been adequate even in their first moment of meaning to take in the fullness of the world that they'd strained to represent. I set the coin aside now to bring with me, a shibboleth; perhaps something would accrue on it that would make it cease to be simply a copy of a lost original.

I brought a few boxes of belongings to Elena's for storage. Her apartment seemed even emptier than usual, with the damp, cavernous feel that our house on the farm used to take on in summer, the sense of not being quite lived in. She and I hadn't talked much about my trip: I had tried to put it as a spur-of-the-moment thing that Rita and I had arranged when Rita had phoned: but she seemed to have understood that there was more to it than I would say, and that made any casual reference to it awkward.

"I'm not sure what you guys hope to accomplish there," she said.

"I don't know. I was born there. It's normal to want to go back. Maybe things are different for you."

"You mean because I'm adopted. Because you think my parents left me in a trash can or something so why would I want to know about that."

"That's not what I said. I just meant –"

"Forget it."

She was feeling abandoned, had that angry, restless energy she took on when she couldn't admit she was hurt. Getting close to her when she was like this was like scratching at an irritation, not knowing if you would soothe or inflame it.

"You've never talked about your parents," I said. "Your real ones, I mean."

"You've never asked."

"So I'm asking."

She gave a half-laugh.

"Here we go. True confessions."

"We don't have to do this," I said.

"No. Fine. It's not as if it's some deep, dark secret. They didn't molest me or anything like that."

"So you knew them, then."

"I was with them till I was five. I guess my dad was a bit of a drunk and he smashed me around a couple of times. End of story."

"And they took you away."

"Yeah, well, you know how they did things back then. Very quiet. I doubt my folks ever even knew what hit them. Then they moved away and I never heard from them again."

"And you've never tried to find them?"

"Why bother? They probably feel bad enough as it is. And then I'm sure they'd be really pleased to find out their daughter's a lesbian. It would be just one more set of people I'd have to lie to."

"Maybe they wouldn't care about that."

"Wouldn't your family?"

She was getting an edge in her voice from having revealed too much. There was a hard look in her eyes that in a different person, one less wilful, might have been a prelude to tears.

"I ought to get going," I said.

"Sure. Send me a postcard."

She saw me to the door. There was a mat there where a pair of Rita's winter boots had sat since her departure.

"Are you still seeing Suzanne?" I said.

"I suppose. Not really. It's pretty casual."

"Oh."

She laughed.

"I guess you thought lesbians mated for life."

"Something like that."

We stood awkwardly a moment but then both in the same instant reached out for a sort of hug.

"Hope you find what you're looking for," she said.

I hadn't told my family yet about my going. When I was a child, a return was always a matter of a certain ritualized formality like a funeral: those returning would sit in wait in their kitchens or rec rooms the night before their departure and all evening long people would come to them like petitioners with their envelopes or little packages to be carried back to their relations. It had always struck me how little joy there had seemed to be in these events, as if a return were a matter of grave risk or threat or as if it were a sort of judgement against those who remained behind, a source of quiet humiliation. Once I had gone with my father to see off his cousin Alfredo: he had brought a small package with him wrapped in brown paper and string to be passed on to his mother, but he hadn't been able to look Zi'Alfredo in the eye as he'd handed the parcel over to him. It was probably merely some token, a shawl or a piece of cloth that my Aunt Teresa had picked out; but my father had carried it as if all his shame, his own failure, inability, to return was somehow enclosed within it.

It was less than a week before my departure when I called Aunt Teresa.

"I'm going away," I said. "To Italy. I thought you should know."

I could never tell with my aunt from what set of mind she would respond to me out of the competing ones that seemed to play in her head. She could be smug or gruff, could put on an informed, cynical tone that appeared to come from her church group or revert to an old-world atavism and incomprehension as if a gap of centuries divided us. Or sometimes she responded with perfect, lucid understanding.

"It won't be easy for you," she said. "People remember things."

"I know that."

"Go to your Aunt Caterina, outside the town there. She always had a lot of respect for your mother."

There were only a few days to wait. All that remained in my apartment were a backpack and duffel bag full of clothes, a mattress, a kitchen table and chair. I spent my days reading novels and drinking coffee in cafés like an exile living a spare but leisured life in some foreign city, awaiting the revolution or coup that would send me home.

It only occurred to me at the last moment that I had to make arrangements for my car. I took it in to a used-car dealer just up the road from my apartment who looked it up and down, impressed with the bulk of it. It was only eight years old but already had the look of an antique, of a car you drove only for show.

"Pretty hard to move a car like that these days," the dealer said.

"It was my father's. He hardly drove it."

He offered eight hundred dollars. By the time the paperwork was done, someone had already parked the car on the lot amidst the rest. A sign in the windshield read SINGLE OWNER, as if my own brief tenure of it had been erased.

Two days later, possessing little more than I had arrived with twenty years before, I got into an airport cab and started back.

XX

I awoke out of groggy airplane sleep just as the Italian coast-
line was coming into view, a curving strip of gold against the
swimming-pool blue of the Mediterranean. Tiny white-
crested waves were breaking against the shore; tiny ships,
trailing thin lines of wake like spittle, were heaving out from
a dozen ports. Beyond the coast, the country stretched out
hilled and green, with the moment's illusion that it was something I could possess whole and entire in a glance, if only I had
eyes enough to take it in.

On our final approach, the plane swung around to follow
the shoreline. The beach there was dotted with bits of colour,
red and yellow and blue, from hundreds of beach umbrellas
lined up in orderly rows in the still of early morning like mock
soldiers awaiting some humorous war with the sea. The
umbrellas made it seem like we were arriving in a permanent
holiday country, a place that had never known hardship or
work, as if those of us who had fled here years before had been
fooled somehow, been packed off on our grim ocean voyages

while behind us the bands played and the streamers waved in the wind.

At the passport control a young man in khaki thumbed through my own with a languid circumspection, his eyes resting for an instant on the details of name, place of birth, but then moving on with what seemed an almost wilful withholding of any welcome as if to say there was nothing special in me, he saw dozens, hundreds like me every hour. He stamped a corner of a page with a small box of almost illegible print, "Roma Fiumicino" and the date. I'd heard stories of young men who'd been conscripted into the army on their return here; but the officer seemed to have no interest in me of that sort, I was free to go, his eye had already turned to the next person in line.

The bus into Rome followed an expressway through rolling countryside and then threaded its way through the city's outskirts toward the centre, past warehouses and factories, highrise apartment blocks, older low-rises in stucco with iron gates that gave fleeting glimpses into plant-green courtyards. Finally we passed through the walls: it was as if we'd burrowed through the concentric rings of a tree to the ancient core. Great palaces and churches loomed up; ruins were strewn about like abandoned construction sites. As we rounded the curve of a wide, car-choked avenue, the Colosseum suddenly reared up to one side like an apparition, a massive ghostly array of arched hollows and ancient brick that hovered briefly in view and then disappeared again as the bus veered around a corner and barrelled up a sidestreet.

We were dropped outside Termini station. It was still early morning but the air had grown muggy, overladen with smells – exhaust fumes, the oily odour of asphalt, but also a thousand indefinable hints and half-hints of things as if the air here remembered everything, had never been cleansed. Several cabbies set upon us as we descended, lifting suitcases before anyone could think to refuse them. One, an older man in jacket and cap, hovered nearby as I gathered my bags.

"Taxi?" he said.

I had picked out a cheap hotel from my guidebook, thinking to spend a few nights in the city before going on to the village.

"I'm going near the Piazza Navona," I said, in Italian.

"*Ah, è italiano.*" But it was clear from his forced smile that he'd in fact surmised the opposite, that I was a foreigner.

The taxi made its way into traffic already grown frenetic and thick, weaving through its laneless flow, the car wheels thump-thumping against the cobblestone paving.

"*Americano?*" the cabby said.

"*Sì. No.*" I had to struggle to dredge up my Italian. "*Canadese.* But born in Italy."

"Ah." He cast a glance into his rearview mirror to get another look at me. "Your first time back?"

"*Sì.*"

The car shot through vast, fountained squares, past cupolas and colonnaded façades, as if the city was merely so much space to traverse, to make a beeline across. Passing through it, I felt a double foreignness, that of not knowing the names of things, what their history was, but also of not being able simply to take them for granted. I might have been anywhere, just a traveller who'd picked up a few stories of a place, a few words of the local idiom, before arriving there for the first time.

The cabby looked as if he was coming to the end of a shift, his face grizzled and lined with fatigue.

"I thought of moving to Canada myself once," he said. "It must be beautiful there."

I didn't know how to respond. It was like comparing apples and oranges, these ruins and fountains, this stink of history, to a near-odourless newness.

"Yes," I said.

He lit a cigarette, then offered the pack to me.

"*Fumi?*"

"*Sì. Grazie.*"

We drove on in silence. We passed the Pantheon, men in suits walking briskly through the little square that fronted it. Across the way, a small café was just opening up.

"The Pantheon," the driver said, almost timidly, as if it were some insufficient gift he was offering up.

"*Sì.*"

At the hotel, he helped me with my bags.

"Watch out for yourself. People try to take advantage. It's not like before."

There was an instant when I paid him that we were simply cabby and client again, just another transaction in a long night of them. He thanked me with a nod and pocketed the bills I'd given him with that tinge of shame I'd seen in peasants as a child when they were given a thing by a superior. But then he held out a hand to shake my own.

"*Bentornato,*" he said. Welcome home.

My hotel was located amongst the maze of sidestreets that came off the Piazza Navona, a narrow, ancient building with an air like that of some faded, small-time society matron, fixed up with marble facing and a bit of canopy at street level but rising up beyond that to rusting balconies and crumbling stucco. Inside, the same contrast was repeated, the tiny lobby done up in gilt and ornamentation but then a narrow stairwell leading up to dim corridors and small, musty rooms like rooms in a boarding house. My own room had a tiny balcony overlooking a courtyard that stank of garbage and food. My first night, I awoke out of jet-lagged sleep to the sound of voices echoing against the courtyard walls – they seemed to be coming up out of a tremendous chasm or well, from some place that was not of the earth, hovering at the brink of meaning like a secret message or code I could not quite make out.

I spent a few days wandering the streets of the city. The concierge at the hotel – just a boy, really, fresh-faced and charming and dapper, dressed every day in the same immaculate white shirts and pleated trousers – made suggestions to me for possible itineraries, tracing the routes on my map and warning me to stay clear of the Gypsies. Half the time, in his zeal to provide me direction, he would make statements with perfect, confident authority that would turn out to be patently untrue, that got dates off by centuries or that mixed the facts or lore of one monument with those of another. He spoke an English sprinkled with American idioms, though he had probably seldom been outside the confines of Rome. With me, because I was someone who had returned, an *americano*, he showed that same hint of longing I'd seen in the cabby I'd met when I'd arrived, the same instinct to leave this place, to imagine other possibilities. But then I would see him sometimes standing smoking in front of the hotel in his white shirt and polished shoes and he would seem utterly at home here in a way he could not have been anywhere else in the world, as if every cobblestone in the street, every inch of mortar and pocked marble and crumbling stucco the city held, had been carefully placed just to provide him his proper setting.

I had learned from Aunt Teresa that one of my uncles ran a restaurant in the city just outside the centre, on via Catania; but the days passed and I didn't look him up. There would be all the awkwardness of my father's death to deal with then, the false, bright conversation, the sitting around with him and his family in some dingy back room while they waited only to get on with their lives. With Valle del Sole it was the same: now that I was actually near the place, within reach, all sense of urgency, of purpose, had left me. It had been nearly three weeks since Rita and I had spoken; perhaps she had already come and gone or had decided not to come at all, had awoken to the full horror of what had happened between us or had simply seen the pointlessness of any coming together. With each day that went by, each passage I made through the city, I felt this leaking away of intention: I could simply remain here in this place, disappear here, and nothing would change, no one would come after me, none of the questions I'd carried with me would need to be answered.

My mother had come here just before we'd left Italy back when Rome had been just that, a place you disappeared in, the young men who came here for work, the women you heard of whose lives, when they arrived here, turned unspeakable. When my mother had come, ostensibly to arrange for our reunion with my father in Canada, I had thought of her as lost somehow, not gone to a physical place that could be reached by a train or a bus but off in a sort of ether or dream world, a place that only an effort of will could transport you to, or back from. She would have been young then, my own age, pregnant with Rita but still undefeated, walking these same streets that I walked, that had known since then only an instant's more history. She might easily have vanished then just as I'd feared, met up with a blue-eyed man and gone off to some foreign country or still be living here now in one of these narrow, anonymous streets, poor and grown old and hanging laundry to dry on her balcony rail. Just here, she might have stepped, just here, weighing her options. There was the child she carried with her in her womb, who still had a chance; there was the one she'd left behind. Or perhaps it had never occurred to her to make a choice like that, to settle for less than everything.

Wandering out near the university once, I came on a vast cemetery that had the look of a fairy-tale kingdom, with arched and pillared mausoleums like miniature palaces lined up along broad, white-gravelled avenues. Further afield the graves grew more modest, simple headstones or stelas with a statue here and there or perhaps an oval photograph of the deceased in sepiaed enamel. There were a few Innocentes among the lot, distant offshoots perhaps of the family tree, among them even a Cristina, my mother's name, though I couldn't remember now if she'd taken my father's surname or kept her maiden one as was usually the practice then. But this Cristina had never lived to marry: she had lasted but two days, from April 11 to April 13, 1919. A simple legend at the bottom of the headstone read GOD, GIVE US STRENGTH.

There was a far section of the cemetery that looked a bit shabbier than the rest, a few weeds cropping up here and there and the headstones no-nonsense and modest, the inscriptions so worn that it took me a moment to realize that they were in a foreign script. Some of the stones had small, age-blackened candelabra affixed to the tops: menorahs. One stone, laid flat in the ground, bore beneath its foreign markings a single line in Italian: DIED AT AUSCHWITZ. The stone had sunk slightly into the earth as if to show that there was nothing beneath it, that it was only a marker. There was no way of telling how many of the other stones, with their runic scripts, airy and slight as though already predisposed to the decay of the elements, told the same story. Back in our village, the war our own stories had spoken of had never seemed the palpably evil event that stared out from this empty grave: bombs had fallen, villages had been burnt to the ground, and yet in the retelling, the horror of these things had always had a touch of the light-hearted to it, as if simply to have survived, to have got beyond, had made the horror small. There were those soldiers who had come to our very house, who my mother had joked with, who had shot a spider off the bedroom wall; it was hard to believe that they had been part of the same war that had produced this empty grave.

The sun had started to set. I walked to an exit and came out in an unfamiliar part of the city, the streets hectic with the twilight energy of end of day. Then suddenly I was on via Catania: it was the street on which my uncle had his restaurant. I walked up a few blocks and there it was on a corner across the street, a simple place with a few tables out front neatly arranged with checked tablecloths, and then arched windows looking into more tables inside. The only sign was a small backlit one above the door that read DA GIOVANNI.

It was coming on to the height of the supper hour, and the place was crowded. A couple had just claimed one of the last empty tables on the sidewalk; and then, while I watched, a young man in a black-and-white waiter's outfit came out to serve them. I felt a tremor go through me: he looked like my double, like a Romanized, younger version of me, the same set of shoulder, the same jawline, the same eyes. A bit shorter, perhaps, a bit trimmer, more elegant, and with a body language – a certain way of holding himself, a bit slack and inattentive but also on top of things, in command – that was distinctly Italian; but as he moved away from the table to go back inside, doing a quick, instinctive scan of the street as if to make sure that everything was in order there, that there was nothing new to catch his interest, I felt the tremor pass through me again, the instant's sense that I was staring into a mirror. For a split second his eyes rested on me and I thought he'd recognized me; but then he turned and went in.

My uncle's son; he'd been just an infant when I'd left. Inside, there was probably a man who looked like my father, with some tone of voice, some expression or mannerism, that would make him seem my father's ghost; and then all the trappings of this different destiny I might have had if a single decision had never been made, if my father had never packed his bags, and set out. I might have worked in a restaurant such as this, attended the university perhaps and lived in some cool, dingy, marble-floored flat in one of the old mustard-coloured *palazzi* in the student ghetto. I would have had friends who came by on motor-scooters, would have dressed well; in the summers I would have gone back to the village and perhaps met a girl there who would be my wife. All the slow disintegration that that first departure had set in motion would never have happened: I would simply have been at home, in my element, would have looked up into the street from time to time as I waited tables on weekends for my father and thought, This is my kingdom, where I belong.

The young man had come out again, bearing a tray of antipasti. He didn't look quite so familiar this time, as if our lives had come together for an instant only, then grown alien again. I could see the boredom in his gait now, the youthful chafing against his work, the evidences that he too had had his own different fights, his lost opportunities, his sense of what he'd been denied. Perhaps he would speak of America in the same wistful tones as the concierge at the hotel, though I envied, in a way, even that, the innocence that could still imagine it a better, more perfect place. He cast a glance out at the street again and caught sight of me, this time holding my gaze an instant and giving a small, inquisitive tilt of his chin as if to ask what it was that I wanted of him. For a moment the question seemed to hang between us like a pause in the evening's rhythm, the rush of traffic, the bustle of supper hour, a tiny rent that some message might be able to slip through. But then someone called to him, his gaze faltered, the question lapsed, and I turned away and walked on.

XXI

I had rented a car for the trip out to Valle del Sole, an old
pastel-blue Opel I'd got a line on from the concierge at the
hotel. The car had the same general stink as the city, the same
exhalation of shadowy odours. It stalled a few times as I made
my way through the city's outskirts; but once I was on the
expressway it seemed to get its wind. The man I'd rented
it from, a thin-haired and unctuous used-car dealer in the
Trastevere, had required only a month's prepayment, in
cash – no credit cards, no documents, no surety I wouldn't
simply drive off with it and never return.

Outside the confines of Rome, the heavy air of the city
gave way to a sun-scoured clarity. The hills that cradled the
expressway were dotted with craggy villages and towns, pic-
turesque and quaint as if they'd been arranged for a travel
brochure. The villages were probably not so different from
the one I was travelling to, would have their winding main
street, their bar, their church on a hill, their old people
staring out from second-floor balconies; and yet there was

nothing in them that struck me at once as familiar, as if their prettiness were a sort of scrim, something that held back their real natures. Seen from the expressway, they looked hopelessly inaccessible: there was no way to get there from here, no turn in the road that could cross from this gleaming asphalt into the mystery they seemed to hold in themselves.

I passed the monastery of Monte Cassino. The hill it stood on looked as if it was still recovering from the devastation of the war, scrubby and rubble-strewn and barren. Mr. Amherst had fought here with the Allies, he had told me once. It seemed an odd quirk of history, that he'd been a soldier here while my father was just a hundred miles away, still a boy in the fields, and while my mother, perhaps, heard the bombs fall from Valle del Sole and thought of those other young soldiers who had passed through our house once, and might be dying. At the top of the hill now, the monastery itself stood newly risen and whole, a white, glittery fortress, a tour bus just inching its way up the hill to reach it. All that had happened there would now be a matter of a paragraph or two in a guide book: this many had died, these walls were destroyed and repaired. Gone would be the single bulletholes, any evidence that such a one and another, their destinies perhaps connected in ways they couldn't know, had faced each other across a divide and sought one another's lives.

At the turn-off for Venafro I came onto a wide, newly paved highway that ran through a plain of green fields toward more mountains in the distance. This was the road that my mother and I would have travelled to get to Naples when we left the country two decades before. It didn't seem recognizable now except in a vague, generic way, as if any landscape of mountain and fields could have served the purpose as well as this one. I stopped for gas at a sort of truck stop, with a small coffee bar and shop to one side, then the pumps, a garage in back. Except for the different dimensions of things, the little cars, the not-quite-definable aura of Europeanness, I might have been anywhere, on any windswept highway where gas was pumped and travellers stopped to drink coffee or have a pee. At the road, incongruous, swinging in the breeze, was a painted yellow sign in English that read CASH 'N CARRY.

Even as I entered the mountains the highway continued broad and unswerving and level, smoothed out by an impressive succession of bridges and mile-long tunnels. Up on the hilltops, sheep grazed and dreamy villages lay folded into the slopes; but the highway continued on its straight-line path as if it had nothing to do with these things, was only a way through, a way past. There was just the barest sprinkling of traffic, an occasional lonely vehicle speeding along in the other direction or glimpsed distantly across a divide, and then beyond that only the still silence of the mountains.

It was just after noon when I reached the turn-off for Rocca Secca. The road grew more narrow and serpentine now. A sign announced the town and I felt the first flutter of memory, a stirring in the brain as if something was struggling to come alive there. But the road passed through outskirts of apartment blocks, feed depots, garages, that bore no resemblance to the Rocca Secca I remembered, a place of cramped shops and thick-walled houses pressed up hard against the street. I drove by a huge, curving structure of grey concrete and had to stop to make sense of it: it was a church of some sort, built to resemble a ship, the walls bowed and the roof and façade angled out to form a prow. Looming out like that at the outskirts of the town it looked ominous, like some last chance for salvation or escape.

I reached a junction. One branch led to the town centre, the other led onwards. A weathered sign pointed the way: VALLE DEL SOLE 7. So the place still existed; I had this proof now. There was still time to turn back, to forget everything, and yet everything, in a way, was already forgotten, this road I had travelled a hundred times, this valley I had stared into. I was searching for the turn-off that would lead me down to Valle del Sole from the high road when I rounded a curve and came suddenly on the outskirts of a village; and then in a minute I had passed through its straggle of stony houses to open country again. I stopped the car to check the sign I'd missed on the way in: VALLE DEL SOLE.

I got out of the car. From where I stood the village lay spread out before me, tiered up along the hillside a mix of earthy greys and mossy browns like a hundred others I'd passed along the way, as unremarkable. Everything about it was wrong: the road had never come in this way, the houses had not been cramped into so paltry a space, the church above the square had not looked so forgettable. And then the simple feel of the place, the unlikeliness that anything memorable or of import could ever have happened here, that all the history I'd carried crammed in my head could have had its seat in this half-ruined assortment of mountain-strung homes.

I left the car where I'd parked it and walked the short distance back to the edge of town. There was not a soul in the street, nor had I passed anyone on the way in. The houses were a mix of ruin and tidy repair, some newly stuccoed and painted, others with boards over their windows or with roofs and walls fallen in. Of those with the look of still being inhabited, most had flowers out front, potted geraniums and hibiscus and oleander or trellised rosebushes spilling bursts of pink and red. The flowers gave the street an air of poised expectancy, like a movie set sitting in wait: any minute the crews would come, bring cameras and men dressed as peasants, prod donkeys and goats to parade down the street for a take.

There was a stone bench built into the wall of the house that stood at the very edge of the village, just a narrow slab of grey with a worn spot in the middle. To one side was a scar, a small furrow, that some boy's hand must have worried away at with a nail or a bit of wire. I could see him, his hand, could feel the hot July sun beating down on him; though it took an instant for this image to shape itself into a memory, for the boy's hand to become my own, for the bit of wire to become a five-*lire* coin that someone, a neighbour or aunt, had given me. This was my grandfather's house, the one he'd bequeathed to me, where I had lived, where everything had happened. This was the door, its worn threshold; these were the stairs that led down to the stable; this was the bench, though not as I remembered it, not some numinous, mythical thing, but merely this real, mean, inscrutable slab of stone. The place hadn't crumbled as I'd expected: the roof still stood, the walls were intact, the front door was still on its hinges. There was a padlock on the door as if someone had tried to seal the place against change, had decided time would not enter here.

I heard a sound behind me: an old man was rounding the corner from the direction of the square, a hoe over one shoulder. For an instant I felt certain I knew him, could feel his name urging itself to my lips; but then nothing. He put a hand up against the sun to survey me as he approached, nodding curtly in greeting. There was a moment then when something had to be said, when some explanation for my presence had to be arrived at.

His eyes went to my car down the road, squinting to make out the plates to see where I had come from.

"Are you looking for something?" He spoke with the careful formality reserved for outsiders, the strain to put things in proper Italian.

It seemed precipitous simply to reveal myself.

"I was wondering about this house," I said, stumbling.

"That's the *podestà*'s old place." That was the title my grandfather had always been known by, "*lu podestà*," the mayor, after the post he had held from the time of the Fascists. "It's been empty twenty years. Marta keeps it up, up the street there."

He kept his eyes on me.

"Coming from Rome?" he said.

"Yes. Yes."

He was still taking in the details of me, my accent, my clothes. Nothing fit, and yet he seemed willing to grant that this house might be important to me, in some foreign, citified way.

"You want to know more about the house, you speak to Marta," he said. "Just up the street, like I told you. Number 12."

And he turned and walked on.

The door at number 12 was open, the doorway barred only by a curtain of coloured plastic strips to keep out the flies. The curtain brought back a surge of memories: this was where my great-aunt Lucia had lived, and where my grandfather had

moved when my mother and I had gone and his own house
had been closed up. Sundays, when I was small, we'd sometimes had our meals here – I remembered pots over an open
fire, the smell of cooking, the air of formality those meals had
had not so different from my Sunday meals with the Amhersts
in Mersea, with that same feeling of things held in abeyance.

I heard movement inside but couldn't make anything out
through the curtain.

"*Permesso?*" I called out.

"*Chi è?*"

The voice was hostile and sharp, as if I'd interrupted some
important task. Before I could respond there was another
shuffle of movement and a bony arm parted the curtain. The
woman staring up at me came barely to my chest, wizened
and gnarled like some stunted thing: my aunt's daughter
Marta.

My eye went instinctively to her leg, my unconscious mind
remembering what my conscious one had forgotten, that she
was club-footed. A crude brace sheathed one of her calves.

"*Scusi,*" I said. She stared up at me with a narrow-eyed,
eremitic intensity that seemed to mirror me back distorted
somehow, to make strange all the usual terms of reference.
"I'm Vittorio. Your cousin. The grandson of *lu podestà.*"

There was that glint in her eye of the madness that had
always seemed to threaten in her when I was a child.

"Well come in then," she said finally, making grudging
way for me as if I were a beggar who had come to the door.

Inside, without a word, she set about making coffee at a
small gas stove in the corner. I stood hovering near the doorway, not sure how to proceed, if she'd understood who I was

or had simply fit me into some arcane private order of things that had nothing to do with me. The room before me looked only dimly familiar: there was a kitchen counter along one wall; there was a blackened fireplace with the remnants of a fire still smouldering in it. To one side, in darkness, was a sitting area with an old couch and a few wicker chairs. A television was on there, tuned to what appeared to be an American western, the sound turned down to a barely audible hum.

All the windows in the room were shuttered over, the only light coming from the translucent strips over the doorway and the blue glow of the television.

"I don't know if you remember me from when I was small," I said.

She kept up with her preparations.

"You can sit down if you want," she said, and motioned with her chin toward the kitchen table.

I sat. It was only now as my eyes adjusted to the light that I realized there was someone else in the room with us, an old woman sitting in a wicker armchair in front of the television. Even as I noticed her she began to turn toward me, shifting her hands on the arms of her chair with a vegetal slowness and scanning the room in my general direction as if trying to pick me out of a fog.

"Marta, *chi è?*"

But Marta ignored her. She poured a single cup of espresso and set it in front of me.

"You'll have to put your own sugar in it. I don't know how much you want."

The old woman stared out a minute more, then finally turned slowly back to the television. I could only assume she was my Aunt Lucia: it seemed impossible that she was still alive, she who had always struck me as hopelessly ancient even when I was a child. Yet there she sat unchanged, as if the past twenty years had been merely the twinkling of an eye. I wasn't sure how to acknowledge her, if she was lucid enough to realize who I was or was touched with the same half-madness as her daughter.

Marta was still standing at the counter.

"I suppose you'll want to see the house," she said. "I kept it up for you, like your grandfather wanted."

This was the first sign she'd given that she'd in fact understood who I was. With that established, the tone that I had taken for hostility began to seem a kind of timidity, like a child's sullen evasion of some not-quite-familiar relation.

"Yes, I'd like to," I said. "There's no hurry."

But she had already taken a keyring down from a nail in the door frame and stood waiting for me while I finished my coffee. It seemed wrong not to greet Aunt Lucia in some way before leaving the house; but the instant I had set down my cup Marta was out the door. I followed her. She moved swiftly, one hand guiding her bad leg over the street's cobblestoned unevenness. At the door of my grandfather's house, with the air of a ritual she had repeated many times, she turned a small key from her keyring in the padlock to remove it and then a larger one in the door itself to click back a deadbolt.

We stepped inside. Marta flicked on a light. I had expected dust and decay, but the room we looked on stood in pristine order. There was a scarred wooden table in the middle of the room, a counter against the back wall with some rough cupboards and a rust-stained porcelain sink, a fireplace to one side with a plain stone mantel above. Everything was as I remembered it and not, was familiar in some wordless, visceral way and yet utterly foreign and shrunken, too tangible somehow to be real. This was what it came down to, my past here, this barren room, these desolate objects, like a museum's depiction of how things might have been.

"The water's off," Marta said. "There's a tap to turn it on in the stable but I'll have to do it, you won't find it."

"Oh."

There were details I couldn't account for, a marble floor that I remembered as concrete, a side balcony overlooking the valley, the simple dimensions of things, their small unprepossessingness. And something else: I couldn't put my finger on it at first but then it came to me – the light. There had been no electricity in the village when I'd left it, that was how I remembered things – I could call up a dozen memories that depended on the fact, that made no sense without it. Perhaps the lights had been put in after we'd gone. Yet the fixtures in the room, the worn switch by the door, the frayed wire the light bulb dangled from, looked as if they'd been there forever.

"I didn't think there'd be electricity," I said.

Marta shot me a guarded look.

"Electricity?"

"The lights, I mean. I thought no one had lived here since we left."

"That's right."

"Ah."

She led me through the rest of the house, opening doors into empty rooms. There was my grandfather's room on the ground floor, and then upstairs my mother's and my own. I kept expecting some surge of memory to take me over but felt only the same disjunction, the sense that my memory was being not so much stirred as stripped away, couldn't bear being confronted like this with things as they were.

There was not a speck of dust on the ledges or floors, not a single cobweb on the ceilings. It was eerie, this pristine abandonment – it made me think of pictures I'd seen of Pompeii, of whole rooms, houses, streets held forever frozen at the moment of catastrophe.

"It's very clean," I said.

Marta grunted.

"I didn't do any painting. You'll have to do that yourself if you want."

It was growing clear that she had kept the place up ever since it had been left empty, no doubt in some sort of perverse fidelity to the wishes of my grandfather, who had promised me at the time of my departure, though I was only a child then, that the house would be waiting for me should I ever return. It had been to Marta that my grandfather's care had been entrusted when my mother and I had gone: he had still been bedridden then from a fall, and perhaps had remained so, for all I knew, until the end of his life. At the time, there had seemed a sort of gloating in Marta at this victory over my mother, at having wrested from her her father's care.

When we had come back to the front door, Marta handed me a latchkey.

"You'll have to decide what you want," she said. "You can bring a bed over or you can stay up at our place, it's the same to me."

It seemed she was prepared simply to abandon me here, had fulfilled her obligations and was ready now to wash her hands of me.

"Well. I'm not sure. If there's room at your place. For tonight, at least."

"Suit yourself."

And she started back up the street toward her house in her grim, purposeful way as though she'd just dispensed with some long-put-off errand.

I was left alone. The place seemed infected by Marta's strangeness, by this weird sense of mission with which she'd maintained it. I wondered what it had taken to keep the house from crumbling as so many others had. Perhaps it had been simple force of will, as if it was only the realization that there was no one who cared any more whether they stood or fell that made houses crumble at all.

I stepped outside and followed the crooked stone steps that led down to the back of the house, where the stable opened out beneath the main floor. Someone, no doubt Marta, had kept up the back garden: there were neat rows of tomatoes and lettuce and fava beans, shored up between furrows cut deep into the earth to control the water flow along the slope. A little terrace of broken stone connected the side steps to the stable door, which was weathered and old but still intact. I pushed it open. Here, too, there was a light switch. I tried it and a bulb came on from an ancient outlet attached to a ceiling rafter.

The room had the look of a grotto or cave, the walls spongy with moisture and sediment, the floor of plain, beaten earth. There was no light except from the dim light bulb, no ventilation except through the cracks in the door. If anything had happened here, back when the place had been rife with the smell of animals and shit, it would have had to have been some crude, unromantic thing, dirty and quick. Apart from a few farm implements in a corner now, a hoe, a spade, a watering can, the space was empty – it looked as if someone had scoured it, cleaned it down to bare earth and stone, then left it to moulder.

I sat down on a stump that someone had placed outside the stable door. The sun was shining, in that way it had, that I remembered, with a dry, dreamy mountain heat. It would be possible, in this heat, to forget things, to walk out to some sunny corner of pasture, and fall asleep. The landscape itself, stretching lazily down to the valley, was busy forgetting: where I remembered an unbroken sweep of carefully tended fields the wild had begun to take over, great patches of gorse and tangled undergrowth hemming in the occasional still-tidy holdout of vineyard or vegetable plot. It was as if this place itself, the land with its wilderness, the village with its ruined houses, had grown senile and old, was gradually nodding toward some eternal sleep.

I felt eyes on me suddenly and looked up to the back of a neighbouring house to see a young woman standing on a balcony there, staring toward me. She kept her gaze on me though I had seen her, in a curious, questioning way as if my being here in her familiar view, her familiar world, meant I could pose no threat.

I nodded in greeting, awkwardly.

"*Buongiorno*," I said.

She was dressed in a loose summer dress, legs bare but her

feet in heavy-soled work shoes that looked bumpkinish against her bare legs.

"You're the grandson of *lu podestà*," she said.

I wasn't sure if she'd simply hazarded a guess or if the word had already somehow got around.

"*Sì.*"

"*Bentornato.*"

She was very pretty, I saw now. Her hair, wavy and dark and long, caught glints of red from the sun.

"You used to play with my older brothers and sisters," she said. "They've all moved away now."

"Ah."

"*Mi chiamo* Luisa."

"Vittorio. *Mi chiamo* Vittorio."

"Yes. Maybe you'll come by sometime for a coffee."

"*Sì.*"

She smiled. This was the first normal conversation I'd had since I'd arrived here, the first sign of welcome.

"I'll see you soon then."

And she turned and went in.

I had supper at Marta's. Somehow I had ended up simply turning myself over to her brusque ministrations: after a long walk in the countryside surrounding the village I'd found myself making my way back to her house with the tired, lonely sense that there was sanctuary there, that I'd be safe. The instant supper was set out, Aunt Lucia got up from her place in front of the television and made her way to the table, infinitely slow but with no other apparent sign of infirmity.

At the table she looked me over as if trying to place me.

"Is this the one?" she said. "But this is the boy from before, the mailman's friend. Tell him to come closer."

I brought my chair around next to hers and took one of her hands. It had the veined translucence I remembered from childhood, glossy and smooth like a water-smoothed stone.

"It's Vittorio," I said. "Your nephew. You used to give me five-*lire* coins."

And she looked me up and down and nodded her approval before finally turning to her food.

Against one wall of the kitchen was an old curio cabinet with some framed photographs inside. There was one of my grandfather, in his reservist's uniform, his war medals neatly lined up along his breast pocket; there was one of Aunt Lucia and a man I took to be her husband, though I'd never known him. Tucked away in a corner was one of a young woman and child standing sombrely before the doorway of a house. The woman, it seemed, was pregnant.

"It was the day you left," Marta said, seeing where my eye had gone.

The woman had a plain, peasant look, her hair long and dark and limp, her dress hanging formlessly over her belly. She was holding the hand of the boy beside her.

"I don't remember this," I said.

"If you remember it or you don't, there it is."

The doorway we were standing before was Aunt Lucia's. I recognized the keystone, the plastic strips. But everything that might have made sense of the picture had been cut out of it, whatever was going on at its periphery, whoever this woman was that Marta seemed to claim was my mother. I could hardly fathom this image of her: it was not just her plainness that struck me, how far she fell from the ideal of her I had created, but that she stood so vulnerable, so grave, with such a look of the mountain peasant that I could hardly imagine I'd ever known her.

"You can have it if you want," Marta said finally. "It was only you we kept it for."

And in my room that night I hid it away in one of my suitcases as if it were a piece of evidence to be concealed.

XXII

The room Marta had given me was one that my mother and I had shared for a few nights before our departure, after our own house had been closed up. I remembered the crucifix over the bed, the old wooden armoire, the double doors to the balcony. It had been Marta's room then, and possibly still was now, though there was little to show that it had ever been occupied again after our departure, none of the usual trinkets or adornments of human habitation. Even the bedspread looked unchanged, fusty and heavy and old, with silky embroidering in faded crimsons and reds. My mother had been well into her pregnancy at the time: I remembered the warm bulk of her, the drag of her belly against the sheets. It was odd to think that Rita had existed then, that she had been floating there in my mother's womb just an enigma, a possibility, knowing nothing of what she was or would become.

In the morning, when I awoke, I heard muted voices from the kitchen. There was a small, kerchiefed woman at the kitchen table when I went down, another much larger one at the door. From the hush that fell over the room when I entered it I had the sense that the women had been expecting me.

"So who might this stranger be?" the one at the door said, with a sort of timid heartiness. I knew the voice, knew these women but couldn't pull their images up out of my memory.

Marta was making coffee.

"You can see for yourself," she said.

The woman gave me a look to show she was stringing Marta along.

"See what? All I see is a handsome stranger."

"He came back for the house," Marta said. "Like I said he would."

Another look.

"And which house is that?"

Marta was growing impatient.

"Don't be an idiot. How many houses are there? If it's not this one, then it's the other."

"You don't mean the old mayor's house?"

There was an air of intrigue in the room that had begun to seem familiar: I could picture these women, or ones like them, in my mother's kitchen when I was a child, passing innuendos and hints in this same probing, joking way, trying to get to the bottom of things.

"*Dai,* Maria, leave her be," the woman at the table said now. "Anyway, I knew it the minute I saw him, you can tell by the eyes. Come, *giovanotto,* you must remember Maria and me. Giuseppina. We used to come by your house sometimes."

"What does he remember, he was only a child," Maria said.

"It's true. How many years ago was it now?"

Maria had finally moved into the room to take a seat.

"It was exactly five years before his grandfather died, I remember that," she said. "It was sad how that happened. He went a little crazy in the end."

They went on like this, a mix of candour and circumspection and squabbling, like chattering birds not certain where it was safe to alight.

"It was Marta who kept up the house for you," Giuseppina said. "After your grandfather left it for you in the will. It's true that she always said you'd come back. She sees things like that sometimes."

"That's got nothing to do with it," Maria said. "He came back because he was born here."

"All the same."

"So you were my mother's friends, then," I said.

"*Sì, sì*," Maria said quickly, and then, "You must remember my Vincenzo, the two of you used to play together. He's in Rome now."

"Ah."

When they'd gone they seemed to leave a residue like the trace of some interloper who'd got into the house. It was as if they'd come to test me, what I remembered, how I might implicate them. Or perhaps they had simply come to get a look at me – this was the one, her son, this was what happened next. Time was different here, people had patience, twenty years wasn't so long to wait for a story to reach its conclusion. In the village's eyes, I might be like some soldier who had returned after years of war – everything that had happened to me during my absence was irrelevant, wasn't part

193

of the tale, didn't take on any meaning until the moment I stepped back into the village, and was home.

Not long after the women had gone the village mailman stopped by the house, a pale, thin-limbed young man in a uniform of shorts and cap that gave him a slightly comical air.

"*Postino*," he said, as if explaining his uniform to someone who had never seen such a thing. "How you say, post-man."

He set his mail bag in a corner and then he and Marta disappeared mysteriously up the steps to the second floor. I heard a mumble of terse conversation, and a moment later he was in the kitchen again.

"I came to help with the bed," he said. "I think we can manage it."

"Sorry?"

"Marta said that you're moving down to *lu podestà*'s old place."

"Oh. Yes."

So that was the plan, then. It seemed for Marta like a point of faith in the creed of some intricate private religion that I be installed there, that her years of tending the place reach this fruition.

The young man led me upstairs to a tiny spare room that held an old bed frame and flowered mattress.

"We'll do the mattress first," he said. "You take the front."

When we'd reached my grandfather's house it took a bit of manoeuvring to get the mattress up the narrow stairs that led to the second floor. We set it against the wall in the bedroom that had been my mother's.

"You don't remember me, admit it," the young man said.

"We used to take walks together up on the mountain there. On Colle di Papa."

It seemed I had been friends with everyone: Maria's Vincenzo, the brothers and sisters of Luisa next door. But this was different.

"You're Fabrizio," I said.

"So you remember."

"We used to smoke cigarettes together. Before I left, you gave me a jack-knife."

"See, I was right, then. We must have been friends."

I was thrown off by this possibility he was allowing that we might have forgotten one another. In my memory of him he was larger than life, as much a part of the landscape of my childhood as this house, these stone walls. But to him I might be simply some boy he'd known briefly who had gone, like dozens of others.

"So you stayed on, then," I said. "In the village, I mean."

"I was in Rome for a couple of years, I worked in a restaurant there. That was a lark. We Molisani, we pretty much run the restaurant business there now. But you can't beat a government job. And the air here – in the city it's not the same."

He gave the same impression he had as a boy of being a sort of vast conduit for information which, however, always emerged from him slightly skewed, slightly tinged with an indefinable residue of him.

"Anyway, it's good you remember me," he said. "Some people come back and it's like they'd never set eyes on the place before."

When we were done with the bed, he left to finish his rounds.

"I'll come by for you after," he said. "We'll have some laughs."

He came around again at the tail end of lunch, changed out of his uniform now into jeans and an old flannel shirt. Without waiting for an invitation he made himself at home, seating himself at the table and wrapping a friendly arm around Aunt Lucia.

"*Ciao, zia!*" he shouted at her. "You're a good girl, you always clean your plate!"

Marta set a dish in front of him and he began in a casual way to mop up our dregs.

"So things must look different from how you remember them," he said. "They changed the road – remember it was just that old goat path before? It was like the end of the world here."

"I was wondering about the electricity," I said. "When it came in."

"What are you saying? That was way back in Mussolini's time, he did the whole country then. And before that there used to be an old waterwheel down by the river that made it."

None of this accorded with how I remembered things.

"But there was that festival one year, when the band had to bring its own generator. They put lights up all over the square. You must remember that."

Fabrizio shrugged.

"Maybe it's something else you're thinking of."

After lunch he took me out to a patch of land he had in the *contrada* of Bellavigna, beyond the slopes of Colle di Papa. It was spread over the mountainside in a precarious series of dips and plateaus, two or three acres at most, hemmed in by the tangled growth of various abandoned plots that bordered it. There were a few olive trees, several rows of vines, some tomatoes and beans. He had bought the land with the money he'd saved while in Rome, though there were family plots, his parents too old to work them now and his siblings gone off to Switzerland, to Turin, to Rome, that had gone abandoned.

"That way no one can tell you anything," he said. "All those family fights, they happen all the time over here. But maybe it's different in America."

He had built a small shack in one corner of the field, a sturdy place in mortar and stone with a propane stove and a cot for sleeping. At the back of it, hardly noticeable from the outside because of the way the mountain swelled and fell around it, was a small garden fenced in by walls he had built from rocks he'd dredged up from his land. There were fruit trees, a grape bower, an abundance of roses. In a back corner, taking its source from a nearby spring Fabrizio had diverted, was a tiny waterfall, a trickle of mountain-clear water sliding over stone into a small, placid pool beneath.

"The Garden of Eden, I call it," he said. "It's my special place. Nobody bothers me here."

The garden was like some secret folly or fantasy, rustic and secluded and lush. In the distance the mountaintops rose up, green and grey, encircling the place like a rim holding up the sky.

"We used to have our special places on Colle di Papa," Fabrizio said. "Remember that?"

"Yes."

"Back then I always thought I'd follow you to America some day. But I'm still here."

"It's not so bad here," I said.

"I don't mind it."

He took me around his field to show me his crops. The blue of the sky here hurt my eyes, so pure was it: the air had a smell of clover and mown hay. For an instant we seemed children again, I tending the sheep in the high meadows near the village and Fabrizio coming out across the fields to keep me company.

"So I suppose people have been talking now that I am back," I said. "About my mother and so on."

He gave a dismissive shrug.

"You know how people are. All the foolish things they come out with."

I pictured him on his rounds quietly collecting the town's gossip.

"So it's true, then. They've been saying things."

"This and that. Just nonsense, really. Like the time your mother tore up that money your father sent back from Canada with Alfredo Pannunzio."

It had been the night of the *festa della Madonna*. There had been an argument of some sort, and then my mother had shredded a bill of some fairly large denomination, fifty or a hundred dollars, in *Zi'*Alfredo's face. In my memory of the event it had been an entirely private thing, unwitnessed.

"What do people say?" I asked.

"Nothing, really. Just gossip."

He had grown awkward. I remembered how we had fought once as children when he had tried to explain to me, in a child's simple animal terms, why my mother had become a pariah.

"Tell me," I said.

"Oh, you know. How she made such a big deal about tearing the thing up and then someone saw her bring it into the bank in Rocca Secca the next day all taped together again."

We fell silent. Fabrizio wouldn't look at me.

"I'm not saying that's how it happened," he said finally. "That's just what people say."

It was plausible that things had happened that way, though there were a hundred other ways they might have happened that were just as plausible. Seen from this distance my mother could have been anyone, hero or hypocrite, sinner or saint.

"And the man," I said. "The one she went with. Do people ever talk about him?"

"Everyone has some story. Some people said it was what's-his-name, Giuseppe *Cocciapelata*, because he went a little crazy after she left."

"People thought it was someone from the village?"

"Where else?"

"It's just that I had the idea it was a soldier. A German."

"But the war had been over for years by then."

"I just thought. From something I heard once –"

"You were just a kid," Fabrizio said. "Maybe you thought that because of all those stories about the war that your grandfather used to tell."

"Maybe."

I couldn't bring myself to press him further. Every contradiction of how I remembered things was like having a part of me torn away.

"I can ask around if you want," he said. "Quietly like that."

"It's all right."

On our return to the village he brought me up along the spine of Colle di Papa to show me where the old high road had passed. Most of it had been dug up now to make way for a new road just under construction, part of the network of impressive straight-line highways that burrowed their way through the region now.

"They spent millions before to change the road so people had to pass through the village and now they're spending millions so they can avoid it again," Fabrizio said. "Anyway, it's all corruption. One way or the other it doesn't make any difference."

He led me down the slopes of Colle di Papa, following a tangled maze of narrow footpaths through the scrubby woods that covered it. At a small hollow amidst a clump of pine trees, he stopped.

"We used to come here together, remember?" And he pointed out a slab of stone – I had no recollection of this – where we had carved our initials.

I felt strangely moved. So he had brought me here to show me this place. I remembered the cigarettes we'd shared that he filched from his father, the idle hours we had passed, two knock-kneed boys joined in their delinquency and loneliness. But something else: I had betrayed him here. He had come to rescue me once, from some scheme of the village bullies I'd fallen into, and I had abandoned him, ashamed of my humiliation, ashamed to have him as my only friend. There had always been that shadow between us afterwards, that knowledge of the small hatred I bore him.

"I suppose I wasn't much of a friend to you back then," I said.

But I saw at once, by how this seemed to hurt him, that he
didn't remember things as I did.

"What are you saying? We were tight, you and me, all the
times we had. But I didn't think you would remember."

XXIII

Marta had set me up for the night in my house, had dressed my bed in stiff linens, brought in a night table and chair, had replaced the canister on the ancient propane stove in the kitchen and set out coffee and a small espresso pot for my breakfast. I still could not quite get my mind around the thought that the house was mine now in some way, that I possessed it, that somewhere a will existed that named me, a deed that had been signed over to me. Being in the house I felt a strange sense of dislocation, as if just beneath the surface of things something deeper was trying to urge itself on me: my body would suddenly remember the turn of a stair, the feel of a doorknob beneath my hand, with a rightness the mind could never get back to; and then the feeling would be gone. That was the hard thing, this not-quite-presence of all my history here, what was everywhere hinted at but nowhere delivered up. And yet it was odd that what seemed to make the past most palpable, in the end, most real, was exactly this mute unreachability, the way it beckoned, and beckoned, and beckoned, and could not be touched.

In bed in my mother's room, I remembered again the dream of soldiers I'd had as a child, the sound of their voices on the balcony as they smoked, the scrape of their rifle barrels against the balcony rail. My mind had made connections then, a child's intuitive leaps, whose intricacies I could no longer trace. It was as if reality – the logical grid I saw things through as an adult, the where and the who and the how, what could be proved, remembered, deduced – had somehow come in the way of a lost, higher order of understanding I'd had then. My grandfather had shown me a mark on the bedroom wall where he'd said the soldiers who had passed through during the war had shot at a spider; but I couldn't locate it now amongst the wall's many fissures and scars. Perhaps the story had been just some amusement he'd made up, an old man's exaggerations to feed the imaginings of a child.

In the morning, I drove into Rocca Secca with the hope of tracking down an old friend of my mother's. A wide, welcoming avenue I had no memory of led into the town centre from the highway, with a treelined centre island and newish shops and low apartment houses ranged up along either side. It was only when I'd got past a bustling central square that the avenue ended suddenly and the landscape began to grow somewhat familiar: I had passed into the old town, the streets here winding and narrow and steep and the buildings leaning into one another precariously. The memories began to come back, of Saturday visits with my mother to the local market, of a trip we had made once to the crumbling Giardini estate on the town's outskirts. Amidst the run-down buildings and abandoned shop-fronts I passed now, the old image we'd had of Rocca Secca seemed to hold, of a place that couldn't be trusted, that hid its decrepitude behind a façade of attractive welcome.

Just off a square in the very heart of the old town I found what I was looking for: a restaurant whose window showed the small figure of a hunter with a rifle slung over his shoulder, the Hostaria del Cacciatore. The place looked so much more modest and plain than I remembered it, tucked away here off a square that seemed as if it might have been an important focal point once but now had the sleepy, forgotten air of a place that time had passed by. In the centre of the square was a large stone pedestal that must have once held a monument of some sort but stood empty now, a lone pigeon preening itself at the edge of it.

I parked the car. A couple of metal tables were set up in front of the restaurant on the cobblestones there, an older man with the slightly corpulent look of someone who had spent his life amidst food sitting at one of them, peering out through reading glasses at the pages of a newspaper.

I went over to him, not yet certain if he was the one.

"I'm looking for Luciano."

He glanced up at me over the tops of his glasses, set down his paper. It was him, I thought, though older than I'd imagined, with the tired, distracted air of someone nursing some ancient worry or grievance.

"Then you've found him," he said, looking me over.

I felt my heart race at having tracked him down so easily, sitting here in the sun as if he'd been waiting for me, biding his time these past twenty years till I returned.

From my pocket I took out the old one-*lire* coin I'd brought with me from home and set it in front of him.

"Do you recognize that?"

There was a small flash of panic in his eyes, an old man's panic, as if some task he would once have been up to, but was no longer, might be required of him.

"What's this about?" He picked up the coin and turned it over in his hand. "It's an old one-*lire*. What's it to do with me?"

I had hoped for some moment of recognition, some tiny epiphany.

"You gave me a coin like that once."

He looked me over again, bringing a hand up to remove his glasses. I could sense his mind straining to figure out some connection to me.

"I'm sorry –"

"It was years ago. I was with my mother, Cristina. From Valle del Sole. The daughter of the *podestà*?"

"Cristina? But she died ages ago, what are you saying?"

"I'm her son. Vittorio."

He was squinting up at me as if he could not quite make me out, a hand against his brow to block the sunlight.

"You mean to say you're Cristina's son? The woman who died, that's the one you mean?"

"Yes."

"But I thought – yes, yes, of course, you've come back, is that it?" Understanding slowly washed over him and he rose, extended a tentative hand. "But look at you, how could I have known? The little boy she had, of course, I remember now. I'm sorry, your name –"

"Vittorio."

"Vittorio, yes. Please, please, sit down. You have to realize I'm an old man now, I don't remember things."

There was the small panic in him again. He pulled a chair out for me, fumbled to clear his paper away from the table.

"After so many years. Here, what am I thinking, I'll get the boy to bring you a coffee."

He went to the door of the restaurant and called in, waited an instant, but no one appeared.

"*Dai*, come inside, I'll get it for you myself. It's my grandson who's helping out, Antonio – the father's in Rome now but he sends the boy out here for the summers to keep him out of trouble."

I followed him in. The interior of the restaurant was done up in a slightly overwrought rustic motif, with exposed rafters and wall beams in dark, varnished wood and undulating stucco work done up to resemble stone. It was well before noon and the place was deserted, the chairs still up on the tabletops. Luciano went to the bar and prepared two coffees at the machine, pouring a quick shot of brandy into his own.

He led me to a table near the window.

"After all these years," he said again.

"Does your wife still do the cooking here?"

"My wife? You remember her?"

I had an image of a large, falsely friendly woman whose eyes had shot daggers at my mother when we'd had lunch here one day.

"I think I met her once."

But Luciano's eyes had gone wet.

"She died five years ago now," he said.

"Ah. I'm sorry."

"These things happen. But I don't have to tell you what it is to grieve for someone."

We sat silent. Luciano took up his cup and drained it in a single draught, like someone taking medicine.

A young man in black-and-white waiter's garb emerged from the kitchen door and began setting chairs down from the tables.

"Antonio, get us some more coffee here. And bring that bottle, the one on the counter."

From up close it was clear that Antonio was little more than a boy, fifteen at most, looking stoic and earnest and innocent in his trim waiter's outfit as he set out our coffees. He poured a bit of brandy into Luciano's.

"No one was more upset with what happened to your mother than I was," Luciano was saying. "I can tell you that."

"It was so long ago now."

"Yes, that's how it happened back then. For every little sin. It's not as if she was the only one, with all the men off in America like that. The orphanages were full in those days. Or sometimes you'd just find the thing frozen to death in the fields."

"I didn't know that," I said.

"Anyone will tell you about it. Nowadays, of course, it's different. If a girl wants the baby, she keeps it, and if she doesn't, well, she just goes to the doctor and cuts it out."

He drained his cup again and absently refilled it from the bottle of brandy Antonio had left behind.

"What about yourself?" he said. "Do you have a family?"

"Not yet."

"Maybe that's for the best. You find a woman now and you don't know where's she been before you. In my day, you saw a girl at a dance, she smiled at you, but then before you so much as asked her her name you had to go to the parents. I remember your own mother and father – I don't know if you know this but I was the one who introduced them. It was terrible how it turned out with him in the end. People here say it was because of your mother, what he did, even after all those years. But nobody knows what's in a man's heart when he does a thing like that."

"I didn't realize you knew him."

"He used to come in sometimes to sell us a bit of this or that from the farm. Your mother I knew from the market, just to talk to her like that. So once I see her across the square while your father was here and I go out and tell her there's a young man I want her to meet."

"My mother told me that they met at a festival in Castilucci."

But Luciano was insistent.

"You're wrong there, I remember it like yesterday. I can still see the expression on your father's face when I brought her in. You know how it is, he wanted to act like it was nothing. But I could see right away that she was the one for him. After that they used to meet here sometimes when your mother came in to do the shopping. To get around their parents, you understand."

So he had been my father's friend. None of this fit with the memory I had of him, as a sort of confidant for my mother's indiscretions.

"You know," he said, "the funny thing is that what your father liked about your mother was that she was educated. All she had was grade eight, that's nothing now, but back then anything more than grade five and you were a professor. That was the thing your father most regretted, that he never got an education. Before he met your mother he was even ready to go into the seminary just so he wouldn't have to spend all his life farming his few hectares of stones for a living. But after they were married, he could never forgive her those couple of years of schooling she had over him. It was the very thing that brought them together that wrecked them in the end, that's what I say. It's funny how things work out like that."

He stared into his cup.

"Ah, well," he said. "All the things that could have been different."

"I was wondering about the man," I said. "The one my mother was involved with."

"Eh? Yes, of course, there's that."

"Do you know who he was? Where he came from?"

"I'm sorry. I can't help you there."

"You mean you didn't know him?"

"I don't think anyone knew him, except your mother, of course. People knew *about* him, or at least they said they did. But you know how it is, what people don't know they make up."

"But you never actually met him?"

"No, no, I can't say that I did."

"But I heard you talking about him once. It was in the market – my mother and I had come in and you were buying your vegetables. The day you gave me the coin."

"Yes, I was wondering about that. I'm not saying it's not true, but for the life of me I can't remember the thing."

"You said the coin was a lucky charm. That it stopped a bullet from entering your heart during the war."

"Ah, there, you see? It couldn't have been me, then. I never served in the war, they never called me."

"But you just made the story up, don't you see? Because the coin had that mark on it."

"Are you sure it's me you're thinking about? You know how the mind is, it plays tricks. Maybe you mixed me up with somebody else."

The kitchen door opened again, and a scowling, heavyset man looked into the restaurant. His eyes took in the bottle at Luciano's elbow and he shook his head and retreated back to the kitchen.

Luciano hadn't seen him.

"You see how it is," he said. "You have your story, I have mine. The truth doesn't even enter into it."

He poured some more brandy into his cup.

"Are you sure you won't have some of this?" he said, though it was the first time he'd offered it.

"No, really, thank you."

There seemed no way to bring him around to my version of things.

"I had the idea that he was a German," I said. "My mother's lover, I mean."

"A German? What made you think that?"

"From what you said that day. And then I saw him once, coming out of our stable. From how he looked then. His blue eyes."

"That's not much to go on. You'll find plenty of people around here as blond and blue-eyed as any German. It was the Normans, you know, they came through here. There's still a church they put up in the town, you can see it, up near the old Roman gate there."

"But I remember it so clearly," I said. "He was on the run. You said someone from the German embassy had come looking for him, because he'd been a deserter or something during the war."

"A deserter? But who would have cared about that, after the war? You see how it doesn't make sense? He would have been a hero for that."

We were at an impasse. Perhaps I'd got it all wrong, every bit of it.

"Anyway, why do you want to go digging up all these old stories?" Luciano said. "What's past is past, it only hurts your head to go thinking about it."

"I just thought things would be clearer to me now," I said.

"You know what it is about the past. It's like a woman – from far away it looks like a lovely thing, but then the closer you get the more you see the imperfections."

Antonio had finished arranging careful place settings on the tables for lunch.

"*Nonno*, we're going to open soon," he said.

"Eh? *Sì, sì.*"

Luciano had taken on an air of reverie now. He absently tilted the brandy bottle to gauge how much remained, poured a bit more into his cup.

"Not many people know this but I have a story, too," he said. "Not so different from your mother's. I was young, just seventeen, and there was a girl I was crazy about. A cousin, in fact. We were going to run away together, because of the families, you know, but then one thing led to another and she got pregnant. After that it was out of my hands – her parents kept her locked up in the house so no one would know, and then when the thing was born they sent it off to some kind of orphanage. I never so much as laid eyes on it. When you're young you think you'll get over these things, you made a mistake but you move on. But I could never forget what had happened. There was always this little thing at the back of my head about that baby. So finally – it was almost fifteen years ago now – I went to the parents of the girl. They were the only ones who knew what had happened to it – even the girl herself didn't know, and anyway they'd found her a husband in Argentina, that's how they did things then. The parents said, leave it, it's all in the past now, but I had to know. In the end they gave me a name – Aurelio, they'd called him – and an address, of a hotel in Termoli it turned out. When I went to the place and asked after the boy they sent me back to the kitchen, and there sitting in the corner was this sort of half-wit, you could see that at once, you know that look they have on their face. I have to tell you, for a minute I thought I would just turn around and go home, seeing him sitting there like an animal – it turned out they just kept him around like that to do the odd little job here and there. But then something, I can't describe what it was like, but it was as if someone was squeezing my heart, because, you know, I could see there, even wrecked the way he was, that he was my son. After that I went to see him twice every month. Always on the same day because he could understand that, he liked everything to happen always the same. I brought him things, I even bought a little apartment for him so he didn't have to stay in the hole they kept him in at the hotel, and I paid a woman to come by to keep an eye on him. Even through all that I don't think he ever realized what I was to him – he was like a little child, a baby really. But I never loved anything the way I loved him. What he gave me not all the riches in the world could give me.

And then one day, just a little thing, he was crossing the street after a ball or something, a butterfly, for all I know, and a car got him. Just like that. By the time I found out, he'd been buried already. No one had even thought to call me. After that it was never the same for me."

His eyes had gone wet again.

"I'm sorry," I said.

"Ah, well. Everyone has their cross to bear."

He had pulled back into his private hurt. A couple of customers came in and a weak, reflexive smile of greeting washed across his face, then faded.

"You must have to get to work," I said.

"Eh? Oh, the others just keep me around now to make me feel important. My wife's brother, he's the chef now, he's the one who really runs the place. I thought my son might take it over, but he'd rather work in the city for a stranger than for his father."

He saw me to the door.

"And what about the girl?" he said. "It was a girl, wasn't it? I always wondered about her. If she would turn out strong, like her mother."

"In some ways," I said.

"To tell you the truth, I was always a little in love with your mother. It was such a waste, what happened. Maybe the girl can have the life your mother didn't."

"Yes."

Something caught his eye on one of the tables outside as he showed me out.

"You forgot your coin," he said, and he picked it up and pressed it into my palm.

XXIV

I had supper that night with Luisa and her parents next door. From childhood I had a dim recollection of her house as a run-down hovel of a place always teeming with dirty-faced children; but now, probably through the interventions of the brothers and sisters who'd moved away, the place had been completely modernized and refurbished, with a large marble-floored entrance hall and a cavernous dining room clearly used only for special occasions and a bright kitchen crammed with modern appliances. Luisa's parents, work-hobbled and elfin, sat huddled up around the kitchen's fireplace while Luisa finished supper, seeming in hiding there from the unfamiliar newness of the rest of the house.

"Your grandfather was always very good to us," her father said. "Your mother too, she always helped out with the children or whatever we needed."

It came out over supper that Luisa was friends with the daughter of my Aunt Caterina, Maria. She offered to take me to my aunt's farm the following day, and well before eight she was at my door, dressed in the same willowy summer dress she'd had on when I'd met her. The dress gave her the air of being much younger than her twenty-odd years, perhaps because her body looked so undefended in it, like some precious thing whose value she hadn't yet realized.

"I called ahead, they're expecting us," she said. "We'll stay for lunch."

"Your parents won't mind?"

"Why would they mind?"

Of my aunt's place I knew only that it was somewhere in the countryside beyond Castilucci, in what as a child I had always imagined as a sort of outback. I had no memory of ever having been there when I was small, most of my contact with my father's side of the family then having come at my grandparents' house in Castilucci proper, and could call up only this sense of it as a place primitive and remote, the way we had thought then of whatever lay outside the confines of town. Luisa and I set out in the Opel along the Castilucci road but forked off it after a few miles onto a ridgeway that looked out over our own river valley to the south and toward the high mountains of Abruzzo to the north. There were farmhouses spaced out at intervals here, more spruce and trim than I would have imagined them, with little courtyards out front and trellised rosebushes up their façades. Down toward the valley, a great combine was already mowing down the first of the summer's grain.

My aunt's farmhouse was perched above the road atop a steep bit of hillside, a cement driveway crudely ribbed against slippage leading up to it. The house, long and narrow like an Indian longhouse, had a look of raw incompletion, here and there the walls only half-stuccoed and a lone part-wall stretching out at the far end to suggest a room that had never been built. There was a flurry of movement as we drove up to the small courtyard the house looked onto, the barking of dogs, a scattering of chickens; and then doors began to open and people to emerge, children, women in aprons, coming out in small clusters from the separate quarters each door seemed to lead into as if the place formed a little village.

It was the first time since my return that I'd had any contact with my father's side of the family. People were shy and decorous in their greetings, everyone seeming modelled on the same frugal proportions, wizened and small, so that among them I felt like a stumbling giant. The children had crowded up behind their mothers; two of them, a boy and a girl, beautifully blond-haired and blue-eyed, looked like changelings that had been dropped here, staring out at me silent and still as if I had come from another planet.

From the end doorway of the house Aunt Caterina emerged, tiny and thin as a schoolgirl.

"I would have recognized you in an instant." There were tears in her eyes. She reached a hand up to my cheek as if to assure herself I was real. "I see your father in you all over again. He would have been your age when he left."

I tried to imagine what he might have been to her, this young man, her brother, setting out. After he'd gone she had never set eyes on him again.

"But come. You must be hungry."

Luisa went off with my cousin Maria while my aunt served me breakfast in the kitchen of her quarters at the end of the courtyard. Drying onions and meats hung from hooks in the ceiling; a pot simmered on a low fire in the fireplace. In a corner, cloaked in shadows, an old man sat shelling chick peas into a basin: my aunt's husband, Nicola. His hair had gone completely white since I'd last seen him, and his face had taken on a wrecked look, carbuncled and red. From the point he seemed to be making of ignoring us I thought at first that he might have gone simple.

"So you've come back," he said finally.

"*Sì.*"

"Well we're not going to turn you away. That's not how we do things here."

"Who said anything about turning him away?" my aunt said.

He pretended not to hear her.

"What happened with your mother there. People don't forget things like that."

"For the love of Christ, Nicola, what's that got to do with him?"

"I'm just saying."

He went back to shelling his peas. He seemed to be struggling with some feeling of offence he couldn't quite give a shape to.

"Just ignore him," my aunt said. "The wine has started to rot his brain."

She served up some bread and a few slices of salted ham. Uncle Nicola, despite himself, looked over assessingly at what she'd set out.

"You should have served the other stuff, it's not as dry," he said gruffly.

"You made this yourself?" I asked him.

"Eh? That's right."

"It's very good."

"Six months, we let it cure. You won't get it like that in America."

"It's very good."

"Yes. Well."

He drew his chair a bit closer to the table to take some bread and meat.

"Bring him the other stuff for lunch," he said to my aunt. "We'll see how he likes that, if he thinks this is good."

Afterwards I followed Aunt Caterina around on her chores, down to the stables to feed some boars they kept, rough, feral things, to make a local salami, and then across the road onto a promontory that overlooked the river where they had some hives for honey. My aunt kept up a brisk pace, worried about a storm that was supposed to be coming in, though above us the sun shone in an almost cloudless sky.

"I know it's been hard for you," she said. "The thing with your father. He always had that in him, the moods he used to get into, but still it was a shock. Like having something cut out of you."

"Were you close to him, when he was here?"

"Close?" She laughed. "I gave him the back of my hand sometimes, if that's what you mean."

The wind had picked up and a low bank of clouds had begun to roll in by the time we reached the hives, which were arranged in a rough semicircle against the bank of a sheltered hollow, swarms of bees hovering around them in arcane activity. Aunt Caterina approached them in naked vulnerability, carefully prying loose the lids and then one by one removing the honeycomb frames inside to scrape their honey away into her bucket, her face furrowed in concentration as if her pillage were a sort of intense, delicate interweaving of her own will with that of the bees.

"You're not afraid of them?" I said.

"What difference would it make if I were?"

By the time she had finished, the clouds that had been coming in were practically upon us. We began to make our way back toward the house, fighting the wind the whole way, Aunt Caterina angling into it with her skirts gathered up in one hand. I had taken her bucket from her, but now it seemed that there was nothing anchoring her down against the wind's sudden force, that in a minute it would balloon up her skirts and carry her off.

Well before we'd reached the road it began to rain, just a few fat drops at first and then a sudden pelting like stones being flung at us. Hail.

"*Addio!*" Aunt Caterina cried, hiking up her skirts and beginning to run. There was a sort of shanty along the side of the path we were on and Aunt Caterina ducked beneath it and beckoned me to her.

"We didn't get you here all the way from America to have you die in the hail!"

We had just missed the worst of it: it was coming down now in great golf-ball-sized chunks that rattled the tin roof of our shanty. Nearby, a patch of wheat looked already beaten down, as if a horde of spirits had raced through it.

"It's the grapes that get off the worst," my aunt said. "The rest'll come back."

In a few minutes the hail had given way to a steady downpour. Aunt Caterina hunched down onto the bench that ran along the back of the shanty and wrapped her shawl more tightly around her shoulders. From somewhere in her skirts she pulled out a wrinkled apple and offered it to me.

"No, thank you."

"Then I'll eat it myself," she said, and took a bite.

We settled in to wait. Great runnels had already formed in the gulleys of the pathway that passed in front of the shanty.

My aunt pointed out into the rain.

"Just down the hill there is where you were born. Where those trees are. You were three weeks late, I remember that."

I wasn't sure what she was referring to.

"I thought I was born in Castilucci," I said.

"No, it was here, I remember. We had the place in town, it's true, but this was where your grandfather built his farmhouse, in the middle of the bush like that. It was like the end of the world there. And your poor mother, waiting day after day with no midwife for miles because it was harvest time and your grandfather couldn't be bothered to keep her in town."

I gazed out through the rain toward the cluster of trees she'd pointed out a mile or so down the hillside. There were no roads here, no power lines, only fields and scraggy pasture.

"You can still see the house there," my aunt said. "What's left of it. If you want, I'll get Maria and Luisa to take you down after lunch."

She took a last bite of her apple and tossed the core out into the rain.

"Did they get along back then?" I said. "My mother and father?"

"Oh, you know how it is. We didn't even think about that sort of thing in those days, not like young people do now. But it was hard for them, living out in the bush like that, and with your grandfather the way he was. And then the baby they lost. But you probably don't know about that."

"What baby?"

"There was a girl before you. Marina. One night the three of them were coming home on your father's bicycle from some festival in the town and they hit a rock and went over. It was nothing, we thought, there was just a little bruise on the back of her head. No one thought to go to a doctor back then for that sort of thing. But that night she went to sleep and never woke up. Your father never got over that. Everything that happened after, with your mother and the other girl – Rita, you call her, isn't that it? – it was just part of the same thing, the way I see it. They couldn't look at each other afterwards, the two of them. There was always that baby between them to remember."

The rain was still coming down. But over the mountains to the east a sliver of blue had appeared; and then, as we watched, the sliver widened and the rain slowed to a final spattering like a towel being flung dry, then died. In the amber cloud-reflected light it left behind some mystery seemed to hang, some revelation.

I was still trying to make a place in my mind for this new piece of the past.

"I didn't know anything about that," I said.

"You see how it is," my aunt said. "You go all your life thinking things are one way and then you find out all of a sudden that they're another."

Through some conspiracy my cousin Maria had arranged for Luisa to accompany me down to my grandfather's old farm-house alone. We set off after lunch, following the same path that my aunt and I had for a distance but then veering off onto a much steeper one that passed through pasture and a bit of vineyard. Luisa took my arm along a particularly treacherous stretch to keep from slipping in the muck left behind by the morning's rain. She was wearing loafers today, not the heavy-soled work shoes I'd first seen her in, though they might have served her better along the muddy path.

There had been more than a dozen of us at lunch, ranged around a table that had been set out in the open of the court-yard. Uncle Nicola had taken on a boozy protectiveness toward me by then, as if he had projected his own bias against me onto the others.

"No one can hold it against you, what happened, or against your father either. It was your mother, she was the one. I've always said that."

In the silence that had opened up I had seen Luisa's eyes dip with embarrassment for me.

"Am I saying anything that isn't true? Tell me that."

The old homestead was nearly halfway down to the valley, nestled against the hollow of a hill so that it only appeared when we were upon it, trees and tangled growth masking its ruined forms like camouflage. Along the approach to it was a small outbuilding that seemed still to be in use by someone, its structure intact and its door padlocked shut. But the house itself was a ghostly wreckage of fallen rafters and walls, the front of it crumbled away to reveal its insides like a cutaway. On the ground floor there could still be made out the rudi-ments of a home, a fireplace, some crude shelving built into one wall; on what was left of the second, an empty window frame looked out onto the bushy slope of the hillside.

"I guess your grandmother just left the place to rot after your grandfather died," Luisa said. "Since they had the place in town."

Of the house in town I still had some memories I could call up, images of rooms, of fireside meals, of a view from a window; but of this place, nothing. It was as if there was a dark spot in my brain where those memories should have been, a place that was there but could not be got to.

We had come down to the little courtyard that opened out in front of the house, the weedy remnants of a stone terrace embedded there. Luisa wandered in among the house's ruins. At the back of what must have been the kitchen was a sort of sideboard in raw, rain-bleached wood. Luisa tried one of the doors; it opened. Inside, sitting alone there on a shelf like a religious icon, was a plain clay bowl with a shard broken away, the missing shard still lying at the bottom of it as if all these years the bowl had sat there awaiting the hands that would come to mend it. Luisa set the bowl on top of the sideboard and fixed the shard in its place. It held.

She picked a sprig of wildflower from nearby and set it in the bowl.

"Like home," she said.

We wandered up to a stone bench built into the side of the little outbuilding that flanked the house and took a seat there, beneath the shade of a towering oak. The bench gave a comfortable view of the courtyard at the front of the house. It was a place where a mother might have sat on a summer afternoon, to watch over a playing child.

"It must be strange to think you were born here," Luisa said. "In one of these rooms."

The wind and rain of the morning had given way to a crisp, spring-like clarity and warmth. From this tree-sheltered hollow, the slopes and the valley below, the ring of mountains in the distance, seemed like a cradle designed to hold just this place, this ruined home, this dappled light. A breeze rustled through the hollow and for an instant the life that had gone on here seemed suddenly possible, real, my father out in the fields, my mother preparing a midday meal.

Luisa picked up a stone and lobbed it idly at a lizard that had begun to scutter toward us.

"You must feel, I don't know, like a stranger here after all those years in America. It must be so different there."

"I suppose. Except now that I'm here, I'm not sure any more where I feel more like a stranger."

"Maybe it's not so different for those of us who stayed behind," Luisa said.

"How do you mean?"

"I don't know. It's just the stories people tell of the past – it all feels so long ago, when people had to live like that. Even this house. It seems a thousand years since anyone lived here. Sometimes I feel like those of us who are left here are just playing at things – we still go out to the fields sometimes and have our few olives and grapes, but everything's different. Things don't matter the way they did then."

We sat silent. For an instant we both seemed to feel the same small sense of insufficiency, as if there was some kernel of a thing we couldn't quite get to.

"If you want," Luisa said, "we could go down to the river. There's a place there I could show you."

"What sort of a place?"

"Just a place. A secret place."

The path down was narrow and stony and steep, skirting the edges of orchards and craggy fields and bordered here and there by weedy stone walls that lizards scurried over as we approached. Luisa went ahead, the path too narrow for us to walk abreast. At one point she broke into a run, calling back to me to follow, though in a minute she was already far ahead of me, disappearing as the path wound around corners and then appearing again on some distant lower slope. Then for a long stretch I could not make her out at all. I felt a lurch of panic. I tried to quicken my pace, but the path had grown more treacherous now, gully-scarred and crumbling.

I rounded a corner and came upon her suddenly, sitting waiting for me on a rock.

"Look at you!" she said. "You're as red as a beet!"

She had hiked her skirt up above her knees and was flapping the hem of it to cool herself. I felt a shiver pass through me, coming upon her like that. All this was familiar in some way, this path, this crisp warmth, the young woman sitting in wait.

"You look like you've seen a ghost," Luisa said.

"I thought I'd lost you."

She laughed.

"Come then, I'll hold your hand."

She passed an arm through mine and led me on, the land levelling now and the path starting to widen. When we reached the river finally, swollen and murky from the morning's rain, it began to come back to me: I had made this trip before. We'd crossed over on these same rocks that Luisa now led me across, though they seemed so much smaller than I remembered them; we had followed this same brambled path along the far shore. Luisa continued to lead me on, along a track that was just a narrow ledge between the riverbank and a cliff face; and then we came finally to the cave. A tiny brook, just a stony exhalation of wetness, flowed out from it toward the river.

"It's a hot spring," Luisa said. "Maria and I used to come here when we were small."

Inside, sunlight from the entrance cast looming shadows of us that merged with the blackness the cave receded into. A strong odour of fetid dampness breathed out from the walls. Toward the back was the spring, a small, bubbling pool dully glimmering in the dark.

"My mother used to come here," I said.

"She brought you here?"

"Once. I think she brought her lover here."

I had said this without thinking how intimate a thing it was to share with her. But Luisa showed no sign of embarrassment.

"What makes you say that?" she said.

"I don't know." I had an image of finding something here that time, behind a rock. But there was no rock here now, nor any of the toothy shapes the place had in my memory of it. "How she acted, maybe. Or something else, I don't remember."

"Anyway she wouldn't have been the first. People have been bringing their lovers here for years. Centuries maybe."

"Has anyone ever said anything to you about him?" I said. "About my mother's lover?"

"I thought he was just a stranger. Someone passing through. That's what my parents told me."

"Did they say more than that?"

"No. Just that."

"Maybe they know more than they said."

"Maybe. I don't think so. They're simple people, they don't ask too many questions."

She had entered the cave and slipped a shoe off to dangle her foot in the pool.

"Is that why you came here?" she said. "To find out who he was?"

"Maybe. I'm not sure any more."

"I wish I could help you."

"It doesn't matter."

She moved a bit further in, bending to cup a few handfuls of water to her face, her neck. From where I stood at the cave's entrance she was barely visible now, just a smudge of shadow and grey against the deeper grey of the cave.

"And your sister?" she said. "Does she want to know?"

"I'm not sure. I think so."

"They say it was strangers who took her in."

"That's true. When she was a bit older."

"It must have been difficult for her. Without a mother or father like that."

Her voice seemed strangely altered now, echoing disembodied off the damp stone. In the dark it was as if the cave itself was speaking, requiring an answer.

"I think she's managed all right in the end."

I could not make her out at all now. There was a silence, a rustle of clothing being removed, a pause, and then the suck and gulp of something submerging and at once the indefinable feeling of her being lost to me, in another element, like a spirit suddenly fled. I felt a sense of privation, as if something had come, been almost tangible before me, then vanished again. But a moment later she emerged: a sound of water on stone, of cloth again, and then she was coming out of the dark like an apparition, her hair dripping, her dress clinging to her skin. There was an instant in the grey when she was not quite herself again, when an image from the past seemed superimposed over the present as if two negatives had got crossed.

"You couldn't see me, I hope," she said, laughing. "But then you've probably seen lots of naked women."

It was nearly dark by the time we'd finished the long climb back to the house. The air had turned chill; Aunt Caterina built a fire in her kitchen and Luisa and I pulled our chairs up to it to warm ourselves.

"So I suppose you went down to the hot spring," my aunt said, casting a wry look at Luisa. Everyone seemed to be so openly encouraging of our coming together – I couldn't gauge if this was something new, if things had changed so radically in the years I'd been away, or if there had always been, beneath the veneer of village puritanism, this acceptance, the tacit approval of the sensuality of the young.

My aunt made us stay for supper. Afterwards, before we left, Luisa took me to a little hillock above the house and pointed out by name all the villages and towns twinkling in the dark in the hills surrounding us. It was as if she were offering them to me, offering them back. Each name called up some echo for me from childhood, stories and images, the particular place each town had held in the local lore as if part of some grand drama that daily unfolded in the amphitheatre the mountains formed.

"Have you been happy in America?" Luisa said.

"Why do you ask?"

"I don't know. You look so serious sometimes."

"Would I have been happier if I'd stayed here?"

She laughed.

"Maybe."

There was a low hum of conversation from the house, a flicker of orange light in my aunt's window from the fire still burning in the fireplace. Around us the mountains stretched, grey shadows against the night, and then the villages, nestled into the slopes or strung out along ridge-lines like torchlight processions. The dark they fought back seemed ancient, unyielding, the same dark that for centuries, millennia, people had built their night-time fires against, that they'd struggled through to get home.

Luisa was close enough for me to feel the heat coming off her.

"It's still in your blood, this place," she said. "I can feel that."

And the lights in the distance seemed to blink their greetings as if in assent.

XXV

Only a matter of days had passed but already I felt like a fixture in the village, taking my meals at Aunt Lucia's, setting up my little household. It occurred to me that there was no place in the world now that was any more home than here: this was all I had left, my kitchen table, my stiff-linened bed, my balcony over the valley. Even the villagers seemed ready quietly to accommodate me, growing daily more friendly and more inscrutable, showing me a flawless country hospitality as if to say there was nothing out of the ordinary in my being here. Their kindnesses were like a forestalling: with each day that passed, each kitchen I sat in nibbling pastries or sipping liqueurs, it seemed more unlikely that I would do anything untoward, that I would ask any awkward questions or in any way disturb the quiet surface of things.

I had begun to forget things. Memories that had seemed clear when I'd first arrived were becoming more and more contaminated, overlaid by other people's versions of the past or simply by mere reality, the different slope of a street or angle of a building that forever obscured whatever subtle truths might have been preserved by my own misremembering. I'd hear some new story or fact and at once all the careful architecture of the past that I'd carried around in my head seemed to shift to make a place for it, my brain producing images that might have been memories or pure inventions, just the mind's attempt to connect things. There were those two women I'd met in Marta's kitchen, Giuseppina and Maria – from just the shiver of recollection I'd felt then, whole scenes had since floated up in my mind's eye that they might have been part of, whole histories had taken shape around them. It was as if I'd come here not to remember but merely to put together a plausible story: these were the elements, I was free to arrange them how I wished.

As the chance that Rita would turn up seemed to become more remote I began to feel a growing sense of futility. If only she would come, then things would make sense, might begin to fall into place. I drove into Rocca Secca one night and called Elena, but she hadn't heard from her.

"You making out all right?" she said.

It had been only a couple of weeks since I'd seen her, but already she and the whole world I'd left behind with her seemed not quite real. I could barely picture what she looked like, the apartment she sat alone in, its treelined street.

"I suppose," I said. "No big revelations or anything."

We both seemed to be lonely for some version of the world that we might be able to confirm for each other.

"Do you think she'll show up there?" she said.

"I don't know."

"All this has something to do with John, doesn't it?"

But all I had still were nothing more than my disputed inklings, my half-theories and fabrications.

"Not really. No."

I settled in to wait. I'd see Luisa in the street and could feel the need to speak to her, the desire to, the wish that she'd take my arm in hers again. But a small reserve had come between us now. The very wholesomeness of her affection for me seemed to place it off limits: it was not something I deserved or could ever deserve, I had put myself forever beyond such things. Against the first pleasure I'd feel at the sight of her there was always this instinctive drawing back, this not knowing what I was allowed.

"You can come eat with us again some time if you want," she said. "If you get tired of those old ladies."

But the days passed and I didn't go by.

Marta had continued to care for me with her unquestioning matter-of-factness. The strangeness of her household had grown almost comforting now. No one asked me questions there; no one required a reason for my presence. At meals I'd watch Aunt Lucia in her reptilian slowness and wonder what she could reveal to me if I could find some way of reaching her, perhaps the wisdom of the ages or mere banalities, the trite, predictable observations of a narrow life narrowly lived. She gave me the sense that she knew now, in some way, who I was, and yet she didn't seem to attach any special significance to the fact, as if no great gap separated this young man who took meals in her kitchen from the boy who had begged five-*lire* coins from her years before. Perhaps that was the very insight I could glean from her, that time and change were not such momentous things.

I spent the afternoons with Fabrizio at his farm, where he retreated every day after he'd finished his rounds. With him I seemed to enter a space like the innocent one of childhood, where everything that was pressing and large, that could hurt, was held back. That was his gift, now as when he was a boy, that child's special power he had to hold the world off like a task endlessly deferred, a pain you averted the sting of. And yet it was heartbreaking somehow to watch his small, boyish ministrations to his little acreage, his careful suckering and winding and pruning, the attention he put into things in this corner of forgotten field as if staving off some great sadness or despair.

He still had the same penchant for arcane knowledge he'd had as a child. Much of it now went into his farming: he knew every possible variety and strain of his various crops, every disease that could afflict them, what things to plant in what soil and how to shift them to keep the soil from being depleted. The rest of his attention he had reserved for local lore, for stories of ancient feuds that he passed on to me, of the war, of the old aristocracy who had once ruled over the region. He knew the landscape of the area like the back of his hand: these were the hills which Samnite fortresses had stood on, these the sites of reputed miracles, these the still visible markings of where the old *tratturi* had passed, the grassy highways of old that shepherds had used since time immemorial for the seasonal movements of their flocks.

Often it was nearly dark by the time we returned to the village. Crossing the ridge-line where the new highway was being built, I'd see Valle del Sole in the distance, its houses just grey, ghostly shapes in the dusk, here and there the first twinkling lights coming on. I'd get a sense then of how the village would look once the new road was completed, just a detour again, cut off and forgotten, a flicker in the corner of your eye as you drove past. In a few years the abandoned houses would outnumber the inhabited ones; and then slowly the town would die out. I pictured Fabrizio thirty, forty years hence still working his little acreage, a final holdout against the newly burgeoning wild, reduced to what our ancestors had been hundreds or thousands of years before when they'd first staked a claim on this rocky hillside.

On our way home once, Fabrizio pulled a small object from his pocket: a gold earring.

"I found it near your house," he said. "You should have it."

But I didn't understand.

"Years ago. Not long after you left. It was probably your mother's."

It was just a small thing, a round hoop of dulled gold. I tried to picture what she might have looked like, wearing it, who that woman could have been.

"You kept it all this time?" I said.

"In case you came back."

He was holding it out to me. It didn't seem right somehow to be taking it from him after he'd so long been the guardian of it. He was always the one giving me things, even when we were small, though he'd had so little then, was always the one who'd worn his heart on his sleeve.

"I thought maybe you didn't have anything of hers," he said. "The way she died and everything."

I remembered a slogan I'd seen once on some sentimental poster: Whatever is not given is lost. But I wasn't sure how it applied here.

"Thank you," I said, taking the thing from him. At the back of my mind was the thought that it was something tangible, at least, something to pass on.

We walked on a moment in silence.

"Do you ever think of marrying?" he said.

The question took me a bit by surprise.

"I don't know. I suppose, if the right person –"

"So you don't have a girl over there yet."

"No, no. Not yet."

He looked a bit awkward.

"Me, I'm happy enough on my own for now," he said. "Do you think there's anything wrong with that?"

"No. Not at all."

We parted at the corner of his street. He had yet to invite me to the house where he lived with his parents, even now revealing the same quiet shame of his family he'd had as a child, though the newish-looking place they lived in now seemed a vast improvement over the crude, dirt-floored one I remembered them living in when he was small.

"You'll come around again tomorrow?" he said. "I'll bring some food out, we'll have a little picnic in the garden."

"I'd like that."

As he was retreating down the darkness of his street, he turned and waved.

"Oh, Vittò!" he called out. "We'll have some times again, you and me, wait and see."

I wandered one afternoon along the path of an old *tratturo* that I remembered from childhood, now used as just a local footpath though apparently it had once connected up with a much wider one that came down from Abruzzo. My

235

grandfather had me told stories of the great flocks that had passed in his day every autumn and spring, massive movements that stretched days long along the track and that had seen village-sized camps spring up every night when the shepherds and their families pitched their lean-tos and tents. He had described these movements as if they were great circuses or festivals, every night the sound of music and dancing around the fire, the drone of sheepskin bagpipes and the beat of drums.

The track I followed ran a mile or two along the spine of Colle di Papa before joining up with the old, now-abandoned highway that used to pass by Valle del Sole when I was small. I followed the highway for a distance, all cracked and weedy now, into gloomy woods I had always feared as a child because of the stories of the brigands and thieves who lurked in them. I kept expecting the road to join up at some point with the new one that led back to the village, but beyond each curve the darkness and woods continued. Then finally I came to the junction of an even more ruined road, just a steep, rutted path that led up through the woods toward the crest of a hill. There was an ancient signpost at the corner with a single arrow pointing up the path, its lettering too faded to be read. The whole scene seemed like something out of a ghost story: the dark woods, the ruined path, the single arrow pointing up.

I began to make my way up the path. There were the marks of what looked like recent tire tracks along it, skirting around the worst of the potholes and ruts. After a stretch, the crumbled asphalt gave way to cobblestones and the ruins of buildings began to appear amidst the tangled undergrowth and woods that flanked the road. It came back to me now: this was the old town of Belmonte. According to the story that people had told when I was a child, it had been destroyed by the Germans during their northward retreat, the story always standing as a sort of cautionary tale of how even a town as reputedly prosperous and blessed as Belmonte could nonetheless be reduced to mere ashes and dust. But seeing the village now, just a handful of broken-down hovels, most of them little more than rubble at this point, I wondered if the story had had any truth to it. The place had probably never held much more than a dozen families, hardly worth the bother of destruction; and it had the look now of a sort of afterthought, its cobblestoned street following along only a hundred yards or so before giving way again to cracked asphalt, the decaying houses lined up along it looking as if they had been felled not by bombs but by simple lack of purpose.

Beyond the village, the road wound up along the edge of a hillside. I remembered it led up to a summit where it was possible, because of the way the mountains swung around, to get a good view of Valle del Sole. It was getting toward dusk; already in the shadow of the hillside it was difficult to pick my way along the path. There were car tracks here as well; and then I rounded a curve and there was the car itself, a newish grey Scirocco with local plates. The driver's door was still open, as if someone had merely stopped an instant en route to somewhere else to admire some curiosity or vista. But beyond where the car was parked the road looked impassable, a hopeless snarl of snaking fissures and gullies: this was the end of the line, there was nowhere further to go.

I reached the summit. The land here opened out to a rocky plateau spotted with yellow-flowered gorse. Toward one end of it, with their backs to me, stood two figures, a man and a woman. The man was gesturing out toward the valley as if to point out some landmark; the woman nodded, and then with a familiar gesture brought a hand up to pull back her hair.

They were standing a few inches from each other, a thin line of sunset lighting the distance between them. My first instinct was to turn, to make my way quietly back down the hill, to let this thing be. But then they seemed to sense my presence and almost in the same instant turned to face me. It was Rita and John.

XXVI

John handled the burden of greeting. I couldn't see him now except through the veil of my suspicions: there would be some telltale marker or sign, some gesture or curve of muscle or bone, that would give him away.

"Well." He extended a hand, awkward and yet seeming at some level genuinely pleased to see me. "Rita said we might find you here."

Nothing in the look of him made the thing clear at once – there was the set of his brow, perhaps, but I no longer trusted myself, the tricks my mind played. He had grown a beard since I'd last seen him, tinged with grey like his hair; it seemed to mask him like camouflage, leaving only his eyes to know him by though they were what seemed to make the thing most unlikely, that I could look into them without any flash of recognition.

"How did you find this place?" I said.

"Ah, yes." He looked embarrassed. "Just wandering and so."

There was always something in his embarrassment that was like a plea sent out, that way he had of discouraging enquiry, of making every question seem as if it had touched some injury in him.

"Are you coming from Rome?"

"Actually," he said, "we've been in Campobasso a couple of days."

I was stung that they'd been so near without looking for me. I had no way of knowing now whether they'd planned to look for me at all.

"You should have come to the village."

"Yes, of course."

Rita stood to one side, the setting sun hidden behind her as if in eclipse, lighting a halo around the shadow it made of her.

"You were looking out at Valle del Sole," I said.

"Oh," she said. "We weren't sure."

We both seemed a bit stunned to be reunited here on this gorse-studded summit.

"I have a house. My grandfather's old place. You can stay there if you want."

Her eyes went to John as if to ask his permission.

"We still have our hotel for the night," she said.

"You can come tomorrow, then."

"If you think you have room for us."

We stood a moment not certain what to do next.

"You came on foot?" John said.

"Yes."

"We'll drive you back."

It was nearly dark by the time we arrived at the village. Rita, sitting in back, had her face up against the window to peer out. The streets were deserted, the village seeming peculiarly unwelcoming and bleak in the twilight hush. A dog ran out from an alley and chased alongside us a few yards, barking, then dropped away.

"Which house?" John said.

He would know the house, if he was the one. But already I felt wearied for us both by my suspicions, couldn't bring myself to be always testing him. Now that he was here beside me in the flesh he seemed so harmless, my suspicions so tenuous.

"The one at the end."

The house was shrouded in darkness, sitting just beyond the reach of the village's last streetlight.

"This is where you grew up?" Rita said.

"Yes."

We had barely spoken so far.

"You could stay for supper," I said.

I couldn't make out her face in the dark.

"We should probably get back."

"But you'll come tomorrow."

"If you're sure it's all right."

They arrived toward noon the following day. I had scrambled to make arrangements, scrounging cots and linen from Marta and Luisa. For friends from Canada, I had said, not having thought through how else I might introduce them. Then when their car pulled up outside the house, I felt a spasm of panic: all this was wrong, bringing them here; nothing of what we were could be made sense of here.

John was already unloading bags of groceries from the trunk.

"We brought some things," he said, a bit doubtfully, as if he were asking some favour of me to accept them.

The house felt transformed with Rita and John in it, its air of preservation, of holding intact some ghost of the past, seeming to flee before their backpacks and bags, their travellers' impermanence, as if some spell had been broken. I showed them to their rooms, John to one on the ground floor and Rita to the one next to mine upstairs. Rita and I stood a moment at her door, looking in.

"There's no bath in the house," I said. "You'll have to use my aunt's up the street."

"That's fine."

The room was bare except for the cot I'd dug up for her and an old wicker chair and a small barrel that I'd set up as an end table. I'd set a glass on the barrel with a few wild-flowers in it.

"There's a good view from the balcony," I said.

She went to the balcony door and opened it to stare out. It was the first time I had really dared to look at her, as she stood across the room with her back to me.

"Has it been hard for you?" she said. "Returning here?"

"Not so hard. Not as hard as I thought."

I tried to read her through the curve of her back, the fall of her hair on her shoulders, the way she held herself. That seemed to be how we spoke to one another now, faceless like that, unable to bear the direct gaze.

"And for you?" I said. "How have things been?"

"Oh, the same, I guess. Not so hard."

We kept to our places, me at the door, her at the balcony, as if some force held us just there, at that precise distance. I could hear John downstairs, the rustle of grocery bags.

"I suppose I should get some lunch ready," I said.

"Sure. I'll be down in a minute."

John had managed to find the couple of pots I'd borrowed from Marta and had set water to boil for pasta.

"Is there any problem?" he said.

"No. No problem."

It was hard to gauge how much he knew of what had gone on between me and Rita – something, surely, if not from anything Rita had told him then simply from the strange energy between us. I had the sense that he held himself back from knowing more, almost as a gesture of trust, an offering against his own secrets.

"It's not much of a kitchen," I said.

"We can manage."

We set about making a meal. They'd brought pasta and bottled sauce, some cheese, some lettuce and vegetables for salad. John worked with the no-nonsense competence of a man long used to preparing his own meals. I thought of his apartment, with its fusty not-quite-disorder, of his solitary life there.

"We haven't talked about your trip," I said.

"Perhaps we can wait for Rita. To have her view of things."

"She's been all right?"

I couldn't keep the thickness out of my voice.

"Yes, of course." He said this in a tone that sounded neither guiltless nor completely reassuring. "A little confused, perhaps."

"Confused about what?"

"Oh, the future and so on. It's normal for her age."

When Rita came down she had changed from her jeans to a ruffled long-sleeved dress full of creases and folds as if it had lain unused at the bottom of her pack the whole trip. The dress seemed to change her, to rusticate her, made her look like some peasant girl dressed up in her Sunday best.

"I saw from the balcony that there's an extra floor at the back," she said.

"That's the stable."

"Oh."

I couldn't remember ever telling her the exact details of her past, their exact architecture. And yet her question hadn't seemed innocent.

"It's empty now," I said. "I can show it to you after lunch."

John came with us when we went down. I almost thought that he was trying to tell me now, not Rita but me, that he was trying to find the right wordless way to say yes, he was the one. We stood, the three of us, at the bottom of the side steps and the air seemed ripe with suspense, as if at any instant the stable door must open and John's younger self must appear there.

"Our mother used to work back here," I said. "In the garden. Our cousin Marta keeps it now."

I opened the stable door, to the dank smell of cold earth and rotting stone. Rita and I went inside. For a moment we stood alone in the stable's murky light.

"There would have been animals here," I said. "Some pigs, a few sheep. I used to take the sheep out to pasture after school."

Somehow my mind was fixed on these simple, banal details, the things I could say for certain. Everything else, the open door, the two eyes peering out, that Rita could have been conceived here in this smelly grotto, seemed suddenly far-fetched.

"Do you remember what it was like for you back then?" Rita said. "I mean, really remember?"

"Sometimes. In a way."

We came back out to the open. It was only now that I noticed Luisa staring at us from her balcony. It seemed from her stillness that she had been watching us for some time.

"So these are your friends," she said, her gaze fixed on Rita.

"Yes. They've just arrived."

"Do they speak Italian?"

"No."

Her eye went to John, then back to Rita. She let the silence hang an instant.

"You should bring them around some time," she said finally.

"Yes. Maybe tomorrow."

We made our way up the stairs. Rita glanced back toward the balcony, but Luisa had gone.

"You sound different, in Italian," she said.

"How, different?"

"I don't know. As if you belonged here."

I had to take them around to Marta's to let her know they'd be needing to use the bath there. Marta was just clearing away the remains of her own lunch, shooting a quick, appraising look at John and Rita and then continuing with her work as if she had already summed them up, slotted them into her order of things.

"They're friends from Canada," I said.

"Friends? If you say so."

It seemed pointless to wait for her to extend any gesture

of hospitality to them. Even Aunt Lucia, perched in front of the television, gave no sign of any interest in them.

"They'll need to use the bathroom sometimes," I said.

"So let them use it, then."

I led them out. There had been no missing Marta's animosity. It seemed an unfortunate way to introduce them to the village, not least because the apparent arbitrariness of Marta's actions almost always ended up pointing toward some truth.

"Marta's a bit strange," I said. "Don't mind her."

But we all seemed to have been made ill at ease by her reception.

We continued up the street toward the square. The village had taken on its midday torpor, sun-deadened and still, the only sounds the buzz of flies and the rustle of lizards darting in the shadows of ruined buildings. We passed a couple of villagers, but they seemed shy at the sight of these new strangers, nodding and mumbling some neutral greeting and moving on. But then one of the women I'd met at Marta's my first morning – Maria, the large one – spotted us from her stoop.

"Oh, *americano*! Who are these foreigners you've brought?"

Before I could think of a way to refuse her she had got us into her kitchen, with an almost predatory aggression, settling us at her table and keeping an assessing eye on us as she went about preparing coffee and setting out sweets.

"But is it your fiancée, this one?" she said.

"No, no. Just a friend."

It wasn't long before other women had begun to appear at Maria's door, passing the same appraising eye over Rita and John as if Maria had set them on display here. In the end there were more than half a dozen of them crowded into Maria's kitchen, large and small, ancient and middle-aged.

"They're just friends," Maria explained, to each new arrival. "From Canada. Though the man, he looks like a German to me."

"*Tedesco?*" one of the women said to John. "*Deutschmann?*"

John reddened.

"*Sì, sì, Deutschmann*," he said.

"There's nothing wrong with the Germans," one of the others threw in. "People said, because of the war, but I'll tell you the Germans always respected us. You know who were the worst, the Canadians! It's true, they were the worst!"

It came out in all this that John spoke a few words of Italian, some of the women trying to draw him out in conversation. But the attention to him was only in passing, it seemed, a diversion. Rita was where the real interest lay, barely veiled and strangely intense, the women's eyes always coming back to her. They asked me questions about her, where she came from, what she was to me, seeming to know that I would lie and yet still somehow taking pleasure in my responses, as if all that mattered was that she remain in their sphere.

"She's so pretty," one of them said. "With those eyes."

And there was a mood in the air of almost reverential deference, as if Rita had come with some secret, some arcane knowledge, that they wished to be privy to.

"They must have guessed who you are," I said, when we were outside again. It was the only thing that explained their fascination: they were searching for our mother in her, what spark or power she had passed on to her.

"It was very strange," Rita said. "The way they were looking at me."

"I think they're a little afraid of you."

The women's attention seemed to have changed her in some way: she looked suddenly less foreign here, in her long-sleeved dress and black hair, seemed to have taken into herself some of the stone and shadow of this place.

"I thought I understood a bit what it was like for her," she said. "For our mother. To be in a place like this. To be watched."

John had hardly spoken. The whole time we had been at Maria's he had seemed to want to will himself into invisibility, putting the women off with a reticence that came close to rudeness.

"I didn't know you spoke Italian," I said.

"A few words, only. From when I was young."

"You studied it?"

"No. No. I picked it up here and there. But it was many years ago now."

The two of them spent the rest of the day in retreat at my house, John sitting reading on the balcony off his room and Rita doing some laundry out back in a big copper tub I sometimes used for my baths, spreading clothing to dry over branches and posts like bits of decoration. From the kitchen balcony I saw Luisa come out to offer her a washboard.

"Thank you. *Grazie*."

"I have machine," Luisa said, in stumbling English. "Is better."

"No, no, it's all right. It's nice to be in the sun like this."

"Yes."

Later, that night, taking a walk through the village after Rita and John had gone to bed, I ran into Luisa near the square.

"So it's your sister who's come, then," she said.

"So people know."

"You were right not to say. It's nobody business."

"But everyone knew just the same."

"You know how they are. They said it was the eyes that gave her away. Because they were blue."

"But how would they have known that?"

"It's not that they knew. It's just what people are saying, that it's because of the washing blue your mother took when she was pregnant. Silly things like that."

"I don't understand."

"They used to believe that before. That you could get rid of a baby by swallowing washing blue."

"That's ridiculous."

"I'm just saying what they thought."

"But it's not something my mother would have done. It doesn't sound like her."

"It's what people say. You were small then, how could you know?"

We were walking back along the village's main street toward home. Here and there a light was on in a window, in the background the dance and flit of the ghost that televisions cast up, the fire that people gathered around now.

"And the man?" I said. "What are people saying about him?"

"I don't know. They were making fun of him a bit, because he's a German."

"Just that?"

"One of them said he looked like someone she'd seen on the TV. In one of those war films."

We'd come to the door of her house.

"So you and your sister are close," she said.

"Fairly. Yes."

"I could see that. I thought she was your girlfriend at first. I was even a little jealous."

"Ah."

She laughed.

"*Povero* Vittorio. You think I'm going to try to trap you and make you stay here the rest of your life."

But I didn't know how to answer her, how to make light of things the way she did.

The light was still on in Rita's room when I went in. For a moment I stood at her closed door, heard the page of a book turn, the creak of bedsprings. I could go in to her now and she would be there on her narrow bed, her body a slender swell in the bedsheets. Then as I stood I heard her rise, heard her feet pad across the stone floor till she was just a door-width away, till I could hear the sound of her breathing. She seemed to hesitate there at the threshold as if she knew that someone waited on the other side, that some decision could be made. But then came the click of her light switch, and the sound of her padding back to her bed in the dark.

XXVII

It rained through much of the night, a hard, driving rain that hit like a scattering of pebbles against the glass of my balcony doors. At one point I awoke with a start at the thought of Rita's clothes outside, then remembered she'd brought them in after supper. But through the rest of the night I couldn't get the image of them out of my dreams, those coloured bits of her spread through the garden, saw them picked up by the wind and scattered all over the valley and beyond. It would be hours', days' work to collect them, a hopeless trek through the muck and cold. Rita waited behind at the house while John and I set out; but it was impossible, the rain was too hard, the road too long.

In the morning Rita was at the kitchen table, alone, when I went down.

"John's gone out walking," she said.

Sunlight was pouring in through the balcony doorway, just a few drifting wafers of cloud left behind from the night's rain.

"Will he be long?"

"I don't know. He gets pretty far sometimes. He said not to wait around for him, if we wanted to go out or anything."

It was the first time we'd really been alone together. We both seemed awkward at the prospect of this time stretching out before us.

"So you and John have been getting along?" I said.

"It's been okay."

I couldn't shake the feeling that I ought to be cautioning her in some way, but I wasn't sure against what.

"I don't want to pry. It's just that you've never really talked much about him."

"We're just friends, if that's what you're asking," she said, her cheeks colouring a bit. "Like I told you."

"That's not what I meant. I was just wondering about his past and so on, that's all."

None of this was going quite right, the subject seeming more fraught for her than I'd expected.

"It doesn't really come up much," she said. "I guess he holds a lot back, coming from Germany and everything. The war and all that."

"Did you go there at all? To Germany?"

"A bit." She seemed hesitant about going on. "He took me to his home town, near Munich. I thought it would be this pretty little village, from how he talked about it once. But it was just a new-looking suburb, it could have been anywhere. I guess a lot of it was destroyed in the war. And then it was like he was just a tourist there – there wasn't anyone he wanted to see or anything. It's almost as if we went there for my sake, not his. So he could show me."

"Show you what?"

"I don't know. What he was. How little he had."

She seemed to have understood something about him that she wasn't quite able or willing to put into words but that she was setting up almost as an admonition to me, a warning not to tamper with whatever it was that they had between them.

"Well he seems nice enough," I said stupidly.

We'd grown awkward again. I found myself wishing once more that she hadn't come here: what was the point of all this weight we had to bear around each other, of everything that couldn't be discussed, resolved, of this stricture in my throat as if I were gazing at water, near at hand, unreachable, while dying of thirst?

There was still the whole morning before us to fill, and then beyond that the days, the weeks, the years.

"We could go for a walk," she said.

But I couldn't bear the thought of passing through the village again, of those eyes on us.

"Maybe in the countryside."

We ended up following a path that wound gently down toward the valley from just beyond the edge of town. The air felt scoured after the night's rain, the grass and weeds along the path still dappled with wet. We passed an old man I didn't recognize at work at his little plot; he nodded darkly in greeting, then stared on at us as we went past before bending back to his work.

A couple of miles out Castilucci appeared in the distance, spread out along a narrow promontory that jutted out into the valley.

"Is that the town your father was from?" Rita said.

"How did you know?"

"It's how Aunt Taormina described it. She used to tell me stories about it."

I always felt a twinge of shame at the memory of Aunt Taormina, because of how as a child I'd thought of her as hopelessly plodding and slow-witted. But during the years that her and Uncle Umberto's family had lived with us she had been a sort of surrogate mother to Rita.

"What sorts of stories?"

"Oh, I don't know. Ghost stories, mostly. There was one about a woman who people said was a witch. How they dug up her grave after she died but it was empty."

There was something in this I couldn't quite make sense of, perhaps simply that she had memories of her time with us that were separate from my own, or that she had fit in in this way, hadn't always been hopelessly outside of things. I had the instant's sense that all the while that she'd lived with us, that I'd imagined her as impossibly alien, this other person had existed, someone who had truly been part of the family, who had talked like us and remembered what we remembered and had heard stories like we had at her aunt's knee.

"You must have spoken Italian fairly well then," I said. "To have understood her."

"I guess it's true. I never really thought about it."

"But you don't remember it now."

"Sometimes I think I can almost understand. With those women yesterday, it was so familiar. But it's like in a dream. It's like the words get garbled somehow just before they get to me."

We had come fairly far by now. Behind us, Valle del Sole was just a smudge of mossy tile and whitewash in the hillside.

"This whole place," Rita said. "That's how it feels to me. Like it would make sense except for some little thing I can't put my finger on. It's almost as if I thought I'd come here and the past would just be here, that I'd pick it up and then I'd understand, I'd be someone else, maybe that little girl who knew how to speak Italian or whoever I would have been if things had been different. But I guess it doesn't work that way."

"You sound disappointed."

"It's not that. I suppose it's freeing, in a way. To know there isn't this other identity out there I have to keep looking for as if there were some kind of curse over me."

We were getting close to the river. The vista here was much different from where Luisa and I had come out when we'd gone to the hot spring, the river stretching out bucolic and wide and wheat fields rolling gently down to sandy shorelines on either side, with no sign of the cliff face that Luisa and I had walked along.

"There was a place along here where our mother used to go," I said. "A hot spring."

"Should we look for it?"

But now that I'd mentioned the place it suddenly seemed too intimate a thing to speak about.

"It's a bit far, I think. Maybe another time."

We came to the shore. There was no crossing where we were, just a uniform stream of silver-blue, eerily silent though moving swiftly after the night's rain. Rita took her shoes off and waded into the shallows. Far up along the shore, past the gorge formed by the promontory Castilucci sat on, a tiny figure was moving, a knapsack over one shoulder. As I watched he came to some sort of footbridge and began to make his way across to the other side, from the distance looking as if he were floating across the surface of the water.

Rita and I walked along the shoreline to an outcropping of rock at the river's edge and sat, a little apart from each other, Rita still in her bare feet. Here in the valley the air was almost completely windless and still, the sun shining down on us like the essence of itself, a dry, bone-soothing filament of heat.

There was a sudden calmness between us as if we had come to a crossroad and had paused there an instant in the quietness of decision.

"I remember how you used to visit me when I was small," Rita said. "Me and Elena. Those Sunday afternoons. It's funny how something sticks out like that, as if everything else was just time passing and then there were these moments where you were already thinking, This is what I'll remember. This is what the past will seem like, when it becomes something you can't ever get back to."

"I never thought you cared much back then whether I came or went," I said.

"I used to go crazy when you didn't come. I must have thought you'd abandoned me or something. It's hard to describe now – it's like you were inside me somehow, like you were a lung or a heart, something I couldn't do without. I never thought of it as love or anything like that. It was more – crazy than that. Like not knowing where my own body ended. Just crazy."

"If I'd known," I said.

But I knew it wouldn't have made any difference. Everything had been so wordless then, so outside the realm of what words could give shape to.

256

"Elena said something once," she said. "It was after Dad died. She was so angry then, like you told me. She said people like us – she meant you too – people without a real family, were pathetic. That the whole world was connected that way, and if you didn't fit in, if you didn't have something that was yours, then you were nothing."

"There's the two of us," I said. "There's that."

"Yes."

She traced a line in the sand with her toe and then with a slow pass of her foot erased it.

"It makes my head scream sometimes," she said. "Just thinking of it all. Everything that doesn't make sense."

"It doesn't have to be that way."

But it was true, the way some things could be simply impossible, could never be reasoned through. There was only the searing line they made through the brain, the devastation they left behind.

"Elena said some things about you that worried me," I said. "About school and so on."

"Oh, well. You know her. She has a tendency to overreact."

"She said you were flunking out."

"She said that?"

"It's not true?"

"I dropped a couple of courses, that's all. After Dad got sick. It was all a bit much."

"She made it sound like you were a little messed up."

"Maybe I am. Maybe that's the problem."

But sitting here beside me she seemed entirely sane, clear-headed, strong.

"When I was a kid," she said, "I used to think there were two of me. The real one, the ugly one, that I was on the inside,

257

a kind of freak but also special in some strange way, and then this other one who wasn't special at all, who was just completely normal and average and ordinary, who got average grades and wasn't especially kind or mean and who had average friends and did average things. Then I found out I could fool people, that I could pretend I was just the average one and people would believe me. For the longest time I thought that that was what I was doing, just pretending. But suddenly it was like I didn't know any more which was the real one. It was like I had to choose: this is who I'm going to be."

"And which one did you choose?" I said.

"I don't know. I don't know."

She kicked at the sand.

"Maybe it's just that I can't face that," she said. "Being ordinary. Maybe because I think other people would be disappointed in me. That you would."

She was asking me to set her free, was laying out two paths for herself, one of which could not quite include me.

"Maybe I would," I said. "Maybe that's why you should choose that. It's not as if it's such a bad thing, being ordinary."

A small breeze blew up and Rita's hair fluttered, a nimbus of reddish black in the sun. It was almost unbearable to look at her, to feel this sense that all my life had prepared me for only this one thing, to love her.

"I suppose we should go," she said.

But we simply sat where we were without speaking. I wanted to move in and hold her to me, to feel her body against mine one last time, the way it fit against me like a natural extension of my own. There were just those few inches between us, that bit of air, it could not make any difference;

except the longing in me would only grow stronger then, my arms would only remember more surely the lost feel of her within them.

She rose, finally, as if to release me from the spell of her closeness, and waded into the shallows at the river's edge. Then without looking back at me she began to move slowly away from the shore into the current. The water inched up to her calves, to the hem of her dress. At midstream she stood a moment facing the current like a naiad at the prow of a ship, letting her hands trail in the water's grey. Then, as quietly as she'd gone out, she turned and came back to shore.

"Are you all right?" I said.

"I think so. Yes."

We returned home along a different route, a narrow asphalt road that wound up through wheat fields and tiny, quiet villages that were just a smattering of ramshackle houses. The cool damp of morning had given way to a midday heat that seemed to have wrung the sound out of things, the fields preternaturally silent and still. The road gradually wound away from the route we'd taken on the way down until it was hard to tell any more what direction we were headed in. But then it ascended a slope and we came out suddenly onto the highway that led into the village.

As we entered the outskirts of the village, Rita took my arm in hers as if something had been settled between us. We would walk this last stretch together, she seemed to say, brother and sister, and we nodded to the villagers we passed as we walked on arm in arm toward home.

XXVIII

John was preparing lunch when we came in, intent over a pot on the stove. His bedroom door was open, a small knapsack lying on his bed.

It took me an instant me to realize it had been John in the distance along the riverbank.

"We've been to the river," I said.

"Ah."

"There was a hot spring down there. Where our mother used to go."

His eye caught mine, and I knew for certain that it had been him I'd seen. He had been looking for the hot spring.

"Did you find it?" he said.

"No."

All through lunch there was a palpable sense of the question hanging clearly between us now, that did not even quite need to be posed anymore. Something, I wasn't clear what, had made the thing suddenly bone-sure – that look in his eyes, perhaps, a look that had seemed both an affirmation and an appeal, like a secret passed. I was acutely aware of his body suddenly, of his ruddy physical presence: if I reached over to him, if I put a hand against his skin, I'd be able to feel his flesh real against my own, that he existed, had not all these years been merely a figment of my imagination.

I felt the anger rising up in me now at his deception, wanted only to get him alone, to put the thing to him directly. But then somehow an expedition was being planned, there was the afternoon to fill, and before I knew it we were on the road in my car, the three of us, with the same sense of barely restrained tensions as when we'd been to the zoo a few months before. John had suggested a visit to some kind of archaeological exhibit in a nearby town, giving terse directions from the back seat, a map spread over his knees, while I negotiated the town's tangle of winding streets. I missed a turn and we ended up in a narrow cul-de-sac where I had barely room enough to wheel the car around, the back bumper scraping up against a low stone wall that edged the roadway.

"Maybe we ought to just give this up," I said.

"We should be close now," John said. "Just a ways back."

We came at last to the building we were searching for, a large, medieval-looking place at the edge of the town's old quarters. Inside, a spry, grey-haired man who spoke fairly fluent English – the curator, it turned out – offered to take us around when he learned we had come from overseas, leading us into a cavernous hall where various display cases and information panels had been set out. We were the only visitors; the curator had to turn lights on, move a barrier aside, as if opening up some special, rarely used room of a house for relations who had come.

A sign at the entrance to the exhibition hall read, SEVEN HUNDRED THOUSAND YEARS AGO, THE COMMUNITY OF THE FIRST EUROPEANS. I hadn't quite taken in till now what it was we had come to see: findings of some sort, evidence of *Homo erectus*, that had been unearthed just outside the town during the construction of the Naples expressway. A photo on a display panel showed the site as it stood now, a fenced-off area of bulldozed earth with a few awkward constructions in fibreglass and corrugated steel housing the digs. Next to this was an artist's rendering of how the site would have looked seven hundred thousand years before: it showed a watery meadow studded with willows and poplars, a herd of bison grazing in the background and a man or near-man, small and stoop-shouldered, stoking a fire in front of the opening of a tiny hut.

The curator was giving a running commentary.

"The first people who settled here probably followed the paths made by wild animals when they moved between the mountains and plains in spring and fall. Then over hundreds of thousands of years, those paths became the same ones that shepherds used to move their flocks, the ones you can still find now here and there. So you see how it's all connected, how that little man in the picture there is our father."

John was sticking close to Rita. In the dim lighting and cave-like hollowness and damp of the exhibition hall it seemed we ourselves were reverting to a sort of half-humanness, to basic animal principles of aversion and threat. I remembered the sense I'd had of John that time I'd followed him home, how primal the connection between us had felt to me then. It was as if I'd been tracking him ever since, on his scent, was at the moment now where he was just that single leap from me, where my muscles twitched from his closeness.

At one of the display cases John stood a moment elbow to elbow with Rita, pointing out some detail to her. Looking at them I felt a chill go through me: for the first time I saw the echo of him in her, a ghostly mirroring of him in her shoulders, the line of her back. It was there so clearly suddenly, like some lineament that marked a species.

Almost in the same instant both Rita and John turned, sensing my eyes on them.

"Is anything the matter?" Rita said.

"No, no, it's nothing."

The curator had moved on to a display of what he called the living-floor of a campsite that had been unearthed. It seemed merely a sort of prehistoric dumping ground, littered with broken bones and tusks and primitive bits of cut limestone and flint worked just barely enough to be distinguishable from the rocks they were scattered among. But the curator explained how much could be learned, deduced, across the millennia from these few shreds of things, as if everything of importance had left its indelible trace. I thought of my stumbling attempts to get at the truth of my own past: it seemed that more could be known for certain about these ancient ancestors, about events that had taken place at an unfathomable distance of years, than of what by comparison had happened hardly a moment ago.

"It's eerie to think of them moving around here back then," Rita said. "What they could have wanted."

"They wanted what we do," the curator said. "To eat. To sleep. To have a fire at night to keep them warm."

We came to the end of the exhibition. As we were walking back toward the exit there was a moment when Rita and the curator were in conversation and I was able to draw John aside. My heart was pounding.

"I have to talk to you. It has to do with Rita."

He gave me a guarded look, as if not surprised by the request yet not quite willing to concede that it had been expected.

"Yes, of course."

"Tonight. After supper. We can go up to the bar."

Rita and the curator were talking near the exit. He had pointed out an old device built into the wall to one side of the door, a large wooden wheel with wedge-shaped compartments that let objects be passed through from outside.

"The women used to put their babies there," he was saying, "when they had one they couldn't keep. Back when this building was a convent."

"How do you mean?" Rita said.

"You put the baby in on one side, turned the wheel, and the nuns picked it up on the other, no questions asked."

Rita ran a hand over the rough wood of one of the compartments. The space looked just large enough to nestle a baby in, wedged in between the narrowing sides.

"It doesn't seem like something the Church would do," she said.

"It was better than just letting the things rot in the fields. Every now and again even the Church showed a little compassion back then."

The sun outside was blinding after the darkness of the exhibition room. From the parking lot there was a view of the valley the town looked over, and of the town itself arching around the curving summit it rested on toward the long, impressive bridge that formed part of the Naples expressway. John stood a moment staring out, with that sea captain's look he'd had when I'd seen him gazing from the window of his apartment months before, as if he were assessing some coming storm that only his eye could make out. But then seeming to grow suddenly aware of me and Rita waiting for him, he gave an apologetic bob of his head, and we climbed into the car and headed back to Valle del Sole.

XXIX

John managed to get the two of us out of the house after supper without seeming to arouse Rita's suspicions, proposing a drink between us with little more than his usual awkwardness as if merely making an overture of friendship. Outside it was still light, the sky singed with the last golden glow the sun gave off as it sank behind the mountains. One of the village dogs, a spotted, mangy thing, trailed along to the far side of us in a sort of cringing beseechment as we walked toward the square.

Now that the moment of revelation had come I'd begun to have doubts again.

"Rita told me you visited your home town," I said.

"Yes."

"I was wondering about your family. What happened to them."

"The war took some of them," he said. "Most of the rest are dead now, I suppose."

"You weren't very close to them?"

"The Germans are not the Italians." He forced a smile as

if to offset the sombre tone of his voice. "We tend to go our own way."

The bar was deserted except for the young man tending it, the grandson of the owner I had known, dead now, when I'd been a child here. We ordered a couple of beers and sat down on the terrace that fronted onto the square. The trees on the embankment above the bar were just catching the last rays of the sun, lit up orange and red with its dying light. Those same trees must have stood there when I was small, must have caught the evening light just so, as they did now. I couldn't say why it hurt so much to think of them that way, if because they hadn't changed in all these years or because they had changed so utterly.

"So have you found what you're looking for here?" John said.

There was a sadness in his voice that seemed at once to be inviting me forward and warning me back.

"How do you mean?"

"I just thought. Coming home again. One always looks for something."

"Yes. I don't know."

Our beer sat before us in its bottles like props we had set out to orient ourselves, give us context: we were two men on a terrace, sharing a drink.

"Rita must have told you what happened with our mother," I said.

"A little bit."

"There were some things that were never clear to me. Some questions."

"You were small then. It's natural. You couldn't have understood things."

267

"Yes."

"But now perhaps you find that people don't tell you what you want to hear, is that it?"

"Something like that."

He poured some of his beer into his glass, slowly, letting the foam rise till it formed a small mound above the rim.

"It has to do with Rita's father also," he said. "I think that must be one of the questions."

"Yes."

Light was slowly leaking away from the square as the sun sank more surely behind the mountains. At the far end of the street, already wrapped in shadows, an old farmer was just walking in from the fields.

"I thought he might be a German," I said. "The father, I mean."

John wouldn't look at me.

"Do people say that? That he was a German?"

"No."

"But that's what you think."

"Yes."

"Why?"

"I don't know. Things I remember."

"I see."

I had the feeling that the truth of my suspicions somehow depended on my proving them to John.

"The Germans came through here in the war," I said. "They stayed in our house."

"But that was years before Rita was born."

"I know that. Maybe one of them came back. For my mother."

"Ah. Over love, you think."

"Partly, yes."

"But so many years had passed."

"He could have been waylaid. Maybe he had a family at home that he went back to, then left behind again. I had the idea that someone was looking for him here, the authorities, I thought. But maybe it was his family."

His beer had sat untouched, the foam gradually dissipating.

"What sort of a family?" he said.

"I can't say. A wife. A child."

We seemed on the verge of a painful intimacy.

"And what happened to them?" he said.

"Maybe there was some kind of tragedy. Something he was running from. Or maybe he just abandoned them."

"I see."

There was a defeated tone in his voice now. In the face of it I couldn't bring myself to pose the question directly.

"Could it have happened that way?" I said.

"It's possible, yes."

"But you're not convinced."

"It's not me who you have to convince."

"I suppose I don't."

"But you would like to know the truth."

"Yes."

"Maybe the truth wouldn't be so interesting."

"That's not the point."

The light was almost gone now, John slowly becoming just a shadow across from me. From inside the bar came the sound of a soccer game, the blue glow of a television.

"And afterwards?" John said. "What became of this man?"

"I don't know. He went to Canada, hoping to meet my mother there. But she'd died."

"So that would be the end of it, then. The end of the story."

"Maybe."

He looked out into the square.

"You would like to find him, this man," he said. "Is that why you came here?"

"I'm not sure. What would you want?"

"Is it for you? Or for Rita?"

"For both."

"But if you found him, what could he be to you now? Only a villain. Someone who ruined your mother. And to Rita, merely someone who abandoned her, who did nothing. If the things you say of him are true, then he's twice a villain, someone who left one family and destroyed another, perhaps for no other reason than his own vanity or pleasure."

"That's still not the point."

"So what is the point?"

"Knowing the truth."

He was frowning now. He stared down at his hands.

"I'm sorry," he said finally. "I don't know how to advise you."

The boy inside the bar turned the exterior light on and a grainy yellow haze bathed the terrace. The light gave objects a sepia tone like things in an old photograph, as if this table, these chairs, were only memories of ones that had sat here years before. It had been on this terrace, at a table like this, in these chairs, that I'd found my grandfather and old Antonio Di Lucci the day a stranger had emerged, blue- or grey-eyed, who could say any more, from the door of our stable. What could it matter now, what had happened back then, what with the wash of years in between, the unutterable way in which things had shifted and swerved, and moved on.

"During the war," John said, "things sometimes happened that afterwards it was very difficult to live with. My own town, for instance – it was on the rail line that led out to Dachau. Afterwards, people said that they'd seen nothing, that they didn't know, though the truth, of course, was much more complicated. But how could people admit that, when to admit it was to be a monster? Sometimes there are truths like that that are too difficult to explain. It's easier to say nothing."

"But not right," I said.

"Not right, perhaps, no. It was one of the things that made me leave Germany finally, that silence. But I often thought about the children who were born there after the war. Who were innocent. Maybe for them, the silence was better. Or maybe it would have been better not to have been born there at all, not to have been burdened with their parents, with what they had done or not done. So perhaps it's like that for Rita and her father. That she's best to be free of the burden of him, and he of whatever lies he might have to tell her."

He was asking me for my trust, even as he gave me reason not to grant it to him.

"He could be anything, this man," I said. "From how you talk about him. He could be evil."

"Yes. Perhaps. Or perhaps just a man. Not a hero. Someone with things he no longer has the will to explain. Every life has those things, things that others could never understand. Perhaps even your own."

He looked at me then and I was suddenly certain that he knew about me and Rita, perhaps not the details, the actual facts, but enough to know that something had happened, that a line had been crossed. I had the sense that he was not so much countering his secret with my own as trying to extend to me the trust, the suspension of judgement, that he in turn asked for.

We sat silent. Two old men were walking up the street in the direction of the bar. They called out their greetings as they came up the terrace steps and then lingered a moment in conversation before going inside.

"You never told me where you learned your Italian," I said, when they'd gone.

John caught my eye as if trying to gauge my intent.

"I served here during the war," he said finally. "Like your soldier."

I could go on or not. I had the sense that he would answer every question I put to him truthfully, that I could slowly transform him back into the man he did not want to be. Or perhaps he would simply rise and disappear again as he had twenty years before.

"Rita will be wondering about us," I said.

We started back. It was night now, the streetlamps casting their bit of yellow light in the narrow street. It had grown cool again, almost chill, some of the houses we passed showing the glow of fireplace fires in their windows.

"Perhaps we'll be leaving soon," John said.

"Yes."

"Will you stay on here?"

"For a while, I think. I'm not sure."

He seemed more a stranger, oddly, now that the thing was certain, this man who had changed irrevocably the course of my life and yet about whom I knew almost nothing. I wasn't sure what sort of a pact we had made, how safe he imagined his secret was or whether I intended to keep it.

There was still a light on in the second-floor window when we came to the house. We paused outside the entrance.

"You know I wouldn't do anything to hurt her," John said. "I think you know that."

"Yes."

But I wasn't sure any more if I'd done the right thing, who this man was I would send Rita off with, or how I, who had made such a mess of things, could be trusted now to decide her best interest.

XXX

Rita's bedroom door was open when I went up.

"Is that you?" she said.

She was sitting up in bed with a book, still dressed though with a blanket over her legs against the cold, an old woollen thing that I'd borrowed for her from Luisa.

She shifted a bit when I came to the door, pulled the blanket in.

"How was your drink?"

There was a small tightness in her voice, as if she'd been concerned after all about our going off alone.

"It was all right."

"Just man to man, I guess."

"Something like that."

I'd remained standing at the threshold of her room.

"You can come in if you want."

I sat in the room's only chair. Rita raised herself up a bit on the bed, folding her legs beneath her and draping her blanket around her shoulders.

"John said you might be leaving soon," I said.

"Oh. I guess we haven't really talked about it." But she didn't contradict him. "There was an idea we had. It's a little crazy, but I suppose we'd have to leave pretty soon to do it. About going home by sea."

"He didn't mention it."

"To see where I was born and all that. It's kind of symbolic. John has a friend in England who works for a shipping company who's going to try to fix something up."

The thought of her on a ship in the mid-Atlantic filled me with a peculiar despair. I had an image of her alone at the ship's rail gazing out over endless grey sea as I had years before, of the salt spray against her skin, of the great tomb the ocean was where somewhere our mother's bones lay.

"Will you land in Halifax?" I said.

"I'm not sure. Wherever."

"You might end up in Argentina or something."

She smiled.

"Maybe."

I could meet you there, it was on my lips to say. Everything would be different there, on the other side of the world: there would be palm trees and pampas and endless sky, December summers, anonymity. It almost seemed possible for a moment, this fantasy, that we could leave everything, everyone, behind, every unanswered question, and start again.

"I guess I haven't been all that helpful to you here," I said. "There's so many things –"

"It's okay. I didn't expect answers from you."

"All the same. There are things we never talked about."

"What kinds of things?"

"I don't know. Your father, for instance." My voice had gone thick. "Your real one."

"Why? Do you know anything about him?"

"Maybe. A few things. Nothing for certain."

"Is that why you're here?" she said. "Is that what you're looking for?"

"Partly."

A shadow seemed to have fallen across her.

"So what have you learned?" she said, though with a note of warning in her voice as if she was trying to discourage me from going on or was testing me, knew more than she was saying.

"A few things. That he wasn't from around here. That he was just someone passing through."

"What else?"

"That he might have gone to Canada. That he planned to meet our mother there, to run off with her. With us."

"It sounds a bit romantic," she said.

"A bit."

"I guess things would have been pretty different for us if our mother had lived."

"Yes."

"But you're saying he might still be there somewhere." She wouldn't look at me now. "In Canada, I mean."

"Maybe."

We fell silent. Rita rose and went to the balcony door and stood looking out into the night, her blanket still around her shoulders.

"John and I talked about this once," she said. "About my father. Whether I'd want to know who he was."

"Oh." There had been the warning tone in her voice again. "And what did you say?"

"I said I wasn't sure."

"Why?"

"It's just how I felt then, when he asked me."

I could see the reflection of her face in the glass of the balcony door, inscrutable, hovering like an apparition against the darkness outside.

"I've thought sometimes about kids who were adopted who find their real parents when they're older," she said. "What it must be like for them."

"And?"

"I'm not sure. I suppose it can be good if that's what everybody wants. You hear stories of how great it is. But then I think of what it would be like to be a daughter again. Maybe failing at that. Or maybe just not wanting it enough. Or not thinking the other person did."

"But if you could know. It might make things clearer."

"What things?"

"Where you come from. Your past."

"You and I are different that way," she said. "It's hard to explain. It's as if you were born in the past, you have to go back to it, but when I was born the past was already over. It's not the same thing for me, to look back. It's not where the answers are."

"But your coming here. And this boat trip. It's the same."

"Maybe you're right. Or maybe it's just curiosity. Not really wanting to know, only playing at it."

I wasn't sure if I should go on. She seemed at some level to know where I was leading and yet everything in her was resisting my spelling the thing out, as if she and John had some pact between them, had made a decision to keep the thing forever known and not, like some bond that would be broken the instant it was acknowledged.

She was still staring out into the night.

"You're part of it too, in a way," she said. "I don't know how to put it. You and me. Not having to think that there's someone I have to keep that from, what happened between us."

"There's Elena. There's Mrs. Amherst. It wouldn't be any different."

"It's not the same somehow. They're not my family. I don't know how to explain it."

There was something in her voice that made me fear for her suddenly. It was as if she were drawing a line, a limit of what she could bear, of the secrets she could hold. Perhaps it was not my place after all to force this thing on her, to meddle with whatever it was she and John had established between them.

"It doesn't matter," I said. "We don't have to talk about this. Maybe you'll feel different later on. When you're older."

"Maybe."

It had begun to rain again, a few dull splats hitting the glass of the balcony door and then more until Rita's image there seemed to be melting in the wet. She had pulled the blanket tight around her shoulders, huddled up to the rain and dark as if to a fire.

"There's something you should have," I said. "Marta gave it to me. A picture of our mother."

"Does she look the way you remember her?"

"No. Not really. Plainer, I suppose. More human."

"I was trying to imagine what she was like when we were in that woman's kitchen yesterday," she said. "With all those old women gathered around. If she would have ended up like them if she'd stayed here."

"Maybe. Maybe she wasn't as special as I remember her. Just a woman who had an affair."

"I guess it's not as if she was the only one," Rita said. "When I saw that wheel at the museum – I suppose I could have ended up like that."

"That's what her father wanted. To put you in an orphanage. But she wouldn't agree to it."

It sounded like some fate out of a fairy tale that she'd been saved from. All her life, even now, had that quality to it of narrow escape, of being on the verge always of being reclaimed from the normal, workaday world into strangeness.

She had turned from the window.

"So can I see that photo?"

I fetched it from my room. With Rita there before me, I could see the clear connection between them, the spectral sameness of their features as if the woman in the photo were some preliminary model of which Rita was the final version. Even the eyes were the same, the black-and-white ones of the photograph and Rita's blue, the same gaze as if there was something just beyond the obvious, the everyday, that they were fixed on.

"She looks so serious," Rita said.

"Yes, it's odd. It's not how I remember her."

It was eerie to see the bulge in my mother's dress, to think of Rita unborn there, of this single portrait we had that was all the proof that we had ever formed a family. I thought of everything that was missing from it, the fathers who weren't there, the child unborn and the other forgotten one, already dead, who I'd never known.

"She looks sort of ancient," Rita said. "I don't know how to put it. Not old but like someone who wouldn't have fit in somehow if she was still alive."

"Maybe that's it. Maybe that was what made her special."

The photo was still in the old frame that Marta had had it in, just a plain wooden thing whose glass had a small imperfection near the bottom, a tiny almond-shaped bubble.

"You should keep this," I said. "It's probably the only photo of her."

"No. It means more to you than it could to me. I would always feel, I don't know. Like I couldn't live up to it somehow."

It was getting late. Outside the rain was still falling.

"I think we should probably be going in the morning," Rita said. "There's a train out of Campobasso for Rome around noon."

"If that's what you think."

I felt the urge again to touch her, to hold her, here in this room with the rain outside and the dark, the black night, as impenetrable as the past, as much the element we moved in. I had the sense that when she left this time, something would be over between us definitively, that there would be no going back to it.

"Goodnight, then," I said.

"Yes. Goodnight."

We stood facing each other, she with the blanket still

clasped around her, and I touched my fingers, the palm of my hand, to her cheek, to her brow. She closed her eyes, standing perfectly still as if to let me read her like Braille, to memorize her. Her eyes were still closed when I leaned in to kiss her brow and left the room, shutting her door behind me.

XXXI

I awoke around dawn to the continuing patter of rain against my balcony door. For a moment, in the room's wash of grey light, I wasn't certain where I was, back in my apartment in Toronto or simply in a sort of limbo without dimension, without future or past. For a long time I lay awake under the sheets unable to drag myself up into the morning's damp cold, listening to the noise of the rain outside, the repetitive scrape of a branch against the balcony rail as it swayed in the wind.

At some point I heard Rita stir next door, then her footsteps on the stairs, the sound of her and John in low conversation in the kitchen. When I came downstairs their packed bags were already sitting by the door, the room gloomy and tense with the air of departure.

John had got a fire going in the fireplace.

"So Rita told you about our plan," he said, awkward. "About returning by sea."

He seemed to want to assure me, to let me know again that Rita was safe in his hands, that nothing had changed. He spread a map out to show me the route they would take across the ocean, their possible points of departure. He had done this once before, he said, on a merchant ship carrying oil from the North Sea.

"They have a bit of space sometimes for passengers. Or perhaps you work a bit."

It seemed his element, the sea, where he belonged. He had that mark on him of the exile, of someone who couldn't quite bear the weight of the world; even now, from here, he was running again, making his quiet escape.

They needed to use the bath at Marta's. I went up ahead of them to set the water warming in the bathroom's small electric heater, then sat minding Marta in her kitchen as they each came by in turn.

"So they're going," Marta said, though I hadn't mentioned this.

"Yes."

She gave a small, satisfied grunt, as if everything had turned out as she had foreseen.

"It's just as well."

They had to drop their rental car off in Campobasso before catching their train. I offered to drive in with them in my own car to see them off at the station, but we all seemed anxious now to be free of each other, seemed to have reached the point where there was nothing more that could be comfortably said.

"It's a long drive," John said. "With the weather –"

"Yes, of course, you're right."

The rain was still coming down in a steady drizzle as they loaded their trunk, the slopes surrounding the village lost in a haze of low cloud. The village looked like an enchanted place cut off in the mist like that, a pocket of the past only some magic spell could get you away from, where I was being left to languish now while Rita returned to the present, to what was real, what had to be got on with. She had only been a visitor here, in the past. I thought of my own trip to the sea years before, of the great immigrant ships at the port, those black-toothed chestnut vendors with their little pots of glowing coals. How the bay of Naples had looked from the sea, no larger than a cup you could hold in the palm of your hand, until it had disappeared from view and the only vista was the endless blue of water and sky.

There was a moment as John finished packing the car when Rita and I were alone in the kitchen. I had a flash of panic then, as if I were a parent who had failed to take proper precautions for a child, was unwittingly sending it off to some doom. Outside, John was fussing with things in the trunk, his hair slicked from the drizzle, his beard dripping rain.

"You don't have to worry about me," Rita said.

We both seemed aware of John outside, of this stolen moment when something ought to transpire between us, when some message ought to be passed.

"Maybe I'll see you in a month or so," I said. "You'll be home by then?"

"I think so."

John appeared in the door.

"I think we're ready," he said.

We didn't kiss or touch. There was only the instant our eyes met as the car pulled away, the way they'd met sometimes in the schoolyard when we were children, the furtive glance that acknowledged the shame and the love of being siblings. As the car disappeared around the corner past the square I noticed Luisa watching from her own front door.

"You never brought them by," she said.

"No."

"And now they've gone."

And up on the road that rose out of town the car appeared again briefly, a glint of metal, before vanishing in the mist.

The rain let up around noon. The fog had settled into the village by then, but after the rain had stopped it took on an eerie glow as if somewhere not far above us the sun had emerged. Through the kitchen doorway the street outside looked brilliant and white like some passageway to the beyond, a vapoury curtain of stilled, refracted light.

I went out. Up the street, an old woman was struggling up from the steps that led down to her stable, carting a bundle of dried gorse; from an alleyway a loud, riding-lawnmower-sized tractor appeared with a red wagon in tow and headed toward the square; a few houses over, two hands emerged from the fly curtain of a doorway bearing a water-filled basin, thrust the water out into the street in a silvered arch, and retreated again. Then for a moment the street was perfectly quiet again, deserted, as if all of these gestures had been choreographed exactly to lead back to this silence. Spread over everything was still the strange light-infested mist, the village nestling itself against it as though settling in for some infinite, heavenly sleep. Minute by minute the light increased and yet the mist did not disperse, until it seemed that the village, the whole mountain face, must dissolve in its ghostly white.

I walked. Up to the square first, deserted, past the bar, which seemed more often closed now than open, though when I was a child it was open daily from early morning till late at night. Up the steps that led to the church: I had not been inside since I'd arrived, though when I tried the door now it was locked. I tried to get a view in through the side windows, with their bits of stained glass, could make out the Stations of the Cross, the gaudy statues of saints in their arched niches along the walls. The space looked so intimate and small, with room for little more than a dozen pews. It was hard to believe how vast a place it had once occupied in my imagination, how it had seemed God's very home, though we had been just us insignificant few score who had huddled together there.

I continued along the path that led behind the church and up Colle di Papa. Behind me, the village had disappeared in the fog; but up ahead, the light continued to beckon. I passed the hollow that Fabrizio and I had frequented as children, but afterwards lost my way, no longer certain in the fog what direction I was headed in. For a long time I continued to climb, coming out finally to a summit I didn't recognize. A crumbling farmhouse in faded crimson stucco sat solitary there, parts of the roof caved in and its doors and shutters rotting away from their hinges.

I wandered inside. Toward the back was a crude kitchen that still showed signs of use, fresh ashes piled in the fireplace and a few utensils and blackened pots sitting on an old wooden counter; it probably served some local farmer to prepare his midday meals while he was out in the fields. Off the kitchen was a room where various bits of junk had been piled: rotting old trunks, a few battered suitcases, an old armoire. The room looked as if it had been pillaged at some point or perhaps used by children as a secret hideout, the ground littered with all manner of refuse, bits of ragged clothing and sheafs of mildewed letters and papers but also candy wrappers, cigarette butts, old grade-school textbooks. Tacked on the wall beside the doorway was an old calendar, 1963. It took me an instant to realize what was so familiar about it: it was from the Roma Grocery in Mersea, the small specialty store where we had bought Italian foodstuffs when I was child. A faded colour photo showed the storefront on Talbot Street, in all its early-sixties innocence and charm, great salamis and cheeses hanging in the window and a man in a white shirt and dark, slicked-back hair standing smiling out front next to the tailfinned back end of a chrome-studded Chevrolet. The photo called up a whole vision of what America was, of the entire civilized outer world, of what it must have seemed like from here in this crude peasant farmhouse at the edge of nowhere.

I looked through the papers on the floor. There was a series of letters still in their envelopes, from a Gelsomino Mastroantonio on Orange Street in Mersea to a *signor* Domenico Ingratta. The letters were mainly litanies of greetings to and from other relations, with the occasional mention of some special event, a wedding, a festival, a death; though within them there seemed expressed an intricate subtext of longing and loss. It eventually dawned on me that the letters were to in-laws, that the Rosina they passed on greetings to, and whom I'd taken at first for a cousin or sister, was a wife. It was only in the later letters that Rosina was addressed directly, usually in an appended final paragraph and usually with polite, formal wishes for an imminent reunion. But in one of the final ones, Gelsomino dropped his restraint. "All these years I have missed you with all my heart," he wrote, "and lived only to see you again."

287

I wondered what had become of them, these two. Perhaps I had seen them at the weddings and festivals of Mersea, not remarkable in any way, never quite living up again, in their mountain reserve, to the bald emotion of that single line, one that perhaps Rosina herself, shielded from its heated urgency by watchful parents, had never seen. It seemed amazing that a hundred, a thousand times this same story had been repeated here: the husbands had gone, the wives had bided their time. Whatever had been individual in this seemed almost irrelevant now, just as we remembered of those ancient half-humans who had come up from Africa along the animal roads only the broadest strokes of what they had suffered or known. And yet everything that mattered was lived in the spaces in between, in the tiny details, whether Rosina had been robbed of the pleasure of that profession of love or had cherished it all her life, how she'd imagined her husband without her in America with his own slicked-back black hair and American car. I remembered the letters that had come from my own father when I'd been a child here, all the mystery that had seemed tied up in their indecipherable loops and swirls, how my mother had seemed briefly lost to me when they came as if even she and my father had had their own private life, had been bound in some way I could never know. Perhaps it had been her realizing how time erased things that had kept her from being true to that bond, her not wanting to fade into the ranks of the unremarkable, though that seemed what those of us she'd left behind had spent our lifetimes trying to get back to.

The fog hadn't lifted yet when I came out of the farmhouse, only kept up its eerie glow. I set out along the ridge I was on but utterly lost now, with no way to get my bearings. For a while I had the sense of a presence dogging me, of something or someone hovering just outside my field of vision. But it was only the weight of the fog, perhaps, being cut off like that by its soft walls, not knowing where I was headed. I remembered how when I was a child here the world had seemed peopled by spirits, how every cranny and field had had its ghosts, how the dead had not so much gone from us as simply crossed over, always beckoning from the other side. Perhaps my own dead were calling to me now, had some message to pass on or would lift some weight from me, restore an old innocence like in those childhood stories of saints, the blinding light that brought you to your knees and then the forgiveness of sins and life everlasting.

The path dipped suddenly and I stumbled and fell. For a few minutes I simply sat there on the stony ground, feeling a vertigo overtake me from the disorientation of walking so long in the featurelessness of the fog. It was only now that I noticed how winded I was – I had probably been climbing for some time and not walking level as I had imagined. Then, as I sat there, the fog thinned a bit and the landscape grew suddenly familiar: I was near Fabrizio's farm. A few minutes' walk and I made out his shack in the mist, a line of smoke rising from its little chimney.

"Oh, Vittò!" Fabrizio was at his door; he must have seen me approaching. I felt a swell of emotion at finding him here, as if I'd been wandering lost for hours, for days.

"You're just in time for lunch," he said.

He led me into the shack. There was a fire burning in the tiny fireplace there, and a pot of stew cooking on his little propane stove. Without a word he went about preparing a place for me, moving a small card table up near the fire and setting out bread and wine, a bowl of stew, and then taking a seat across from me, our knees bumping beneath the table. The smell of the stew filled the shack, a steamy cooking smell that put me in mind of our Sunday meals with Aunt Lucia when I was a child, the crowded kitchen, the burning fire.

"So how are your friends?" Fabrizio said.

"They've gone. They left this morning."

"Ah."

I could hear the same small note of hurt in his voice as there had been in Luisa's at my never having brought them around to see him. It hadn't been that kind of a visit, I wanted to say, and yet what seemed truer was that at some level I had purposely kept them away from my old life here, had wanted to protect it somehow from them, from the present.

"You must know what people were saying about the woman," I said. "That she's my sister."

"I won't say I didn't hear that."

"I thought you should know that it's true."

"Well. It's none of my business. But I'm glad you told me. As a friend."

We ate a moment in silence. The stew had great chunks of sausage in it, spicy and coarse like the sausage my grandfather used to make after we'd slaughtered one of our pigs.

"She seemed very pretty, your sister," Fabrizio said. "Like her mother."

"You saw her?"

"Once or twice. In the street like that."

He mopped up a bit of stew with his bread.

"People say that they took her away from your father there," he said. "That she grew up with an English family."

"It wasn't quite like that." Though that was what it came down to: we had failed her, she'd been taken away. "It was a sort of agreement."

"All the same. It must have been hard for you. Her being your sister and everything."

But what I remembered now was the small relief I had felt when it had been clear that she was gone, the small hope that it might be possible then to be a normal family.

Fabrizio replenished our wine and dished out what remained of the stew.

"That German fellow," he said. "People told me he spoke Italian."

"Yes. A bit."

"I was wondering about him. If he was her father."

He said this so matter-of-factly that I wasn't sure at first if I'd understood.

"What makes you think that?"

"I don't know. Just what you were saying before. That you thought the father was German."

"Yes. That's right. I thought – I don't know. I might have been wrong, like you said."

"It's funny though, him speaking Italian like that. Even a little dialect, people said."

"Yes."

"Me, if I was the father, I would just say. But maybe he has his reasons."

"So do you think it was him?"

"I don't know. No one remembers him. But then maybe your mother was better at secrets than people thought."

I wasn't sure what to do. It still seemed important some-how, not so much for Rita's or John's sake as for my mother's, that the secret be kept intact, that there remain this bit of mystery about her.

"Anyway," Fabrizio said, "maybe sometimes it's better not to know. There was that guy in Bagnoli people talk about – it turned out his father wasn't his father at all but some uncle was or something. He went a little crazy when he found that out."

"This isn't the same," I said.

"Maybe it is. Maybe this guy, this German, did some bad thing in the past and your sister would have to live with that. As it is he's just another stranger. What he did is his own business."

It seemed that in his uncanny way he had seen through to the truth and was trying to reassure me, to let me know the secret was safe, that I'd done nothing wrong. But I had the sense in that instant that the opposite was true, that it had been wrong to let John go without confronting him, that somehow both Rita and I had been coerced, had merely traded our own moral ambiguities for his.

The wine had begun to go to my head, warming after the fog and wet but also clouding my thoughts, setting off small explosions in me of confused emotion.

"I should have brought my sister around to meet you," I said.

"It's all right. Next time. I'll come and visit you in Canada some time, like I always said I would."

"We were very close, you know. Are."

"It's normal." But he seemed to sense there was something more to what I was saying. "She's your sister."

"Yes. Maybe not so normal."

I had to stop myself from going on. In a moment I would tell him everything.

There was an instant's awkwardness. Fabrizio got up to clear our dishes away, then set about making a pot of coffee.

"Do you remember that day up on Colle di Papa?" I said. "When we were kids? When you saved me from some of the other boys?"

"Sure I do. It was Alfredo Girasole and his gang."

"Yes, that's right. I couldn't remember his name."

"He's up in Rome now, he works for a bank. You'd never know what a bandit he used to be."

"Do you remember what happened? The way I ran out on you?"

"What are you saying?"

"You came to help me and I deserted you. The boys ganged up on you and I ran away."

"What are you saying? We fought them together, don't you remember that?"

"No. That's not how it happened."

"But it was so many years ago now, how can you know? Maybe you just don't remember it right."

"I don't know. Maybe. It's just – I always remembered that, after I left here. It was one of those things that stuck out, that made me feel that maybe I wasn't any good. Not like other people, not like you. And then with my sister, you know. I used to think that maybe God had given her to me as a sort of test, that she was my chance to be good. If I could find the way to do it."

"But you must have done that. If she turned out all right the way people say she has."

293

It looked like the rain might begin again soon. Through the window of the shack I saw that the fog had thinned but not lifted, its glow of light given way to grey again as if whatever better weather had been going on above us had passed.

"Anyway you can't go thinking about these old stories all the time," Fabrizio said. "Everyone has things they regret."

The coffee came up, a slow bubbling stream and then a final cough and sputter of boiled air. Fabrizio lifted the pot from the burner onto a little counter, careful to avoid spillage, then set out two little cups and carefully poured the coffee into each. I remembered now that he had worked in a restaurant in Rome. But he had probably been hopeless there, to judge by this caring, careful intensity of his, his treatment of every object as if it were sentient.

He set the cups on the table and took his place again. From his seat he reached over with a poker to stir up a bit of flame in the fireplace.

"There was something else," I said. "When I left here. There was something I should have given you."

I pulled out my one-*lire* coin. The whole time I had been in the country I had carried it in my pocket as if still in some boyish hope of its powers.

"I've seen this type before," Fabrizio said, taking it from me. "With the mark like that."

"My mother's friend gave me one like it when I was small. As a good-luck charm. I had it in my pocket that time you gave me your jack-knife. I ought to have given it to you then."

He eyed the coin.

"And did it work? Did it bring you good luck?"

"No. Not really."

"Then maybe if you give me this one now that will make things right for you."

He made it sound as if it was actually possible to correct things like that, across the years.

"I'd like that," I said.

He fingered the coin a moment before setting it next to his coffee cup on the table. There was an odd sense of deflation between us suddenly, as if we had come to some threshold but weren't quite certain how to move beyond it.

"Will you be leaving soon?" he said. "Now that the others have gone?"

"In a while, I suppose. Though I'm not exactly sure where to go."

He poked at the fire again, but most of the wood had burnt down to ember. I got up to leave, afraid of remaining with him, of what more I might tell him.

"I'll come with you," he said.

"It's all right, I can find my own way."

Partway home the rain started again; by the time I got to the house, I was drenched to the skin. The house had the cold, empty feel of recent abandonment: I seemed to realize for the first time that Rita had gone, that something was over. No looking back. I changed out of my clothes and hung them over a kitchen chair to dry, then set about building a fire, huddling up to its first licks of flame while outside the twilight came on and the rain continued to fall.

XXXII

Shortly after Rita and John's departure Valle del Sole began to fill with former villagers returning from the city for their August vacation. Houses that had been shuttered and dark were opened up again; women in skirts and high heels and children who spoke what seemed, after weeks of dialect, a precocious textbook Italian began to appear in the streets. There was something utterly foreign about this returning group, even in the people I remembered vaguely from childhood – they were citified in what seemed a peculiarly Italian way, with a certain sheen of instinctive elegance but also a certain parochialism, an immediate distancing from the unfamiliar as if all they could need, all they could want, had already been defined by their city lives.

The arrival of this group seemed to take the village away from me in some way. It was as if an era had passed, as if the village had briefly resided in a sort of timelessness, a space where it might have been possible to go back, to step through a doorway to the past, and now had suddenly been brought into the mundane present, just a quaint back-country village which people returned to for their summer vacations. I began to fall in with Luisa again, who seemed as put out by these new arrivals as I was, reduced by them from someone in her element to a simple country urchin, not quite to be taken seriously. Her own house was full of returning siblings now, brothers and sisters and their families back from Turin and Rome. They treated her with the unthinking imperiousness of older siblings, expecting to be catered to, looked after, perhaps feeling at some level that they had abandoned her here and for that reason not able to let themselves see her as an equal.

None of the siblings appeared very approving of Luisa's attentions to me, the earlier acceptance I had felt in her house when it had been just her and her parents giving way to a slight undercurrent of mocking condescension as if to say it was not so much after all, to have gone off to America, they had done as well or better here at home. Luisa showed a stubborn loyalty to me in the face of this, coming by alone to the house, walking with me in the street and sometimes taking my arm even though the old villagers, the younger returnees, would stare after us burgeoning with speculation. I could see the direction all this was moving in and yet lacked the desire or will to try to put a different complexion on things. But the first flirtatiousness that there had been between us had been replaced by a kind of solemnity now, as if we could no longer ignore the fact that we were young, that we were attracted to one another, that there seemed nothing in our lives to impede a natural coming together.

We drove out one day to see the Samnite ruins at Pietrabbondante, an old fortress town perched on a stony summit that formed a lookout over the entire valley. The road up followed hairpin switchbacks and passed through villages that were replicas of Valle del Sole but without the veil of familiarity to obscure their actual strangeness, the sun-baked, prehistoric stillness and silence, the mangy dogs in the square and the children who stared at the sight of our passing car. At the end of the road, Pietrabbondante sat high and remote on its great heave of rock like some lost Andean hill town. Up that high, the wind came down with an elemental purity and force, bits of the sky itself seeming caught in it, small wisps of its cool, unearthly blue.

The ruins were at the town's outskirts, along a slope of craggy hillside dotted with gnarled crabapple and olive trees. A gravelled path led down to them from the roadway. We had to sign a register at a tiny gatehouse that an old man in a rumpled suit and tie presided over.

"Watch that your wife doesn't slip on the stones on the way down," he said.

The path continued for quite a distance before we rounded a hill and the ruins finally appeared before us on a small plateau. Great squares of white stone formed the foundation of what seemed to have been a temple; spread out around it were the low, rectangular remains of smaller, more minor buildings, their bits of wall showing the same stone and rubble construction as the houses of Valle del Sole. There was a feel of abandonment to the place as if someone had begun work here and then lost interest, a few fenced-off areas that showed the tentative beginnings of new excavations over-grown now with weeds. Littered throughout the site were massive blocks of cut stone, great giant-sized bits of rubble spread out in a seemingly random dispersal as if whatever great form had once existed here was gradually reverting over the years to a state of perfect, utter disorder.

"They keep hoping the tourists will come," Luisa said. "But who ever sees tourists here in the middle of nowhere?"

Beyond the temple, hidden from view until we were actually upon it, a small amphitheatre lay sheltered at the bottom of a grassy hollow. It was a surprise after the meagre offerings of the rest of the site, its half-dozen rows of stone benches sitting so placid and still, so human in their dimensions, they seemed to be awaiting an audience that must arrive at any moment. The whole construction was an odd mix of delicacy and brawn, a retaining wall along the edge of the upper rows built up of huge, uneven blocks pieced together without mortar, but then the ends of the bottom rows graced with carvings of subtle, griffin-like figures and the seats themselves forming a perfect symmetry of smooth, rounded slabs of cut stone. The seats had been gently contoured to accommodate the curve of a back, a feature that struck me as unexpectedly tender, that these fierce mountain people had taken that care.

As a child I had hardly known of this place, though I'd lived just across the valley almost in sight of it.

"Do they teach you about these things in school now?" I said.

"Oh, well. This and that. About the Samnites and so on. Because we came down from them."

We took a seat in one of the front rows. It was like being up against the sky here, against the gods. Beyond where the stage would have been the land fell away toward the valley, gently at first and then more steeply; two thousand years ago one would have sat in this place and gazed out over what might have seemed the whole of the known world. A few hundred people could have been accommodated here, no more – that was what a civilization was, back then, a few hundreds huddled together against the dark watching some scene unfold that might have been simple-minded or trite or more primal, more pure in its pain, than we could imagine.

"So what can you tell me about them?" I said. "About your ancestors?"

Luisa shrugged.

"We beat the Romans once. We had them trapped in a valley but instead of killing them we just made them pass under our swords to show they'd lost and then sent them home. But after, they wanted to wipe us out, because they'd been shamed like that. They came back and wrecked everything, and then when they built their roads they made sure that none of them passed through here so we'd just be left to die out. But we didn't die, you see? We're still here."

I laughed.

"You're very proud, you Samnites," I said. "Very tough. I can see that."

"You, too. Don't think you're any different. You're still one of us."

There was a sound of wind and beyond us, on the hillside, the trees swayed like bending dancers. But in our sheltered hollow the air remained perfectly calm and still.

"It's funny," Luisa said, "but I always thought of your mother whenever they talked about that, about how proud we were. I was just a baby when you left, but that was always how I saw her, from what people said. *Una vera Sannita.*"

She seemed to be holding the memory of my mother out to me like a gift.

"You would have liked her," I said. "She wasn't so different from you."

We were sitting almost touching. I could feel the heat of her, could smell her country odour of soap and sweat. There was something in her profile that looked suddenly familiar beyond words, the ancestral trace there, the distillation of lineages that went back and back and back.

"I wonder, sometimes, if things had been different," she said. "If my family had gone. Like you did."

"But this is your place. You're at home here."

"Yes."

A small despondency had come between us. We both seemed to have felt the moment pass when I ought to have touched her, taken her hand.

"I suppose we should be going," she said.

The days passed. As if by agreement Luisa began to come by less often; nothing was said, but it was clear that we were taking our leave of each other. I went by Aunt Caterina's once and walked down to the old homestead again, drawn to the place as if there was something I'd missed, some answer I might still stumble upon. But its ruins seemed as remote now, as unfathomable, as the bits of scattered rubble at Pietrabbondante. I felt a sense of desolation go through me at how lost to time things were, at the irreducible foreignness of this place though I had come from it. The clay bowl that Luisa had repaired sat still intact on its weathered sideboard, a bit of rainwater collected in the bottom of it – in ten, perhaps a hundred years it might be sitting there still, as much an enigma to those who came then as these fallen rafters and stones, the hard, mysterious lives that had gone on here, were to me now.

Just under two weeks had passed since Rita's departure when I decided to leave the village. I felt no sense of destination, only the impression that my time here had run out. Marta came by to close up the house, turning the water off and bolting up the shutters.

"Don't expect it to wait here for you another twenty years," she said.

The day of my departure Luisa and Fabrizio came by to see me off. It occurred to me for the first time that circumstance ought inevitably to have made of them a couple, yet the whole time I had been here I had never once seen them together. Even now, as they stood elbow to elbow to see me off, they seemed connected only through me, though they'd surely known each other all their lives. There was something in this that tore at me, as if we had each of us in our way missed our fates, our chance at happiness.

"Next time I see you it'll be in America," Fabrizio said, though I knew it was a trip he would never make.

My second departure from Valle del Sole, twenty years after the first, felt more final and more fatal: there had been the future, at least, to drive off into then, all the unknown, limitless world. It took only a few minutes of driving now for Valle del Sole to disappear from view; and then I was on my own again without destination or hopes, with no place left now to go home.

XXXIII

Rome was half-deserted with the August holidays when I arrived there, restaurants and corner shops closed down, tourists wandering disconcerted from closed door to closed door. I returned my car to the dealer in the Trastevere and took a room for the night at my former hotel. A grizzled and unfriendly older man checked me in; I asked after the young concierge who had been there on my previous stay and was told he'd been let go.

"He was good for nothing, that one," the man said.

"He seemed nice enough."

But the man shrugged as if to say he couldn't help it if I'd let myself be taken in by him.

I was given a room on the second floor, the garbage stench from the back courtyard overpowering in the August heat. For a long time I sat unmoving in the room's dingy arm-chair, my two suitcases sitting unopened on the bed. I felt strangely affected, for some reason, by the young concierge's dismissal – there had been something so hopeful in him, so innocent, at least as he had seemed to me then. But when I tried to call up an image of him I couldn't bring it into focus.

I still had my open return for Toronto. But the thought of booking a flight, of tracking the number down for the airline, of dialling it on the tan-coloured phone that sat on my night table, filled me with an infinite exhaustion. It was as if the engine that ran my body, the little mechanism that everything depended on, was slowly grinding to a stop. I could not imagine boarding a plane, traversing an ocean again, stepping off on the other side, all the effort it would take to carry my life so far again, for so little purpose.

Rita and John might have embarked by now or might still be in London trying to arrange a passage. I had not got any details from them, who John's friend was, where he worked, how I might track them down. I chided myself for letting them go off like that, for letting them get away, though I couldn't think what else I might have done, whether there was some other resolution I had missed. There was no other resolution; and yet the thought of Rita still on this side of the world, still not yet returned to the fixity of things as they must inevitably be, gave me a sense of last desperate hope.

The light at the balcony door faded as I sat in my chair, to twilight, to dark, though at the top of the deep well of the courtyard there remained a fugitive shimmer of pale evening blue. I went out into the streets to catch this last bit of light but the buildings closed me in, all long and humid shadow, no escape. By the time I came out to the openness of a square the sky had dulled to black and the streetlights had come on. There were some buskers playing old Beatles tunes on the steps of a fountain, Germans, perhaps, or Scandinavians, blond-haired and bandanna-ed, the lyrics coming out with a telltale foreigner's drawl. Young backpackers had gathered around them, sitting crosslegged on the cobblestones or on the fountain steps – they had the look of a marauding band, scavengers who had filtered into the city after the residents had deserted it. They were smoking and laughing, singing along with the buskers; and yet there seemed no joy in them, only the abandon of nowhere to go.

I walked for some time, finding myself finally in the square off Termini Station. Inside, great swarms were moving about, coming and going; Gypsy women with dirty infants in their arms moved up the lines at the ticket booths, begging alms. The schedule showed a train leaving at midnight for Paris, with a change there for the boat-train to London – it was something, at least, a destination, a way out of Rome, the oppression of its history, its heat. I went back to the hotel and sat in my room, chain-smoking cigarettes to kill the stench from outside. Finally I came to a sort of decision and repacked my bags, putting all my essentials into the smaller one and leaving the larger one behind when I went to check out. The concierge was watching a small black-and-white television when I went down.

"You're leaving?"

"Yes."

He shrugged.

"It's the same to me. Either way you still have to pay for the night."

The train was already packed by the time I boarded it, only standing room remaining, people crammed into the aisleway leaning out the windows in the heat. I stood pressed up against the curtained door of one of the compartments, my bag between my legs; there was no room for it in the overhead rack, and no room to pull down one of the folding seats that ran along the aisle. The train was late pulling out of the station, ten minutes, fifteen, all of us crammed there in a heat growing more and more unbearable until finally shouts and bellows began to go up all along the length of it; but when half an hour had passed and still we had not moved, the train grew strangely quiet again. Someone fainted up the aisle from me, a young woman, and had to be helped past us onto the platform, the crowd quickly shifting to fill the empty place she had left. Then finally there was a hiss of brakes releasing and the train set off, in an eerie humanity-crowded silence, floating out through ugly train yards into the night-dead outskirts of Rome.

It was not till after Florence that a bit of space opened up in the aisle and it became possible to let down the folding seats or make a place for oneself on the floor. People dozed off as best they could, propped against suitcases or knapsacks, the carriage filled with the breath and sweat smell of sleep. I had claimed my own bit of floor, nodding off from time to time before some jolt of the train awoke me again, each time the same sense of panic rising up in me, the disorientation of not knowing for an instant where I was, where I was headed; though once I'd got my bearings the feeling was worse, the sick hollowness in the pit of my stomach as if it could not matter, after all, where I was, one place was as senseless as any other.

Some time in the middle of the night the train began to falter: I had the impression through my dozing of a constant stopping and starting, the hiss of steam, the shouting of train men from outside. As dawn came on it seemed we had stopped for good: an hour passed, then two, and still we sat stalled. There was not a town in sight, just bits of bush and field; there was a smell of the sea in the air, but no view of it through the windows. People had begun to stir, to stumble out to the toilets, irritable at the delay, at the mess of bodies and limbs to be got through. When we had finally set off again it was only twenty minutes or so before we had stalled once more; and then in this halting way we continued until, some time past noon, the train finally hobbled into Genoa, hours behind schedule. An announcement was made: the train would be cleared here, it would not be continuing onward. On the platform people stood amidst their suitcases and bags looking abandoned, cut adrift, as if we had been cast out like stowaways.

There were no other trains for Paris until the evening. I decided to take a mid-afternoon one for Lyons – it seemed important simply to keep moving, to avoid the vertigo that set in when I stopped, the sense of being at a precipice. On the train I found an empty compartment and settled into one of the window seats, my body aching now with fatigue. An old man in a soiled linen jacket slouched past the doorway, came back to it, stuck his head in.

"*C'è posto?*"

"*Sì.*"

A stench came into the compartment as he entered it, of alcohol and days-old sweat. His face was purpled with carbuncles and broken veins, a whole anatomy visible there of drunkenness and nights in the open, of animal want. He huddled into one of the seats near the door, furtive, as if eluding a pursuer.

"*È italiano?*" he said.

"*No. Canadese.*"

"Hm."

And he turned uncomfortably away from me to look out through the compartment door into the aisle.

Other passengers came up the aisle as they boarded, peered into the compartment, caught sight of the old man and continued on. Then a conductor showed up at the door: perhaps someone had alerted him.

"I've got my ticket," the old man said, angry, defensive. "There's nothing you can do, I've got my ticket."

And with a callused hand he pulled a stub from the pocket of his jacket. The conductor looked it over without a word, seeming to weigh his options for a moment before finally handing the ticket back and moving on. The old man shot a quick glance in my direction as if seeking an ally, then seemed to remember my foreignness and silently turned back to stare into the aisle.

The train set off. The old man pulled out some bread and cheese from an oily paper bag he carried with him and then a bottle of wine, offering them out to me. I declined them but his show of generosity seemed somehow to put him more at ease. He began to talk, just a mumbling patter at first, as if he was talking to himself, but then slowly working up to a greater animation. He kept replaying the scene with the conductor, seeming very pleased with himself at having outwitted him.

"Did you see his face? They can't do anything to me, I've got my ticket. Did you see the way he went off?"

I had opened the window but the stench from him still filled the compartment; it appeared to come up from his belly as he talked, a noxious odour of liquor and rot. He was on his way to some town near Turin where there was a festival, he said – it was good for begging, people felt guilty at a festival when they saw people worse off than themselves.

"It's no different than anything, being a beggar. Any business. You just have to find the right way to take advantage."

As he drained his bottle he became more and more garrulous and less and less coherent. I was only half following him, occasionally nodding or mumbling assent but wanting only to sleep, to be left alone. He kept coming back to his little victory over the conductor – it seemed emblematic for him, as if all his life had been this struggle to hold onto the barest human dignity; and yet there was nothing sympathetic about him, nothing that didn't seem tinged with depravity.

"You know, I killed a man once," he said. "At the end of the war. It was one of the Fascists – not that I cared about that, it was only to rob him. But you see what I'm saying, I could see the end by then, how things were going. You have to know how to take advantage. No one came after me for that. They were stringing the Fascists up in the square by then."

I felt sick. I took my bag down from the luggage rack and left the compartment, though the old man hardly seemed to notice my going. I went through to the next carriage to get away from him and found an empty seat in one of the smoking compartments; but I could still smell his stench, could taste it in my throat. I felt contaminated somehow by my contact with him: my body was dirty like his, smelled of days-old sweat, the others in the compartment seeming to shrink away from me as I came in. I tried to sleep but couldn't get the old man's image out of my head, that dull gleam in his eye that seemed just brute, selfish need, the absence there of any humanness or perhaps its essence, what we were when stripped down to our barest selves.

Just past the border into France I finally nodded off. When I awoke it was to darkness, the train quiet and stilled, the compartment deserted. I felt the panic again, more acute, my mind scrambling to make sense of things, where I could be, stopped at a station perhaps, but there were no station lights and no signs, only the darkness and the silence. I made out the ghost of another train through the far window, also dark and still: I was in a train yard. The train must have reached its destination and been shunted off here. I felt a shame go through me at having been forgotten like this, at having been left behind as if I did not merit the kindness it would have taken for someone to wake me. I walked up the aisle to one of the doors, heaved it open – there were more darkened trains, a great expanse of empty tracks. In the distance, a cluster of lights: the station. I climbed down from the carriage, bag in hand, and slowly made my way across the empty tracks toward the light.

It was the following night before I reached London: there had been rain and rough sea across the Channel, and then a haze that slowly thickened to fog as the train entered London's outskirts. It seemed days, weeks, since I'd slept, bathed, had a proper meal, since I hadn't been living my life on trains and station benches, moving toward a destination that seemed now, as I passed by the blocks of soot-blackened row houses that flanked the rail line, like an arrival at nowhere, as much the end of the world as any place could be.

I stood outside the station thinking I might simply collapse there on the pavement: this was the end, there was nowhere further to go. I could hardly remember now what instinct had brought me here, if I'd imagined that Rita might somehow appear to me out of the whole anonymous world or if I'd simply needed to reach this point where there was no going on, where I was sure of that.

Someone had come up to me, there in the fog, a tall, stoop-shouldered bird of a man in a raincoat and spectacles, eyes blinking. He seemed an apparition, some phantom my sleep-deprived mind had called up.

"Are you looking for a hotel?"

I ended up following him through the foggy streets to a quiet sidestreet of slightly derelict Georgian townhouses, discreet hotel signs strung out along the length of it. Though it was barely eleven the street was deserted: we might have been in some quiet, elegant suburb except for the faint boarding-house look of the hotels, the peeling paint, the telltale bits of garbage at the bottoms of stairwells. The man had kept up a mumble of distracted conversation, seeming not quite entirely in his wits.

"There's private bath if you'd like, though it's a bit more expensive, of course."

The hotel he led me into had a stale, animal smell like a private home, a doorway off the narrow lobby leading back into what looked like living quarters, the furnishings crammed tight and the walls overladen with photographs and cheap-looking paintings. The man took out a register and bent in close to scrawl in the details from my passport.

"An Italian name, isn't it?"

"Yes."

"My wife's Italian, you'll meet her in the morning."

I took the room with private bath. He led me up a narrow staircase to a small, musty room on the second floor, faded red velour curtains covering the window and a narrow, thick-blanketed bed pushed up against the wall. Above the bed hung a sentimental watercolour: madonna and child.

He handed me my key.

"Can we expect you for breakfast?"

The question threw me into confusion.

"No. Thank you."

The bathroom was stuffy and cramped, the bare wooden floor there discoloured and warped, seeming to roll beneath my feet as I stepped over it. A short ball-and-claw tub, streaked brown under a steady drip from the faucet, had been wedged between an air shaft and the toilet; above it, on a tri-angular ledge, sat a squat electric water heater. I reached up and flicked a black switch on the heater's side; a red light came on, and the heater began to gurgle.

The water would be some time in warming. I went to the window in my room, pulled back the curtain; but the mist outside held the world back like a veil. A couple of taxis passed by on the street, dim forms pushing through the fog to emerge briefly black and solid below me before disappear-ing again in the other direction.

I sat down on the edge of the bed. I could hear the drip from the faucet; it seemed more insistent now, had sped up slightly or taken on a kind of asymmetry. I sat listening, my eyes following the floral pattern of the room's wallpaper as if somehow to use it to force the drip back to its regular rhythm. But no, the wallpaper too had quirks and irregularities, roses giving way to flowers I couldn't name, these to small, bent figures in frocks and kerchiefs, my vision beginning to blur with the dim, tiny detail of them.

Almost as an afterthought I took a packet of razor-blades out from my toiletries bag, the double-edged kind that were not much in use any more – I had had them since Africa, had packed them against some special need and then they'd remained there in my bag for years, till I took them out now. I had noticed them in passing while packing my things to leave the village; though perhaps the thought had already begun to form then at the back of my mind, required only that I should have come to the proper end of things, that all pos- sibilities be exhausted. I set the package in a wire soapdish that hung down inside the tub, then placed the tub's plug into the drain and tested the water. It was warm but not hot; it would have to do.

I undressed while the tub filled, unaccountably taking great care to fold my clothing and pack it back into my bag. When I'd finished I sat down on the edge of the bed again to wait, naked, my skin tingling. It felt good to have my clothes off after my days of travel, of smelling my sweat. I ran my hands up and down my thighs, my calves, feeling the muscle and bone there, the heat of my blood. This was my body: for a moment I understood with perfect clarity what it meant to have a body, the wonder and the tyranny of it, the strange- ness. For a long time I sat exploring the textured surface of my skin, the lines on my knuckles and palms, the hairs and moles on my chest and arms. I had carried a body for so many years and yet wasn't on familiar terms with it – it might have been some strange thing washed up by the sea, sprouting limbs whose purposes, lost in the recesses of time, would never be known.

A sound of splashing: I turned to the bathroom door to see a sheet of water spilling like curved glass over the rounded edge of the tub. It took me an instant to register the meaning of this, to undertand that the overflow valve must have clogged, that I ought to turn the water off. I rose and shut off the faucet, then reached into the tub to release some excess into the drain. A thin layer of water had collected on the floor; it seeped quickly into the floorboards, turning them a wet grey.

From the bathroom doorway I looked around the room again, at my bag on the floor, at the picture over the bed. For the first time, perhaps, I grew aware that I would do the thing, that I had only to follow out the chain of events I had set in motion, and it would come to pass. I stood naked there, staring out, and could only think to have the thing over, to have the courage, the energy to bring it off – there was no larger thought in me than that, as if the matter were merely some small, unpleasant chore to be got through, and this as much as anything, to be at the brink without an insight, to have learned nothing, made me wish to get on with the thing, and have it done. I turned, stepped into the tub, and lowered myself slowly into it, the water rising in counterpoint to my descent, coming up once again to near the tub's rim. The water was tepid; it chilled me as I sank into it, stripped me down to a second layer of nakedness.

I reached for the package I'd placed in the soapdish. It was soggy now, the water had got to it; it fell apart in my hands as I opened it. Inside, the blades clung together from the wet. I cut my thumb prying one free, and instinctively brought it to my mouth to suck on the wound.

I held one of my wrists slightly submerged and gashed it with a blade, hard, not across but along, as I'd heard it was right to do. I lost heart then, at the blood – there was an instant when I seemed to black out, when there was only the panic, the animal pounding of my heart. I closed my eyes and a kind of calm returned, but I couldn't face that instant's panic again, to see the blood's first pulsing out; and so I sat there with my single cut wrist thinking, it would do, the cut had been clean and deep, I had not made such a mess of it.

With my eyes still closed I lay back in the tub, sinking until I heard water spilling over the tub's sides again. Something was ebbing away from me, I had the sensation of that, though it was not my very self, not the essence of me, merely the waking part, or so it seemed, merely what I could after all do without. I could hear the drip of the faucet at my feet, could feel the slight tremor in the water's surface as each drop fell. The drip seemed to set the timing of my breathing, of my heartbeat, forming little ripples in my mind that then stretched themselves out over the surface of my thoughts, and died. I felt myself slipping toward sleep, felt it beckoning before like a country to reach, like home. Young maidens in kerchiefs and frocks were waiting for me there, had made me a bed of roses and daisies and angels' tears, if only I could get to it, could hold on.

The drip had grown faint and plodding now, moving at the pace of dreams, each sound surrounded by long, lazy silences that threatened to stretch out endlessly. Time had slowed almost to the point of stopping: I could breathe or not breathe, my heart could plod on or stop, it didn't matter. Someone would come, though, in a moment, to sit at the end of the tub and give me a word, a shibboleth. I could hear him knocking already at the door, and calling me by name – the water, he says, and I tell him I died once before, in that way, my corpse already wasting away on the ocean floor.

I was in a cave, in a warm dark pool. One by one their frocks and kerchiefs fell away and they stepped down beside me. They held me in the water and caressed my calves, my thighs. Luisa was there, and Rita, and another too, the third, though I could not make her out; I wanted to bring a hand up, to run it over the smooth curve of breast, of cheek. At the mouth of the cave, rough white pillars tapered down from the ceiling and up from the floor.

They were knocking again. Two of them, two voices, a woman and man – they had broken the window with their pounding, the fog was coming inside. But I wanted only to sleep, those last few precious moments before the clock wound down and began its wild ringing, and it was time to rise. My father would be waiting for me in the fields – there were miles and miles of beans to be hoed, and tomatoes too, we would do them together, laughing and talking and stopping at ten for cheese and homemade bread. All that and more was waiting.

Someone was standing over me.

My god, he said, my god, but I could not hold on for him now; and then the room, the face and voice above me slipped away, and my mind went dark.

~

Tell me your dreams, she might have said, and I would have told her, I dreamt I wrote you a letter and in it was everything. That is what I have wanted, to hold every nuance and hope, every smell, every bit of sky, though there hasn't been a single line I've written here that hasn't seemed untrue in some way the instant I set it down.

Sometimes I awake in the middle of the night and there is an instant when a dream or just the residue of all the images my memory has churned up during the day makes me imagine that I'm back in some moment of the past, a child again in my mother's bed or rising up on a summer dawn on the farm or in my corner apartment in Toronto, listening for the clack of the streetcar or the drifting late-night voices of passersby. There is always the effort my mind makes then to hold the illusion, to work into it the sound of the wind outside, of a branch against the roof, the dank, sweat smell of the bed-sheets, as if it is the mind's job not so much to see things as they really are but simply to make some sort of sense of them, to fit them into whatever general order it has already arranged for itself. In its way, the time I have spent here now writing these words has seemed this same hovering between waking and dream, this effort to hold intact an illusion; except in memory there is no final awakening to the actual truth of things, only the dream, only the little room the mind makes for itself with no doorway to the outside.

I have beached up on an island off the Kenyan coast that I visited once during my years in Nigeria, just a sliver of sand and bush at the far edge of a continent. I do my writing on the verandah of a flat I've rented above a food shop in the island's single town, with a view of a harbour where every day bare-backed men unload boatfuls of mangrove timber that they've culled from along the island's shoreline. Once, I was sitting here trying to describe my childhood departure from Valle del Sole when I suddenly remembered the rain, how I'd heard it building at dawn, how every aspect of that day had been suffused with it though I'd almost forgotten it; and when I looked up then from my writing to see the workers sweating at the docks and the sun reflecting cleanly off the harbour, for an instant I could hardly grasp the meaning of what I was looking at, so much had my feelings got caught up in the swell of remembered rain. But thinking the scene over again afterwards, I realized there was something else I'd forgotten: the photograph of my mother and me that Marta had preserved, taken that very day, or so Marta said, though there is no sign in it of the rain. There is some simple explanation, surely – maybe there was no rain, after all, or maybe the photo was taken at some other time. But the fact remains that the real story is forever lost to me, that I cannot now, or ever, account for the rainless instant that the photo represents. Perhaps there are always these moments that can't be accounted for, that can't be made to fit, as if the story of a life, to verge toward the truth, should always imply at every instant the dozens of other versions of things that must be suppressed to make way for a single one.

When I first arrived here, after two weeks in a London hospital, I thought I had made a mistake in coming, to simply another destination where I was anonymous, where I had no reason to be. But in the end my anonymity has grown on me, is perhaps the thing I will have to fight to abandon as I try to work my way back to my life. It was only after a month here that I was able to write to Rita, and then it was a month more before she replied: she was back in school by then, seemed to have fit herself back into the normal flow of her life, though she was no longer living with Elena. She didn't elaborate except to say that some money had come through from their stepmother, and that they were managing; and then at the end of the letter there were just the briefest few lines that mentioned, as if in passing, that John had moved back to Germany. There was something in her restraint that made me certain that she'd known everything, had known from the start, in some way, not only who John was but that he would go, that it would somehow come to that. At bottom I don't know what she has made of all this, and perhaps never will, since there are doors in her now that appear forever closed to me; but she seems to have accommodated herself to his going as if she'd understood all along that her time with him was simply a sort of gift to him. Of John himself I know even less: he is one of the darknesses in this story that may never be fully plumbed, the point where it recedes back into the unknown. Maybe our paths will cross again and things will be different then; or maybe he will always be the unfinished thing that both Rita and I must contend with, what was never quite understood.

I have had two other letters from Rita since the first, in reply to my own. There is still an intimacy in them but it is clear now that we are moving apart, as if we are growing our own skins again, extricating ourselves from each other; and soon it will be difficult to imagine the point of closeness we once reached, perhaps even to bear the thought of it. I have told her nothing about London; and she, for her part, has not asked me why I am here or how long I will stay, even if there is always the unspoken question between us of what follows, of what we will be to each other when I return. In the meantime I set things down, placing them one after another like links in a chain that might finally pull me back to the world, though there remain always those things, perhaps the most important ones, that are not quite captured or that are held back, where ability fails or where every fibre rebels at the betrayal of putting a thing into words. Language seems sometimes such a crude tool to have devised, obscuring as much as it reveals, as if we are not much further along than those half-humans of a million years ago with their fires and their bits of chipped stone; though maybe like them all we strive for in the end is simply to find our own way to hold back for a time the encroaching dark.

The moonlight here in this place where I've landed is a kind of narcotic: in it, everything seems itself and not, distilled to its essence but also transformed, as if at any instant some great secret must be revealed. One night, looking from my verandah toward the peninsula of bush and sand that the harbour trails around to, I made out in the moon's glow dozens of fishing boats pulled up along the shore, and on the beach the first flames of a bonfire that perhaps a hundred fishermen stood gathered near, small silvered silhouettes against the black of the forest behind them. As the flames rose higher a sound of drums came across the water, and then just the barest chorus of voices like prayer; and then one by one, the bonfire still burning, the little fishing boats began to set off from the shore into the half-daylight of the moon-crusted sea. It took a long time before the last of them had put out, the sea by then dotted with them to the dark line of the horizon, this strange moonlight flotilla like some whispered night-time setting out for the beyond.

Afterwards, the episode had the hazy quality of a thing that you are no longer quite certain actually occurred, that you hesitate to recount for fear that its reality will be diminished. But that night I had a dream: I was walking along a mountain path, and behind me the shepherds had gathered in their flocks and pitched their tents and started their music because the night was coming on, but still I continued to walk, with that peculiar feeling of lightness the mountains give, the sense that just ahead some new vista will be revealed or some new freedom hitherto unimaginable be offered out. The path I was on was neither gentle nor steep, the darkness that was gathering was not the black of blackest night nor yet quite without threat; and the music drifting out from the shepherds' camp had an ancient, primitive sound as if some great sadness was at once contained in it, and lifted away. Then, as I walked, small flickers began to appear in the valley beneath me: bonfires like the ones we would light on Christmas Eve when I was a child, the little messages we'd send out to join ourselves with the scattered villages and farms throughout the valley. There was just a handful at first but then more, spreading across the valley like code, a slow wordless coming-together, and I stood watching from the slopes as the valley lit up with them, ten thousand of them burning away, sending their sparks up into the night that floated an instant, then died, as if bidding goodbye.

Acknowledgements

For their contributions to this book I am grateful to the following: Erika de Vasconcelos, for seeing the book clearly when I could not; Don Melady, Marian Botsford Fraser, Lee Robinson, and John Montesano, for their advice and support; Tania Charzewski, Peter Buck, and Rafy, for special services; Janet Turnbull Irving; Cal Morgan; and, especially, Ellen Seligman.